About the Author

I am an Australian writer with a passion for stories. My desk drawers are full of unfinished manuscripts, and my bookshelf overflows with books and graphic novels. *A Vow to Live Well* is the first publication to be accepted by a publisher, and I hope it is the first of many. If writing has taught me anything, it's that there are no stories that aren't worth sharing.

A Vow to Live Well

Andrew Gill

A Vow to Live Well

Olympia Publishers
London

www.olympiapublishers.com
OLYMPIA PAPERBACK EDITION

Copyright © Andrew Gill 2023

The right of Andrew Gill to be identified as author of
this work has been asserted in accordance with sections 77 and 78 of
the Copyright, Designs and Patents Act 1988.

All Rights Reserved

No reproduction, copy or transmission of this publication
may be made without written permission.
No paragraph of this publication may be reproduced,
copied or transmitted save with the written permission of the publisher,
or in accordance with the provisions
of the Copyright Act 1956 (as amended).

Any person who commits any unauthorised act in relation to
this publication may be liable to criminal
prosecution and civil claims for damage.

A CIP catalogue record for this title is
available from the British Library.

ISBN: 978-1-80439-072-6

This is a work of fiction.
Names, characters, places and incidents originate from the writer's
imagination. Any resemblance to actual persons, living or dead, is
purely coincidental.

First Published in 2023

Olympia Publishers
Tallis House
2 Tallis Street
London
EC4Y 0AB

Printed in Great Britain

Dedication

For my mother, Robin, my most devoted reader. Without you, there is no me.

Acknowledgements

First and foremost, I thank my family for their love, generosity and support. You are the anchors that keep me grounded and the wings that give me flight. I want to acknowledge my friends who are my light in dark places. To my friend, Sam, my most valued critic, for our daily talks and night time walks. To Nathan, who is patient and tolerant, for your counsel and your jokes. To Emma, for being the only person I know who understands pain as I do, your courage taught me how to endure. To Terry, for sage advice that soothes and conversation that motivates. To JC, for kindly offering distraction during difficult times. To Autumn, who loves to listen to me ramble, you are a lifeline. And to Ash, the source of my greatest inspiration.

Chapter One

Friday, 2nd July 2021 5:15 p.m

Josh Dempsey's life is a perfectly balanced routine. A husband and father of two, his life revolves around his job and family. He is employed by a financial planning and brokerage firm as an advisor. It is not a job that he sought to secure as part of some juvenile attempt to fulfil a childhood dream. Financial planning is not even something he is passionate about. Josh's career manifested in the same way it does for so many others who give no thought to their future while they are still young enough to make determinations about the course their lives will take; he got a job to make money, and once he became comfortable and confident in his role, he chased promotions to increase his wages. His job is the result of underestimating the importance of determining his values and selecting a career that enabled him to exercise those values before financial pressures restricted that choice. In the formative years of his life, he never took the time to learn what sort of pursuits were meaningful to him. Growing up, while he still had ample opportunities to decide how best to direct his time and attention, he did as many do when they have more time than sense; he wasted it. Thus, as it does for all who fail to choose in time for themselves, life decided a path for him, and once life set him upon it and necessity made his job imperative to his own survival and, later, that too of his children, the appeal of starting over diminished entirely. He is paid a decent wage, and that's about where his interest in the work starts and ends. What makes his workplace less tolerable is that, while Josh could say decisively that there are other things he would rather be doing with his working days, few around him could boast the same. Many of his colleagues *chose* to be here. They went to school and got diplomas and degrees and subjected themselves to tests by the regulatory bodies just for the right to occupy a cubicle. These people are savvy investors and economic conservatives. People who are always thinking about the bottom line. Engaging with clients, they talk to clients about the benefits of financial education, boasting great incentives and schemes to save and earn money. They talk to each other about much of the same on their breaks. The latest interest rate cut, the rise of inflation, the cost of living versus economic stability. They speak of long-term sustainable growth in their portfolios and debate the risks and rewards of various investment strategies. They seem content to have the same conversations with the same people every day, complete the same tasks every day, virtually *live* the same day, over and over, without complaint. Somewhere along the way, Josh slipped in among their ranks, synchronised himself with their patterns, and lent his voice to the choir of mundane, routine mediocrity.

Then there is the second aspect that dominates his life: family. This sphere occupies all of the minutes of the day before and after work. Before work, it's breakfast and preparation for school. When he finishes at the office, he is behind the wheel of his car, transporting his kids to one of their many after-school activities. Music lessons, swimming lessons, little athletics… Every day is like the last. There is comfort in that. Going through the motions is effortless because it does not require or demand any initiative. He has no regard for the trajectory of his life, instead unconsciously remaining in a state of motion that is sweeping him towards old age, one day at a time. It's a patterned routine that consists of the same activities on an endlessly predictable loop. Even when he sleeps, the characters of his dreams have the same faces as the people he works with, the clients he serves, the parents he is forced to socialise with at his kids' after-school activities. Even his dreams, the last frontier of true originality that by nature should belong to him exclusively, have been surrendered to the prevailing forces in the war of the same. Nothing in his life is really his own. Even his dreams don't really belong to him any more. Not only does this travesty go unacknowledged, but the tragic loss goes unavenged. The days blur together into a predictable tapestry, and Josh operates unobjectionably on autopilot. He smiles when expected of him, laughs when convenient, and agrees with every opinion proposed to him, never offering a conflicting point of view. No scandals. No controversy. Nothing upsets the balance. Everything is agreeable. Like a piece of driftwood, he floats along the river of his life one day at a time, never believing anything unexpected or radical can or will happen.

That is precisely why he was so unprepared when it did.

Friday night drinks after work. Attendance isn't compulsory, but those who don't oblige the social convention are subject to water-cooler gossip and socially scorning whisper treatment at the office. Those who don't or can't attend, the unwilling and the unable, become pariahs treated like lepers by the cliques of the office. In finance, getting ahead in the industry is less about performing well and more about how many arses one has kissed and how many big-wigs have been smooched. Josh attends these events with just enough frequency to satisfactorily avoid the bother a consistent absence would cause later. At dusk, the bar is most crowded. It's that idyllic time on a Friday afternoon when folks have been working hard all day, eagerly awaiting the clock reaching five. Freedom hour. Then, as darkness approaches, the mood shifts becoming observably lighter, and people are keenly attuned to the electric buzz in the air. Friday night: any office worker will testify that the prelude to the weekend is the most greedily anticipated time of the week. If Josh could bottle up that Friday-night-feeling and sell it in stores, he would be the world's richest man and then he'd *really* have something to talk to the finance drones about. Josh sits outside the bar on the pavement's edge with a group of his peers. They're yapping about the latest spike in some newly created cryptocurrency. He drinks the last swallow of beer from his glass as he gazes off in the distance watching the light fade. The sight of the sunset is skewed by the tall towers of Brisbane City's Central Business District. The diminishing light transforms them into poignant silhouettes, their grey bodies stark in contrast against the backdrops of the approaching twilight. He raises the empty glass, visibly shaking it side-to-side to his work colleagues.

'Going to grab another drink,' he said with a controlled smile. It elicits the typical responses from his cohorts. Vague, half-drunken cheers of approval, stifled acknowledgements and naturally, one or two requests for another drink. He made his way inside, careful to avoid collisions with other patrons. He was standing at the bar, paying no attention to what was going on around him while he waited his turn to be served when he heard his name spoken by a familiar voice.

'Josh, is that you?' He turned around. She was standing half a meter away, smiling at him.

'Rachael,' he said, beaming. 'Wow, I can't believe it's you. What's it been, ten years?'

She scratched her chin thoughtfully. 'More like, fifteen. God, where does the time go, huh?' She flashed a flirty smile.

'Yeah.' He chuckled. 'What are you doing here?'

'Same thing as you. Drinking.'

He looked her over. Her skin retained a youthful glow, and her lime-green eyes still possessed the same devilish charm he remembered from years ago. There remained something remarkably alluring about Rachael Wright. 'You look good. Seems like the years have been a lot kinder to you than they have to me.'

'Well,' she said with a casual shrug, 'I *do* have a very regimented skin-care routine.' She leered at his body for a few seconds. 'But I think you're too hard on yourself. You're still looking good.' She closed the distance between herself and Josh and came to stand beside him at the bar. 'Can I buy a drink for an old pal?'

'It would be rude of me to refuse such a generous offer.' The scent of her perfume wafted into his nostrils, and it was like sampling a taste of ambrosia. He worked tremendously hard to prevent his arousal from showing. It created one of those instant reactions in him, the kind where certain scents unlock forgotten memories. Rachael got the bartender's attention right away, ordering them two beers. 'I feel like I've been waiting twenty minutes,' Josh groaned. 'A pretty woman stands beside me and gets a drink in five seconds.'

'That's the way of the world, Joshua, my old friend!' She pats him on the back, her hand lingering for a moment longer than it should. The bartender set two golden beers down in front of them. She presents her perspiring pint glass for a toast. 'Cheers!' The glasses clinked, and Josh took a long swig from his glass. They moved into the back of the bar and spoke until their glasses were empty. They ordered another round. By the time they emptied their glasses of their second drink, most of Josh's work colleagues had elected to move on elsewhere. He didn't mind. He never really wanted to socialise with them anyway and did so only out of a feeling of obligation. Talking with Rachael was fun, and he preferred her company to theirs. Somewhere amidst her third drink, Rachael had become a little drunk, and it had altered her mood, causing her to become introspective. 'Mum is quite ill,' she said with a raspy voice. 'I'm worried she might not live much longer. After losing Dad years ago, well, it'll just be me then…' A sympathetic instinct originating in his limbic system controlled Josh's reaction. An old familiar signal, long-unused, caused Josh to reach for her hand and entwine her fingers with his own, the way they used to when they were younger. It was a knee-jerk reaction but felt so natural that he didn't even think about what he was doing. Rachael didn't flinch at his uninvited touch. She took his hand into hers as if it were a comfortable gesture the two had practised over many years. A thoughtless exercise in casual affection. But it wasn't casual. Nor was it thoughtless. Touching Rachael communicated something no words could ever pronounce. He realised that her desperation to be comforted equalled his conviction to feel needed. He could sense that just holding her hand made her feel comforted and reassured, and he was made to feel vital for the assurance his gesture offered.

'It's going to be okay.' The words came without thinking, the partnership of his words and touch unlocking a desire in each of them that neither even knew was there. She inched closer to him. It became apparent to Josh and Rachael in a way that defies logic that life felt better for each of them while they were together than it did for either of them while they were apart. She stepped closer to him again. The comfort of an old friend was a tempting thing, and perhaps she had not realised until now how much energy she had been devoting to maintaining her composure. The alcohol had dissolved her inhibitions, and his touch was all the permission she needed to go a step further.

'Thank you,' she breathed as her head came to rest on his chest. A few seconds went by as the pair stood together in an embrace among a sea of drunken strangers.

'For what?' he asked.

'For just… being you.' He felt her clench his hand a little tighter. The scent of her shampoo served to conjure memories he didn't know were still buried in the depths of his unconscious mind. Memories of her touch, of her warm, soft skin, her long desirable kisses. Josh recalled a memory that until now had been dormant.

'Hey, do you remember years ago, when we were dating, and you commented that it takes time for a new couple to learn each other's rhythms and preferences when they kiss?'

She giggled. 'So random, Josh. Yes, I remember. What about it?'

'Do you think it would still be the same for you and me as it was back then, even after all this time?'

She lifted her head from his chest and looked at him. 'How about you come with me back to my place, and we find out?'

His heart raced. He knew he should say no. That was the right thing to do. The ethical thing. But it isn't what happened. 'Yes,' he said earnestly. Her body against his felt so good. He couldn't resist wanting to feel more of it.

She raised herself up, sliding her hands over his firm chest. 'Hard to believe I still feel so comfortable around you even after all these years.'

'I feel the same—' She kissed him. It was just once, but long enough that it served as both an invitation and a summons. 'C'mon. Let's get out of here.'

There was the nagging rational brain condemning him for the unconscionable thing he was about to do. He rejected it. For once in his life, he was determined to do whatever his emotive instinct compelled. And in this instance, it was uproariously in favour of fucking Rachael Wright till his cock couldn't get hard again. Rachael needed someone, and he *wanted* to be needed. Tonight, he could be an assuring, desirable, and unapologetic man. Rachael could be vulnerable, sensitive and tentative. Each would get what they needed from the other, and for just one night, they could do as they pleased, no questions asked. It was as simple as that.

They walked down the street to find a taxi. Once inside the car, Rachael stroked his leg in the backseat, caressing his crotch, tempting him with her tantalising fingers. She crossed her legs and leaned into him. He traced the back of his fingers across the smooth skin of her freckle-covered shoulders, softly caressing her neck. That old urge had come again. A feeling of attraction so powerful it was like there were magnets beneath their flesh compelling their union. Josh prepared a text message to his wife, Anne. In it, he explained that he would be home late. Josh had always been faithful, so Anne had no reason to suspect anything was amiss. He took off his wedding ring while Rachael wasn't paying attention and tucked it away in his pocket.

Rachael swept her strawberry blonde hair over one shoulder when they were inside her apartment. It was meticulously combed, but the ends were curled with a natural wave. She unbuttoned her blouse as she led him to the place in her apartment where Josh assumed her bedroom was located. The dark makeup around her eyes gave them a distinctive and seductive quality. Her pink, inviting lips dredged up memories of the even more enticing pink lips between her legs. She kicked off her heels, and as she reached the couch, she paused to unroll her stockings, revealing the manicured black toenails of her feet, which in years gone by, he fetishised with worship. Back then, Rachael had awakened a devilish sexual appetite in him. A hunger that in their years apart had gone unfulfilled. He did things with her that he never did with another woman, even his wife. And tonight, the way she looked at him with that same want in her eyes, he knew that he could do *whatever* he wanted.

Josh could not explain what it was about Rachael Wright that caused him to experience such elevated levels of attraction. It's ineffable. Just softly touching her body and looking upon her was enough to give him an erection so hard the pulse in his pants mimicked a ticking clock. He was so eager to be inside her, so desperate for release, that the feeling of urgency made him frenzied with lust. The sensation of surrealness and detachment from reality made him feel as if he were in a dream. The edges of the world were a little blurred. His every action was automated. He was fully aware of his actions but felt unable to control them in any conceivable way. He was just… doing. Just being. He lunged at her before she reached the bedroom. He unclothed, eagerly discarding his pants and shirt and underwear. He held her hair in his hands like a horse's rein and pressed himself against her as he bent her over the couch. He spread her legs forcefully and took her. His manhood slipped inside her without resistance. Between her legs, she was virtually *dripping.* He fondled her massive breasts as he fucked her. Each thrust inside her was the most heavenly sin. His world spun out of control. Reality and memory whirled together in a hedonistic haze of debauchery. He pulled out just in time to cover her shapely arse with his hot seed. She wiped the sticky mess from her flesh as he collapsed to the couch, his body mildly fatigued with the sudden burst of exertion. She straddled him on the couch while his hands explored the terrain of her body. He touched her shoulders, combed his fingers through her hair, tracing his fingertips over her round, malleable tits. Her nipples were caressed by his tongue, and she whimpered with pleasure. Only minutes after his first ejaculation, he was ready to go again. She kissed his neck, and he cooed with delight. She loved the way he moaned when her mouth touched his skin; the sounds he made caused her to feel as if he were the most excellent lover to have ever lived. As if he were being pleasured by the lips and tongue of the Goddess Aphrodite herself. He shuddered as electric shivers coursed along the nerves of his spine. She raised herself up, reaching beneath her and took his aching, throbbing cock into her hand, guiding it in as she lowered herself onto him. For Josh, the world resonated with a dream-like quality once more. The pressure inside her vagina felt akin to his penis as he imagined the raging waters of the Red Sea did when they crashed upon the Egyptians after being parted by Moses. The sensations of pleasure as she kissed him and he touched her... Incomprehensible, unspeakable; nothing had ever felt so good. Her hands rested on his shoulders while he suckled at her breast, and she raised herself up and down his shaft. Her palms pressed against each of his cheeks, and she drew his gaze. He looked into the eyes of the succubus and found he could not resist her enchantment, nor did he want to.Every sound she made, coupled with every expression of her body, evoked a charming, potent magic that stripped him of any identity or personal history. Inside her, he was just a helpless man who urged and yearned and needed more than anything the satisfaction he craved with maddening desperation that only she could deliver. The speed with which she rode him mimicked the ferocity of their lust, and she approached her climax. Up and down, backwards and forwards upon him like the hypnotic cadence of the plastic horses on a children's merry-go-round. She achieved an orgasm, and it sounded like an orchestral crescendo, the sound of many instruments in an archaic rise to forte! And then, the wave crashes, and her pleasure recedes as water does from the shore after the collapsing of the wave as it is smoothly called back to the deep. She collapses her weight upon him, sighing breathlessly in his ear. His first and second great marital sins had come and gone so quickly there was no time at all to preserve the fine details of the occasion. That is the beauty and tragedy of imperfect memory. It makes sharp all the experiences of the moment but fails to preserve the thousand tiny details of the experience. The look in her eye, the tingling sensations that traverse his spine as her breath caresses his neck. The heat of her body, the exact shape of her breasts and the feeling of her weight upon him. These details can be remembered but never preserved completely. The experience is so spectacular that these memories are stored in all the senses. His skin remembers. As does his nose, eyes, and ears and tongue. He wants to remember it all, forever, so that he can relive the experience whenever the mood strikes. Therein lies the problem. He knows that memory will not serve. The only satisfaction is repetition. It's like *remembering* the high of a drug. It's not the same as getting high. This error of judgement invites intrusive thoughts he cannot repel. Once Pandora's box is opened, what was locked up cannot be returned to the box. He cannot merely ignore his lust for her. He cannot oppose his desire. One time, two; this is not enough to satisfy the fiendish urges that gnaw at him now like a quenchless thirst. He will be back here again; he knows it. As much as he wants to deny it, to bury it. Whatever power she had over him when they were young has not diminished with time. If anything, his original infatuation is restored beyond the measure it ever was. They fuck again and again, with the kind of stamina only known to casual lovers. With Rachael, he indulges every secret fetish, every hidden desire. She allows it because it turns her on to witness how oddly desirable she is to him. It's an ego-boost. She thinks of herself as relatively unremarkable, but he worships her nonetheless, and that makes her feel as though she wields awesome, preternatural power. Their encounter lasts well into the night until Josh's body cannot reproduce the liquids at a rate that is faster than they are being expelled. Soon, the two lovers must wake from this dream. Both find themselves wishing, at least in part, that it doesn't have to be so. That they might freeze this moment and perpetuate it so that they might exist together beyond the confines of time and constraints of their ordinary lives. With dawn comes the responsibilities of their attachments. As the saying goes, time waits for no man. It also makes no exceptions for lovers. For a time, the two lay together in comfortable silence, unwilling to end their embrace before the occasion arrives that they know they must. She holds him close while he strokes her flesh with his fingers. When Josh realises the late hour, he begins to ready himself to return home. 'This was a one-time thing,' he says soberly to Rachael with a guilty conscience starting to lend its weight to his already troubled mind. 'I'm married, Rach.' He slips his wedding ring once more to its appointed place on his finger as if simply adding or removing it does the same for the vows it represents. 'I can't see you again.'

She shrugs. 'Hey, it was fun while it lasted.' He thinks she might be trying to conceal some disappointment beneath a false bravado. Unfortunately, he can't discern whether she is being sincere or sarcastic. 'Maybe we'll run into each other again in another ten years.'

'I don't know if my body could handle it in another ten years,' he jokes. He gives her one last kiss. She takes him by the back of his neck and draws him in with her hands, lengthening the kiss, making it memorable.

'Bye, Josh,' she says, withdrawing from him, touching her own lips as if to preserve the taste of him.

'Bye, Rach.' A significant amount of time on Josh's return home is spent swearing to himself that he won't come back. This was a one-time indiscretion, he promises. Never again, he swears. But that feeling inside, that indescribable attraction he feels, is so strong. He can only hope that his willpower will prove the greater force in the contest between lust and loyalty.

Chapter Two

Wednesday, 24th November 2021 3:52 p.m

Josh sits at the desk in the cubicle he's occupied for the last four and a half years at his office, ignoring the growing list of emails he has yet to answer. He has half a dozen Statements of Advice he should be preparing for clients, phone advice to administer and meetings he's rescheduled with no intention of ever attending. He should be doing all these things, but instead, he's thinking about Rachael. It feels as though that is all he has been able to do since he encountered her nearly five months ago that night in July at the bar in the City. That night, everything changed. It threw him off his axis, and ever since, he has been adrift, moving through each day by habit alone, clinging to the rhythm of his routine. Where before he was ignorant to how directionless and uninspiring his life had become, now he could do nothing to ignore it. It was supposed to be just one night of casual sex, and he was never supposed to see her again. But, the road to hell is paved with good intentions and what often remains when something that is *supposed* to happen inevitably *doesn't* is what was genuinely preferred in the first place. It's like when an alcoholic promises to quit drinking first thing Monday morning while it's still Friday night. It's meaningless talk that seldom eventuates into truthful execution. And it allows the drunk to get hammered all weekend without the burden of a guilty conscience because, come Monday, they *intend* to stop

drinking, and that's good enough to make overindulgence all weekend totally permissible. Josh doesn't have a drinking problem; he has a Rachael problem. If he were an alcoholic, then she is his poison, and that night in July was the relapse that catalysed him right back into the throes of addiction. One week after that night in July, Josh received a message from her on social media. He stares at that first unsolicited message dated five months ago. Three words:
I miss you.
That's all it took to dissolve his resistance. She positioned the words between the red-kissing-lips emoji and a sunflower emoji. The sunflower had been a sacred object between them in their youth. Back then, it symbolised their special connection and served as a sigil of their affections after Josh presented one to her the first time they met. Their first date coincided with Valentine's Day that year, but Josh presented her with a sunflower instead of roses. Rachael swore she would never share the sunflower with another man from that time onwards. In addition to the meaning the sunflower was assigned originally, it now inherited a new meaning in the present, representing the reverence of their secret romantic affair. A one night fling was easy to conceal, but five months of infidelity made the affair dangerous. The longer it went on, the more precarious it became. Yet, after giving it some thought, it became apparent that the presence of risk urged him on, making the juices of the forbidden fruit that is Rachael Wright taste even sweeter. Before their fateful encounter at that bar, his predictable life lacked the sort of dark excitement inherent in doing the wrong thing and getting away with it. Doing the wrong thing with zero accountability gave him a kind of smug satisfaction. It made him feel as though until he met Rachael again, he had been colour blind, and after being with her the last

five months, colour had been restored to him, brightening his world, bringing with it a whole new perspective. All he had to do to keep the greyness of boredom and routine from stealing away his shine was to follow his instincts and continue to do whatever it was *he* really wanted. This was not as easy as he might have anticipated. Being selfish can be challenging for a family man. Rejecting his biological and social programming was difficult. Going against his instincts hard, yet all the more satisfying for rising above it. After years of being a husband and father, which required him to put his family's needs before his own, he had been deprived of his sense of self. For the first time since the birth of his second child, he was the happiest he had ever been. Being selfish and being with Rachael restored his sense of identity, giving him an idea of who he was before becoming a husband and a father. He swiped through some of the photos on Rachael's social media profile. The years had changed her but seeing her through rose-coloured glasses blinded him to anything that might be regarded as a defect of age. Inside this beautiful forty-four-year-old woman lives the spirit of the hedonistic hippy he knew and loved in his twenties. He spent every spare moment he could with Rachael, allocating time that should be dedicated elsewhere, like work and family, to being with her. Every time they were together, they fucked like rabbits. And it was damn good. Only, no matter how much time they spent apart, he could still taste Rachael on his lips, and no amount of showering seemed to dispel the scent of her from his skin. He's an addict. He can't get enough of her. She is a drug more addictive than any opioid and doubly as perilous. Three words and all the effort he put into convincing himself he would stay away was spoiled. Three words, one message from her, and his response to her landed him back at her apartment the very next day. Since then, hardly a day has gone by in the last five months in which he has been unable to resist the call of the siren's song.

When a lot of activity is compressed into a brief period, the impression of the experiences compacted into this time can be difficult for the present mind to record. A lot can happen in five months. In hindsight, a lot *has* happened. Josh felt he had lived more fully in five months with Rachael than he had in the last five years in his marriage to Anne. Rachael had become someone Josh characterised as a Dark Angel. Her very presence awakened something primal inside of him. It was like a signal she broadcast, or pheromones she excreted. Whatever the cause, the effect is profound. He likened it to what the ancient humans in the City of Sodom experienced when they were confronted by the presence of angelic beings – an irresistible lust. For those wretched souls of Sodom, before God smote them from the Earth, just being in the presence of an Angel instilled a lust so endearing that it compelled humans to seek them out to the very threshold of the door of the house in which the Angels were being harboured so that they could defile the heavenly beings. That is precisely how it feels for Josh. Rachael, the incandescent, Dark Angel of his dreams whose presence inspires an unnatural allure. He, the poor, hapless mortal stupefied by her magic. Together, Josh and Rachael could talk, laugh, and fuck for hours and never tire of it. He never had that with another woman, not even his wife. Yet, Angels can be equally as dangerous as they are desirable, as he was sure the parents of ancient Egyptian families in the time of Moses could attest, having suffered God's wrath when the Almighty sent one of his Angels to the homes of the Egyptians to slay the firstborn child of every household. In that regard, he felt like he was part Egyptian and part Israelite, being both parts damned and pardoned. His Dark Angel didn't deliver death unto him like the Angel did to the Egyptians. Instead, she wrought a twisted form of living in which she both sustained and alienated him, wielding a terrible influence over him until the imbalance of power in their relations heavily favoured Rachael's needs over his own. She would use her words to be cruel, tormenting him with harmful taunts. She labelled them *jokes,* the hurtful things she said to him. She masqueraded cruelty this way, discrediting him when he raised objections by alleging she meant nothing by it. There were times he was so hurt by her bullying that he felt he never wanted to see or speak to her again. Yet, whenever she sensed that she had gone too far and hurt his feelings and he would pull away from her, she would become irresistibly affectionate. She would reassure him and comfort him, soothe him and seduce him. Just like that, he was hers again. Little by little, this continued until he became dependent on her to lift him up again whenever she laid him low. She could repair the damage with a kiss or inflict more harm with a few words. She had all the power and nothing to lose. Meanwhile, he's putting it all on the line for her, risking it all to the point of total vulnerability while she remains safely guarded. He knows he should be worried about that. It would be the rational response. But he isn't. Is he crazy? The toxicity of the co-dependence she fostered failed to diminish his fondness for his Dark Angel. She had infected him, obscuring every facet of his life. At work, between meetings with clients, he doodled, writing silly poems. He sits at his desk mindlessly penning his latest little rhyme, daydreaming drearily before he realises what he's doing. He reads it over:

Dark Angel, your body tempts me; I'm turning over,
I'm twisted inside your envy green eyes.
The depths of your Autumn hair are my despair,

I have to worship you.
Your taste, your touch, it's too much…
I can't ever get enough.
You're a drug, and I'm a fiend,
Please, Dark Angel, give me sweet relief!

He screws up the paper and tosses it in the bin under his desk. Get a grip, man! He hasn't told anyone about his affair. Not even his best mates. At first, keeping the secret had been a tantalising endeavour that elevated his excitement. But, as the months went by, maintaining it had become troublesome. Concealing the affair from his wife had proven particularly challenging. Strange that Anne doesn't seem suspicious despite the late nights at work and the increasing frequency he is away from home. When she asks, he offers lame, poorly thought out excuses. At first, lying had not come naturally, but now it is effortless. She doesn't complain about his extended work hours or late-night work events. She hasn't whined once when he has forced her to alter her schedule to be present for the kids after-school commitments to pick up his slack. He knows he should feel guilty about that too. But he doesn't. Not really, because when he is candid with himself about what he wants, what he *really* wants – not what he *wishes* he could make himself *want* to want – he chooses Rachael over Anne every time. He loves his kids; he assures himself of that. But he has chosen to put his needs ahead of theirs for the first time since they were born, and he isn't regretting it. It goes against every parental instinct, but such is the magnitude of his attraction to Rachael. Anything he can do to secure more time with her, he does, risking all manner of condemnation and rapture. He checks his phone for current messages but finds nothing new from Rachael. It's not unusual; sometimes, she is quiet for a few days at a time. Absence makes the heart grow fonder, and all that. They had kept their communication to a minimum to avoid raising any red flags. He prepared a message to her that read:

Next time we're together, I think we should talk. I think I'm in love with you.

Then, he promptly deletes it. No, he thinks. Better to say nothing until he's had more time to think. Josh isn't eager for any kind of confrontation with Anne, but he feels the pressure's mounting. Something has to happen soon. Something has to give because it can't go on like this. It's not fair on Anne, and it's unfair on him too. For the first fortnight of meeting Rachael regularly, he was plagued by a guilty conscience and felt desperate to confess to Anne, believing it to be the only way to relieve himself of the awful guilt. But, as time went by and he saw Rachael more frequently, the guilt lessened until it hardly remained at all. Now, doing the wrong thing actually excites him. Regardless of how he feels, a reckoning is coming. All good things must come to an end, and there is no denying that at some point or another, he is going to have to make a decision about which woman he wants to be with before life makes a choice for him. It can't go on like this indefinitely. Too much is at risk. Josh loves his wife, or, at least, he *used* to love her and believes that he could again with some effort on his part. They have a good life together. A lovely home, stable jobs, and no squabbling. It could be worse. Conversely, now that he is with Rachael, he feels he cannot live without her, or at least doing so is not what he wants. So, he must divorce Anne and be with Rachael or end things with Rach and remain faithful to his wife. A choice equal to an epochal event. A fork in the road will change the direction of his life and that of those beloved to him forever. Naturally, there are practical considerations. Leaving Anne means dividing assets and making co-parenting arrangements for the kids. It will probably cost a fortune. He will have to endure the social fallout and all the thousand messy details a dissolved marriage creates for people. The bitterness of that choice would be a lot easier to swallow with Rachael at his side. Suppose he chooses to stay with Anne and break things off with Rachael? In that case, he worries he will secretly resent his wife for ultimately being the obstacle that prevented him from being happy with his Dark Angel.

He affirms in himself that next time he's with Rachael, he will broach the subject with her. He needs to know how *she* feels. He knows that Rachael doesn't want to lose him. She has said as much, but is her reluctance to lose him the same as wanting him to stick around for good?

Chapter Three

Friday, 10th December 2021 5:13 p.m

Just like Garfield, Josh hates Mondays. But if a man is to endure a hated day, it is a much easier burden to bear in the arms of a beautiful woman.

Josh had intended to speak with Rachael about his feelings weeks earlier, but he was too afraid. Should she not share his desires, then the party between them would come to an abrupt and premature end. He didn't want that, so he took the cowardly approach and waited. Finally, after weeks of building himself up, he summoned the courage to ask: 'What are we doing?' But he chose his moment poorly. He lowered himself from atop Rachael and came to lie beside her, breathless and naked, smiling like it was the happiest day of his life, having just ejaculated for the second time this afternoon.

'I thought that was pretty obvious,' answered Rachael as she wiped her stomach and breasts with tissues. 'Right now, I'm cleaning up the mess you made.' She cast him a wry, sarcastic smile. She discarded the tissues and began looking around the room, lifting the displaced blankets on the bed and rummaging through thoughtlessly discarded items of clothing on her bedroom floor. 'Where are my undies?'

That was a nice segue into another subject, thought Josh. 'You like to get dressed right away, don't you?' Josh stroked his hand along the ridge of her spine.

'I don't like looking at my body longer than I have to.'

'That's a shame, because I do.' He pulled at her shoulder, and with a begrudging grumble, she lowered herself down to him, snuggling up beside him. She kissed him, soft, affectionately, like a greeting. He loved the way her lips felt on his. He traced her lips with his finger. 'When I'm not with you, it's impossible to remember *exactly* how they feel. I think that's what makes it so special, you know? The fact these sensations can't be remembered exactly as they feel in the moment.'

'You're an idiot,' she said teasingly, her eyes glimmering with a certain satisfaction. She wouldn't let him know it directly, but she *loved* how he was so obsessed with her. It makes him freaky in bed, and she loves that too.

'You still haven't answered my question,' he insists.

'You caught that, huh?' If her sarcasm could be weaponised, it would be the deadliest man-killer since the atomic bomb. 'I don't know what to say. You know how I feel about you. You also know I like spending time with you and that we have fun together, can't we just leave it at that for now?' She kisses his nose and gets up. The gesture is a little pandering, but he doesn't mind. At least he had *an* answer. Perhaps not the one he was looking for, but it wasn't the worst-case scenario either. It could carry him over until the desire for more certainty arose on the next occasion.She abandons her search for her undies and instead dons a loose black dress of cheap cotton. To Josh's disappointment, the hem ends at mid-thigh. Her bong and chop-bowl are atop her tallboy dresser drawers, always filled with finely cut marijuana. She packs a cone, ignites her lighter and applies the flame to the weed. Josh watches it burn as the watery chamber bubbles and fills with smoke. She inhales the smoke into her lungs, empties the chamber, and casually returns to the bed, blowing a plume of smoke in Josh's direction as she approaches.

'It still surprises me to know you smoke weed,' he says as he waves his hand through the air to dispel the fragrant white cloud forming around him. 'How old are you now, like, forty-four? forty-five? I thought you'd be over it by now.'

'It's how I self-medicate. Honestly, I'll never stop using drugs. It gets me through the days.' She shrugs as if this explanation is all that's necessary to excuse her addictive tendencies. 'You want some?' She dangled the bong in the air in offer.

'Nah, I shouldn't. Not sure how I would explain being baked to Anne when I get home when I'm supposed to be at the office right now.'

'Maybe a client refused to receive financial advice from someone at your firm unless they could prove they knew how to have a good time…'

'By that logic, I had no choice in the matter.'

She nodded approvingly. 'You were just trying to do the right thing by the company.'

'Serving the client is the most important thing, after all. I couldn't let them down!'

But, as the banter drew to a close, he still refused, citing it was better to be safe than sorry. 'Is it?' Rachael asked with the kind of tone that indicated she was prepared to prove him wrong. 'I actually think that occasionally, it's better to be sorry than safe.' She spoke with such enticement. What was she up to? 'Sometimes, a mistake has to be made so that you know it was a mistake. Sometimes, you can't know something is a mistake before *learning* it's a mistake. You know?' The strange, circular logic of a stoner. Apparently, it's the sort of thinking comprehensible only to those of their kind. Only their kin know their mind, and damn it if stoners don't *love* company.

'How high are you, woman?' Rachael tiptoed around the room, collecting articles of clothing from the floor. She pulled a pair of jeggings over her long, desirable legs. She put a leather jacket over her cheap dress. A pair of sneakers came next. The outfit looked strange, like a child playing dress-ups. 'What are you doing?' asked Josh while he watched her get dressed.

'I want you to get high for me. High *as fuck*. Like we used to. So, I'm giving you a little incentive. For every cone you smoke, I'll remove an article of clothing.' She spins in place, a flirtatious demonstration of her form. 'You already know I'm not wearing any underwear.' She smiles a devilish grin and shyly looks away, biting her lip. He knows that *she* knows; she has him. He's already getting hard again. He's quick to react, getting up from the bed, but as he tries to take the bong from her, she withdraws. She packs the cone herself.

'Not too big,' protests Josh. When she finishes, the cone piece is filled to the rim, and she hands it to him with the lighter. It had been years since he smoked dope, but he found the weed still went down smoothly. Until it came back out – then he coughed. Rachael was seductively removing the jacket from her arms as he blew out the smoke. She made her way over to the bed as Josh packed his second cone. As the smoke of his second passed his lips, she was kicking off her shoes. The third saw the jeggings fly across the room like Alladin's magic carpet. By the time the fourth cone was cinders, she had loosed the black fabric from her body, decorating the floor with her ridiculous outfit. Smoking so many cones in such a short time had knocked Josh about. A static buzz coursed his body. Space seemed to bend before him, warping his environment in a way that made objects appear nearer or farther depending on their proximity to his person. He could hear himself laughing as he began pacing around the room, unable to remain still so long as the good vibes were electrifying his muscles. His mind was numbed and emptied of thoughts. He could see Rachael was laughing and realised that he was laughing too. What was he laughing at?

She curled her finger at him. 'Come here, mister.' He came over to her, the circus of THC parading in his bloodstream. She laughs at him as he approaches on wobbly legs. When he gets near enough, she extends her legs and pushes the flats of her feet against his chest. 'That's far enough,' she says commandingly. He takes her ankles in his hands, stroking the smooth skin of her legs. Had anything ever felt so good? Her skin was satin-covered-velvet. Now he feels that hunger again; his cock is bulging and pulsing, eager to be inside her. Like a starving animal, he's desperate for satisfaction. He spreads her legs with his hands, sighting the prize between her thighs. He tries to position himself so that his waist is between her legs, but she wriggles free of his grasp, turns herself around on all fours, plants her knees into the mattress and presents her arse to him. 'Eat me out,' she beckons. Her voice is like a dog whistle: whatever magic it possesses, he doesn't know or care to understand. He just does as he is told. He lavishes her with his tongue and fingers for over an hour while she climaxes multiple times, each earth-shattering orgasm contorting her body in writhing, sweet agony. He loves the way her body shudders violently when she has an orgasm. It's like a thunderclap roaring in every muscle. Makes him feel accomplished, proof his hard work and tenacity have their rewards. She cries out with no regard for her neighbours or anyone else who might overhear. He envies that about her. She's so liberal that she doesn't care what strangers think of her. In contrast, he is overly conscientious concerning the opinion of strangers. He feels her fingers upon his scalp, pushing his head away. His work is done. 'Your turn,' she says. He presents himself to her, and she gladly reciprocates his affections, taking her time to ensure that the experience is as fulfilling for him as it was for her. She treats his cock as something sacred, and the wet warmth of her mouth attends to his penis with the care and attention of the most delightfully sinful devotion. Her worship secures the donation of his cum in a matter of minutes. While women are capable of many multiples of orgasms that can persist for half-to-whole minutes, men are denied this pleasure. However, while Josh's orgasms are fewer and all of them concentrated into the space of only five to ten seconds, they are of such rare intensity that his whole body endures the ripple effect. For five seconds, nothing else in all the universe exists except that feeling inside. The impact on his body is like the implosion of a star, nuclear fission on such a grand scale it deafens and silences at once, rattling his bones and causing every muscle to falter. He looks down at her as his body quivers with the after-shock of his orgasm. All he can see are her smouldering green eyes like two smoky emeralds. She swallows the parting gift he left in her mouth and pulls at his wrists, urging him down to join her on the bed. For a while, they lay together quietly, listening to each other's breath as it settles to resting rate. Soon, they were talking again, reminiscing about the good old days. Josh listened as Rachael explained how she spent her time after they broke up, fifteen years earlier: 'I had a travel blog for a while. I moved from place to place, making a living by doing odd jobs and writing. I love travelling because it reminds me that there is this massive world out there and that people live in all sorts of ways, by the mode of various customs and under different belief systems. It's like, living in Australia is equivalent to living in a bubble and going abroad is stepping outside it for the first time.'

'I know what you mean,' said Josh. 'So, what countries did you visit? Did you have a favourite?'

'Hmm,' she sounded. 'Let me think. For a year at a time, I lived in the Netherlands, England, Russia and Japan. I spent a little time in Norway, Denmark and Spain, and I did tours in Germany, Italy, Greece and France. Later, I went to the United States, Mexico, Canada. Then, South East Asia; Thailand, Vietnam and Cambodia. My favourite? I loved Alaska. The snow-capped mountains and the gold-and-rust coloured leaves in the Autumn. And the Northern Lights are a hard sight to beat. It's like nothing I've ever seen. It's like seeing the breath of the cosmos.'

'That sounds amazing. Seeing all those wonderful places. I'm sure you met your share of incredible people too. So, what happened? Why did you come back here?'

'It was fun, of course! But also kind of lonely. After a while, I got sick of living out of a suitcase, never feeling like I had any reason to stay anywhere, nothing to anchor me to one spot. While some people have nothing *but* reasons anchoring them to one place all their lives and others actively seek to avoid tethering themselves down, there is a certain appeal to putting down some roots and making a place a home. Sure, ancient humans were nomadic, but they also lived in groups and settled worldwide. Eventually, I guess I just felt like I wasn't doing what I wanted to do and wasn't where I wanted to be. I needed to find my home. So, I returned to Australia and finally put the piece of paper I earned from six years at University to good use.'

'And became a primary school teacher,' said Josh flatly.

'Seems like a bit of a downgrade to me. If I could choose between teaching Aussie kids at a Brisbane school and travelling the world, seeing all there is while I'm young enough to enjoy it, I reckon I would choose the latter.'

'Y'know what they say; the grass is always greener. It might feel that way because you went another route. But, you got what you wanted, in the end too. Had your kids, got married, settled down.'

'*Almost* everything,' he said, touching her face tentatively with his fingers. 'Now, I have you, that's true.'

'Oh, you *have* me, do you?' she teased.

'You tell me.' They held each other's eyes for a moment.

'Maybe,' she said with a half-smile. 'I plead the fifth.'

He smiled. 'Don't get me wrong, having kids is fantastic; it really is. It's one of those experiences that can't be understood by talking about it. You have to experience it to really understand what it feels like to be so intimately connected to another living person. I had no idea until the birth of my son. When Lucas was born, it was like my soul was divided in two, and part of me lives in him so that we're never really apart, even when we are. I didn't think I could ever love someone so much. Then, when Suzie came along six years later, I learned how wrong I was.'

'…Why do I sense there is a *but,* coming?'

'No, it's nothing. I love my kids, and I would die for them, but I just forgot what it was like to be selfish at some point in the last twelve years. I forgot how good it can feel to do what I want without taking anyone else's feelings into consideration.'

He was lying on his back. She curled up beside him on her side and whispered softly in his ear: 'You can do that right now.' She stroked his crotch. He moaned softly as she nibbled at his ear and kissed his neck. Her hands traced his stomach and caressed his over-worked manhood until that satisfying firmness took hold. Just when he was ready to begin to seek relief for the growing discomfort of his arousal, Rachael dangled a carrot. 'I have something new I want to try.' An offer too tempting to resist.

'Anything,' he said, his interest piqued.

'I've always wanted to roleplay, like, a break in. You come in to rob me in the middle of the night while I'm sleeping, thinking I'm not home. You wake me up, and because I've interrupted you and we're alone, and you're a bad guy, you decide to seize the opportunity and… you know…'

'Take you?'

'Mmm,' she moaned. 'Yeah.'

That cheeky smile could be the death of him. He clasped his hand around her throat. 'So, you want me to be rough with you?' She closed her eyes as he squeezed her neck. 'And I'll take what I want.' He threw her legs apart and climbed on top of her. 'Whether you want to give it up or not…' He raised himself up and squeezed her neck with both hands till her cheeks were flushed with colour. She pressed her hands against his chest and tried to push him away, but the resistance only urged him to fight harder to get what he needed. He grabbed her by the hair and pulled so hard it risked ripping hair from her scalp. He drove himself inside her and began thrusting while she moaned helplessly beneath him. This was how power was transferred between them. In their social dynamic, she controlled him, but she was a submissive brat between the sheets. And they both loved their respective powers. Their final bout of intercourse lasted half an hour and produced the final orgasm for each of them for the day.

'That was… spectacular…' sighed Rachael when it was over. 'I had the feeling that you had been holding back until now, and it seems I was right. I liked that. You can be even rougher next time, too, if you want... Just use me. It really turns me on.'

'I think I can manage that.'

'Well, it sounds like a plan.' She glanced at her phone. It was getting late. 'I have end of year report cards to write up tonight, so, how about next time you come around, we try out my roleplay?'

'I'm game. What's the time?'

'It's just past six-thirty.' Josh has been with Rachael since four p.m. He couldn't be too late home tonight, or Anne would be furious. He spent all night last Friday and Saturday nights with Rachael. He couldn't repeat that this week or Anne would give him too much grief.

'I better get going. The kids will be having dinner soon, and I like to be there before Suzie goes to bed.' Reluctantly, he got changed. He dreaded leaving. Hated it. Being away from her for too long felt like going without water too long. Unnatural and dangerous.

'Wait a sec,' she said. She rolls over and reaches into the drawer of her bedside table, collecting a silver key. 'I got this cut for you. You will need it if you're going to' —she makes an air-quote gesture— 'rob me.' He looked at the key. Then, at her. He wondered what the key meant. Was it a sign she was ready to move forward in their relationship? Trusting him with a key to her place, that's got to be a big deal. She interprets his expression, and reading it, issues a harsh warning: 'Don't overthink it!'

She puts the key in his hand, and he kisses her goodbye. As he readies to leave, he takes a look around her bedroom, pointing to various valuable items. 'TV, laptop, phone... I look forward to' —he sarcastically mocks the air quotes she just produced by mimicking them— 'stealing them.'

She gets up on her knees on the bed, so she's level with his eyes. She holds him by the waist and gives him a little peck on the lips. 'As do I,' she says with a wink.

After Josh leaves, Rachael begins reviewing her students' yearly performance and grading their overall standard of achievement. It takes a couple of hours to review two terms' worth of grades for her students and compose report cards that articulate how they're performing. Of her class of thirty, twenty-five have done better than expected. She's warmed by a sense of pride, knowing her students are performing above the standard of the curriculum. It's one of the trade-offs teachers make at the end of the semester. Today is the last day of the school year and the beginning of the Christmas break. She likes to get the last of the hard work done right away to get a head start on her preparations for next semester early. She will send off the report cards in a week or so, and by then, she will have prepared the majority of her content for next term. In doing so, she gets to spend more of the holidays doing as she pleases. As for doing what she wants, right now, that's Josh Dempsey. When she finished marking and composing her reports some hours later, she ordered dinner, and it was delivered to her door in a brown paper bag with black strings. She has been enjoying her time with Josh, but the stamina of that man was exhausting! She missed him when he was gone, but occasionally she revelled in her time alone. The idea of valuing her alone time reminded her of Gun's N Roses' hit, November Rain. She sings the part of the song that describes the unique tragedy that is the loneliness of grief softly to herself while she prepares her bong. As the smoke of her first hit evaporates, she considers that at some points during her life, being alone was the most depressing thing imaginable, while during other periods of her life, being alone had been therapeutic, providing space from the complications of other people. She supposed the song got it right in more ways than one. Sometimes, being alone is a relief. And sometimes, people need someone. For her – with Josh – both are true. That's a complication. Fortunately, she has a very useful solution for complicated matters. A solution named marijuana; a beautiful green ambrosia that quietens the mind and soothes uneasy hearts. Two more very large and satisfying hits from her bong later, and she's sitting on her couch watching reality TV. Growing bored with the television saga, she starts thinking about Anne Dempsey. When she spoke with Josh about their youth earlier, a curiosity emerged in her thoughts. What was Anne like? Who was this woman that Josh chose to marry and bear his children? She taught Lucas at school but had never actually met Anne personally. She didn't even know what she looked like. She pictured Lucas and Josh in her mind and tried to fathom what the woman who dedicated half of her genes to producing Lucas might look like. When her imagination failed, she turned to technology. On her phone, she searched Anne's social media profiles. They were all set to private. Unfortunately, she wouldn't be able to stalk her photos. All she could see of Anne Dempsey was the single profile picture on her various profiles. LinkedIn, Facebook, Instagram. She had dark hair, chestnut brown with blonde highlights. Her eyes were a little darker than her hair, a tawny brown. She possessed high cheekbones and wore massive, round-rimmed glasses. Her smile was naturally warm. By all accounts, she was absolutely gorgeous. She couldn't help but wonder, what was it Josh saw in her that he didn't see in his beautiful wife? Why didn't his wife command the same level of infatuation and obsession he displayed with her? Looking at the pictures, Rachael wondered what Anne looked like when she was younger, around the time she married Josh before they had their first child. Anne must be about her age, she estimated. According to Josh, he didn't meet Anne for several years until their relationship ended all those years ago, and Rachael left to go travel overseas. He had not offered to tell the story of how they met, and she didn't much care to hear it. The less Rachael knew about Anne Dempsey, the better off she was. Her thoughts drifted, and she wondered if she and Josh had not broken up back then, might it have been her who ended up at the altar with Josh? Josh always wanted kids. That was what ended their relationship in the first place. Rachael knew by the time she reached her late twenties, she didn't want to be a mother. But, things are different now. After they parted, they both got what they wanted in their lives independent of each other, and now, fate had brought them back together again. Now that Josh had his kids, there was no relationship-killing reason preventing them from properly being together. Josh had begun to feel like family to Rachael in the last five months. She relished having him in her life. She had come back to Australia to teach and to make herself a home, and while one half of the equation was complete, she felt as she reached her mid-forties that home isn't a place; it resides in the people we choose to surround ourselves with. Maybe she *could* be with Josh now and not have to concern themselves with the time-sensitive matters of courtship that put pressure on relationships. Her biological clock had chimed for the last time already, and she had accepted that. While she didn't yearn for kids, she did feel a growing desire to share her life with someone, a lover, a companion. All she has to decide is whether she wants that or not. It should be easy. So, why doesn't it feel that way? Was she prepared to navigate the turbulent waters of Josh divorcing Anne to be with her? Is that what she wants?

It's nearly eight-thirty p.m when Rachael receives a phone call from her best friend and colleague, Elise. 'Hey, homewrecker,' teases Elise with her typical enthusiasm as Rachael answers the phone.

'Shut up,' prods Rachael.

'So, what's going on? How're things with lover-boy? It's been, what?' She pauses. 'Five months? Sick of him yet?'

'I don't know. He was here earlier and kind of put me on the spot.'

'What did he say?'

'He asked: "what are we doing?" and I didn't know what to say.'

'Good grief, what a monster!' Elise laughed. 'So, what *did* you say?' Elise's tone betrays her over-interest in the matter.

'I just said: "we're having fun."'

'Oh, my God. Babe!'

'I have been thinking about the past, the reason things ended between us in the first place. Back then, he wanted a commitment, and I wasn't prepared to commit to him, so we just sort of went our separate ways. No mess, no fuss, nobody hurt beyond repair; just an amicable ending. Now, I sense he wants the same thing again. I don't think he wants to just be casual any more. He wants us to be together.'

'What do *you* want?'

'That's the thing; I don't know.'

'So he wants to define the relationship. How do you feel about him? Do you love him?'

Ugh, Rachael hates that word. Love. It's so claustrophobically singular. Ever since the emergence of these idyllic, archetypical monogamous romances emerged in the cultural zeitgeist – the Tristan and Isoldes, the Romeo and Juliets

– romantic love is fetishised and hyped up into this disastrously precious thing that has to be reserved and devoted to just *one* person, *forever*. Rachael wasn't sure she ever felt that way about any man in her life. The do-anything-for-love kind of love. She felt a strong connection to Josh; there was no denying it. He was the kind of person who belonged to her tribe. She trusted him completely. He also knew her better than any man ever had, the *real* her, even the parts of herself that she hides from family and friends. She could be herself with Josh, which is a massive check in the plus column. If she's being honest with herself, being with Josh is also safe. He is so madly in love with her that she never fears him betraying her trust as he has done to his wife. But the question remained: did she love him?

'Things with Josh are uncomplicated,' answered Rachael.

'For you, maybe.'

'Ouch!' Elise wasn't the type to bite her tongue, and while sometimes it felt ill-considered as far as compassion goes, Rachael had to respect that very few people are capable of that degree of truthfulness. 'Well, I mean, let's be real for a second, Rach. He's cheating on his wife for you. Risking it all. The least he deserves is a bit of honesty about how you feel.'

'I know,' she sighed with resignation. 'You're right. It's just… What we have right now, it's kind of perfect. It's fun, it's secret, and it's just ours. If we take it further, it becomes so real. He would leave her for me if I asked him to. Then, that poor woman's marriage is ruined, and her kids are still young enough that a trauma like this could still impact their development. What if that happens and Josh grows to resent me? There's just a lot to consider. I don't know what's wrong with keeping things the way they are for a while. Nobody is actually getting hurt. Ignorance is bliss and all that. Leaving out the labels, avoiding putting things in a box… Just going with the flow.'

'I love you, Rach, but we're in our mid-forties, woman. You know what they say: don't waste his time and keep him on the line. Just know that whatever you decide, I'm here for you, okay?'

Rachael had never really had a girl friend like Elise. Occasionally, they bickered, but only because both were straight-shooters. She liked that about Elise. No games, no bullshit. 'Thanks, El,' said Rach.

'We still on for lunch tomorrow?' asked Elise.

'For sure.'

'All right, well, bed for me. It's nearly nine p.m, and I'm an old spinster who needs her beauty sleep. Buh-bye!'

'Night, El.'

After Rachael hung up the phone, she plugged in her charger, set it to silent mode, and lay down to sleep. As she drifted off, her thoughts trailed off into a string of possibilities. She and Josh break up. They get married. So on, and so on. Finally, she cut off the intrusive thoughts… *Hell, I'm overthinking everything, just like he does!* She smiled at that. She knew he was sensitive to being criticised as one who typically over-thinks things. His overused counter-proposal to anyone who suggested that critique was that most people are guilty of *under*-thinking. 'He can be such an idiot,' she says to herself thoughtfully. 'Maybe I *do* love that idiot…' Before long, she is asleep.

She wakes, disturbed by a sound that shouldn't be present in the middle of the night. Even in a half-awake state, she recognises the distinct sound of a door being opened and closed in her apartment. She checks her phone; it's twelve forty-five a.m. At first, she panics. Fear causes her to tremble and fret, but then the fog of sleep lifts and she remembers that she proposed this very scenario to Josh just hours ago. A home invasion. A burglar in the night. She, the helpless victim. He, the criminal intruder. She just hadn't expected him to return *tonight*. It was typical of him to take the initiative. The fact he couldn't stay away for even one night was somewhat tantalising. She was already feeling aroused. She could hear him inside the apartment, his vain attempts to step lightly spoiled by the quiet of the night. She could see the light of a torch in the crack at the bottom of her bedroom door. Footsteps approach from down the hall, the sound growing louder as he approaches her room. The light grows brighter, the sound of his steps louder. Her heart is beating fast, and her skin feels hot. She's anxious. Excited. Curious. A tingling sensation of fear and arousal morph together to create an erotic knot in her stomach. The door opens slowly. A faceless shadow enters the room. The silhouette of a man. His clothes are all black, he wears long trousers and a long-sleeved top that covers his torso to the neck. His face is masked by a balaclava, his hands gloved. He is a menacing sight. She shields her eyes from the bright light of his torch as he enters the room and gasps. 'Who are you!? What do you want?'

The man raises a gloved finger to his lips. 'Shhh…' He switches off the torch, and for a few seconds, while her eyes adjust again to the dark, she is temporarily blind.

'Please, take whatever you want, just don't hurt me…' She tucks the covers up under her chin in an act intended to convey her vulnerability, feigning fear. The shadow moves a little further into the room, closing the door behind him. He moves cautiously as if every purposeful step is made to savour the moment. He finds a pair of her underwear hanging on the side of her dirty clothes basket. He takes them, and Rachael hears him sniffing them audibly, moaning with subtle satisfaction under his breath. 'Oh my God, you *are* a freak...' she teases, momentarily breaking character. Still, she won't give him the satisfaction of openly admitting how turned on his freakiness makes her. The shadow moves faster now, realising the opportunity that has come unexpectedly. A simple burglary has become so much more... He pockets her worn underwear, takes her bed covers into his hands, tossing them aside. Rachael reflexively covers her lower body by crossing her legs and pulling down the loose-fitting T-shirt that barely covers her lower half. A gloved hand reaches through the dark and tentatively strokes her arm. 'Wow, you really went the extra mile, huh?' she says about his outfit. 'The balaclava and gloves are a nice touch... If I knew we were going to dress for the occasion, I might have had time to coordinate an outfit...' Josh gestures quiet, pressing his finger to his lips with one hand. He takes her by the arm and forcefully rolls her to her side with the other. She struggles against him as part of the roleplay. Her resistance forces him to press his weight down. He slides into the bed beside her, holding her arms at her side. He pushes his front against her back. She notices he smells different. Is it a different cologne? He must have worn something new to bring multiple dimensions to the roleplay. She would never have thought of that kind of detail herself. She was impressed with the lengths he had gone to make this real for her. His hands are ravaging her flesh. The gloves feel strange against her, cold, unlike the warmth of his skin but fitting for the pretend hands of an intrusive stranger. She continues to pretend to struggle against the intruder making a little effort to bring some authenticity to the scene, as he has. He becomes more aggressive. His hands run low, seeking to remove her underwear. His free arm coils around her neck and squeezes lightly, a non-verbal cue that he is the one who has the power in the situation. She manages to slip her arm underneath herself and leverages it to roll over and face him. With his chokehold loosened, he grips a hand to her throat. 'Well, Mr Burglar, are you going to take me or just play with me?'

'I'll make you mine,' says an unfamiliar voice. This time, her panic is real.

'What the fuck,' she says, looking into a pair of wild, menacing eyes that she *knows* do not belong to Josh.

'Mine forever,' says the intruder with a deep baritone voice distinctly different from Josh's slightly higher register. She tries to roll away from him, but he has her by the throat. He squeezes it tight with one hand. She scratches at him as he positions his other hand upon her neck. He's choking her with both, and she cannot draw a breath. Her muscles are tense as the natural adrenaline levels in her bloodstream spike. This isn't right. She tries to beg him to stop, but she cannot produce the word. This isn't how it's supposed to be. It's wrong! She wants it to be over. Rachael's hands claw wildly at her attacker's face, scratching and assaulting wherever she can land a blow. Thoughts become vaguer as she is deprived of oxygen. It's real; she's fighting for her life. Absent of her will, she's reacting as her body fights to survive. She lashes out violently, but he is so strong. He tries to draw himself away from her blows but cannot withdraw from her striking distance when they are this close. With sudden and ferocious force, he clambers on top of her, straddling her chest, choking her now with full force. She feels his weight on top of her, crushing her chest. He's so heavy, and she can't breathe! Now that he is on top of her, there is nothing she can think to do that will free her. There is no escape. She knows it, some synapse firing in her oxygen-starved brain knows the truth, but the body acts independently of the mind, fighting and clawing for every second of life. Her hands are fashioned uselessly around his wrists, trying to clear his hands from her neck, but it is no use. She can't move them. She beats against his arms uselessly. He continues to squeeze. Some final instinct takes hold of her dying brain. The mask. She tears at it wildly with the last strength she can summon and manages to skew it from his face.

'You!' she tries to cry, but the words won't come out. Her peripheral vision darkens. Her limbs feel heavy. A grey curtain encroaches her vision as the pain in her neck recedes. She is terrified. Her eyes flutter as awareness fades. She feels nothing, *becomes* nothing.

Her body is still. Her dead eyes are wide and startled, gawking at a face known to her that gazes down upon her with morbid fascination and insidious satisfaction.

Chapter Four

Saturday, 11th December 2021 6:00 a.m

Anne Dempsey's life is a perfectly balanced routine. Her full-time job as a Business Analyst Consultant keeps her busy, but she liked to joke that a husband and two kids keep her exhausted and broke. The work she completes at her job is about studying metadata and using it to inform predictions about trends. She assesses the micro and leverages that information to inform judgements about the macro. Over the years, she has refined this skill to the point that her ability to recognise the patterns that present before the success of a business teeters and begins to fail border on rivalling the supernatural power of psychic premonition. She is so good at what she does that it could appear to an untrained eye from an outside perspective that what she does is magical. But all magic is an illusion. She is no shaman of data; she is merely one who excels in understanding how specific patterns inevitably result in very particular outcomes. Lacking the knowledge that she harnesses to exercise her duties to the uninformed, the total accuracy of her predictions concerning future fortune or misfortune seem miraculous. Yet, sadly, her wizardry as an analyst does not extend to her personal life. If it did, she might have had some chance at predicting her own doom, looming just beyond the borders of her own personal horizon. Doom in the form of the unique brand of insanity that arises from being disillusioned about the distinction between being happy and not being *aware* of being unhappy.

The passage of her life is a cycle centred around a repetitive theme. She works at the office, then returns home where she washes and cooks and keeps the house tidy for a lazy, unthankful husband, a messy, pre-teen boy and her little girl. Then, she does a tour of duty as everybody's therapist for the evening before succumbing to absolute exhaustion. At the end of a hard day, karma rewards her selflessness with one measly hour of solitude she has to herself each night before she succumbs to exhaustion and has to go through it all again the next day. An hour to herself out of the twenty-four in the day means there is an ever-increasing list of books she will never have time to read. TV shows her colleagues are binging every night and yapping about at work as if literal gold is being spun from their LCD screens that she never has the time to catch up on. There are five hundred overdue orgasms her husband has failed to generate for her. Vacations that will never be booked. These, and a thousand other tiny ungranted wishes, unacknowledged desires and ignored needs continue collecting, and yet, although she would be well within her rights to, Anne never complains about the sacrifices she makes for her family. She is dutiful, before all things. She drags herself through each day, a mother, a wife, a number on some company's payroll, never experiencing anything out of the ordinary. Every tomorrow is as easily predictable as it was today because it is just like all the yesterdays that came before. A recurring dream haunts her nights when she sleeps, imposing a feeling upon her waking hours that weighs heavy on her soul. She is on an aeroplane during the dream, seated beside a window. She peers through the little glass square, but in the place of blue sky and white cloud, she witnesses moments of her own life represented in fleeting visions. She watches her kids being born again and observes all the wonderful moments she cherishes so profoundly in their upbringing; their first steps and first words. She watches herself marry her husband, reprising her role as the bride with all the hyper-excitability accompanying that day. Each night is a different slide from the same story. Her story. The tale of how she became a mother and wife and found success in her career. She gained so much in becoming a wife, a mother, and a mentor in her workplace that it was so easy not to realise that she was also surrendering parts of herself that could not be retrieved once lost. Her story is not unique, or for that matter, very interesting. It doesn't contain heroes or villains; it isn't tragic or inspiring; it is plagiarised word for word from the pages of humanity's history as we rose from the depths of the ocean, descended the treetops and clawed our way from the dark hovels of our caves. Day by day, year after year, from the time of the primordial Earth to antiquity, Anne does as all those did before her – she survives. Sadly, few recognise the difference between surviving and living. Life was never meant to be easy, but that does not infer that it was designed to be altogether hard either. Every night on the plane, the flight she takes is smooth. There is no turbulence because the weather is fine, so the passage between the origin and destination goes uninterrupted. Each night she falls asleep, resumes her place in the same seat and watches the reel of her memories through the same window. And when she wakes, the feeling her dream incites is the same. She yearns to disembark a plane that always takes off but never lands. She hungers for variety, for change, because nothing out of the ordinary ever happens.

    That is how she was so easily caught off guard when it finally did.

    She wakes at six a.m, minutes before her alarm is due to

sound, same as always, even on weekends. Her first sensation is a feeling of frustration. She thinks: what evil did I do in a past life to deserve to be punished this way? She wishes her body would be merciful, just once, and allow her a sleep-in. Her next thought: What day is it? But, given that today is as unlikely to be any different than yesterday, does it make any difference?

She had the dream again, and her heart ached because of it. That feeling of sameness clings to her like wet clothes. It makes her feel heavy and cold. Next to her, Josh is still sleeping, a low, rumbling snore rattling from his throat. She retrieves her phone from her bedside table. Half a dozen emails in her inbox remain unread from yesterday. She scrolls through the mailbox, rubbing her eyes. Client email, client email, spam, spam… She blinks, thinking what she saw must have been a mistake. She collects her eyeglasses and looks again.

That feeling of sameness is dispersed. In its place, the most poignant shock of her life. She rereads the email's subject line: **Your husband is having an affair.** The sender's address is rachael.wright@edu.qld.gov.au. Her heart feels as though it has been petrified. She can feel it sinking from the place it should be in her chest. She realises that she has been holding her breath and exhales. Is this a joke? She reads the subject line ten times, daring herself to open the email. Josh is still snoring. She opens it and reads:

You probably already know my name. I teach at the school your son Lucas attends, Claremont College. I'm writing to confess that your husband and I have been having an affair for the last five months. I don't know you, not personally, but I know that you deserve the truth. Josh was with me last night, but it's over now. Your husband and I will not see each other again. I made a horrible mistake, and I don't expect you to forgive me for what I have done to you.

I suppose my religious upbringing still maintains some influence over me now because as I write this, I am reminded of something my Pastor used to say when I was young: Only the truly repentant at heart can enter God's Kingdom. Those who feign remorse for the sake of exoneration should live in fear of the Almighty's judgement. The full extent of His wrath is reserved for those who outwardly appear humble and contrite but in their hearts, which cannot be concealed from Him, are false. I have done the wrong thing, and I know it because they say a guilty conscience cannot rest. While sleep eludes me, I have been reading from the Bible when I found this passage which I think appropriately encapsulates my pertinence:

Anne clicked on the hyperlink Rachael copied into the email, which directed her to a website in her phone's internet browser. There, highlighted, was a passage from the Book of Romans:

To set the mind on the flesh is death, but to set the mind on the Spirit is life and peace.

The email confession concludes with:

As you might suspect, you can see why this passage resonates with me. I have been indulging my bodily urges, and it has caused me only grief, so I seek respite in the hopes of earning some measure of peace by giving my attention to more virtuous endeavours. I know that is of little consolation for my misdeeds, and nothing I can say could satisfactorily convince you that I sincerely intend to make better choices from this time on.

I deeply regret my part in hurting you, and I am very sorry.
May you someday forgive me,
Rachael Wright

As she finishes reading, the home wifi signal cuts out. Anne reconnects her mobile to the router and refreshes her emails. She reads the email from Rachael again, and a third time and a fourth. Josh will wake up soon, so, after the fifth read-through, she locks herself in the ensuite bathroom of their bedroom so that she doesn't have to immediately present a false pretence when he wakes. She needs time for this to sink in. And for that, she needs to be alone. She turns on the shower and sits naked on the shower floor, allowing the water to rain down on her head. In nightmarish fantasies, she had imagined a scenario like this before. In the fantasy, having learned of her husband's infidelity, she imagined herself enraged with a fury so fierce she could collapse mountains with it. She imagined herself exploding with rage. She expected tears, anger and heartbreak. She could never have anticipated that what she felt instead of these things was relief. How is it that she could feel relieved? The thought troubled her deeply. It isn't the natural reaction. It's not what someone in her situation is *supposed* to feel. She looks at her hands and scrunches them into fists, squeezing them until her knuckles are white. She mashes her teeth together, gritting them with as much pressure as she can muster. She frowns and flares her nostrils, trying to stimulate her body into producing the reaction that is supposed to come naturally. She wants herself to get mad! But, the harder she tries to force it, the more distant it feels. None of it feels right, so she relaxes her body and begins to really contemplate her reaction. She loved her husband, so why, of all things, did she feel relieved to discover he has been unfaithful? The realisation dawned on her almost as soon as she had finished asking herself the question. She *loved* her husband. Past tense. She isn't *in love* with him. It seems that time had changed Anne and Josh, and neither of them had the insight to apprehend the changes. Once, Anne had a conscientious, thoughtful, sincere, and romantic husband. In the beginning and for some time after their marriage, things had been good. But, somewhere along the way, the man she married transformed into a skilled liar, capable of such radical deceit that he was able to conceal a five-month-long affair. And why? What reason could he have to do such a thing? To spoil their marriage and ruin her life with such a betrayal? Rachael's confession revealed to Anne the patterns in her life that signalled her discontent that she failed to recognise out of ignorance of the subject matter. She comprehended that somewhere along the way, with every occasion her husband neglected to identify and satisfy her needs, she fell out of love with Josh. Only, she wasn't aware of the change in herself. The routine of her life had made her ignorant of her own feelings and numbed her to the truth. When she inspected her emotions, she understood that what she felt for Josh was the echo of love, in all ways an identical mimicry of the passionate feelings she once embraced and cherished. She remembered what it *felt* like to be in love and had been carrying on as if she still was. Truthfully, the love she once had for her husband only exists now as a memory. Something close to the real thing but not entirely genuine. What concerned her now is how long into perpetuity she might have continued carrying on with her routine life while totally oblivious to the disservice she was doing herself by continuing to allow herself to deny that she wasn't happy or content had Rachael Wright's confession not discharged the spell that ordained she remain unconscious to her own happiness?

Chapter Five

Sunday, 12th December 2021 7:20 a.m

Anne winced at her husband as he stood with his back to his family at the kitchen bench preparing Sunday morning pancakes. Look at him, she thinks. Carrying on as if he's done nothing wrong. Two days ago, he was screwing a teacher from their son's school. Now, he's flipping pancakes and pretending to be the perfect family man. Ever since Anne read the email Rachael sent her yesterday morning, the pieces of a puzzle she hadn't even recognised existed had begun to come together. All the late nights Josh claimed to be working on work projects at the firm. The meetings he scheduled at clients' houses after hours. Most of the financial advice Josh gives is over the phone. If an appointment *is* conducted in person, it would be at the office, not their private residence. Five months, he's been getting away with it. Almost half a year, lying to her face, betraying the sanctity of their marriage. And he makes it look so easy! 'There you go, Suzie-Q,' he says to their six-year-old daughter as he dumps a golden circle pancake on her plate. 'Do you want butter or syrup with it?' Suzie screws up her face at her father. 'Right, right. Of course, syrup. I shouldn't even have to ask!' He squeezes the syrup bottle, lathering a spiral of thick, golden sugary goodness onto his daughter's pancake. Josh snatches his son's mobile phone from his hands.

'Hey!' Lucas protests.

'Phones away at the table, son. Mealtime is family time.' Twelve-year-old Lucas sighs loudly and begins devouring his pancakes. 'Are you chewing them or just opening your gob and breathing them in?' teases Josh. Suzie giggles fondly at her big brother.

'Shu-uh,' says Lucas to his father with his mouth full. Josh smiles at Anne and bites into a bacon strip. She forces a smile back. She can't let him catch on that she knows yet. Not in front of the kids. There will come a moment when she can confront him about the affair. She wants to look him in the eye when she does it, but she's genuinely afraid of what she'll see there when she does. He sits down at the table, casts a smile at Anne and chews on a bit of bacon.

'So, what do you think Santa is going to bring you for Christmas this year, Suze?'

Suzanne perks up at the sound of Santa's name. She raises her fork in the air like some turn of the century dictator. Her eyes glance to the ceiling as she considers her answer. 'A horsey,' she declares first. 'With a pink mane! Annnd' —she squints as if the process of thinking is superbly tricky at such an early hour— 'a dress just like Anna's.'

'Who's Anna?' Josh looks to Anne for help. His daughter frowns at him with displeasure.

'Anna, Daddy!'

Anne clarifies., 'A character from her favourite movie.'

'Oh, I see. Okay. So, a horse and a dress. What will you name your horsey, then?'

'Ummm, I will name him…' Her eyes gaze up at the ceiling while she considers the question. 'Olaf!'

'Let me guess,' says Josh. 'Another character from your favourite movie?'

Suzanne smiles her wicked little grin. 'Yes, Daddy, gosh. Don't you know!'

'Yeah, Dad,' mocks his twelve year-old son, Lucas. *'Don't you know?'*

'That's mighty cheeky from a son who has been bugging me about Santa delivering him a new gaming computer this Christmas. Remind me, Suzie-Q, how long has your brother been telling Daddy he wants Santa to get him a new computer for?'

'Forever,' answers Suzie with trademark exaggeration and perfectly characterised roll of the eyes.

Josh squints at his troublesome son. 'Mm-hmm. *Forever* sounds about right.' Lucas smirks with a wayward glance, gobbling up the remainder of his breakfast. Anne watches it all unfold. Why couldn't the time they spend together always be like this? Everyone is cheerful. There are no tears. Nobody is speaking harshly. It's perfect. Why would Josh want to throw this away?

There is an unexpected knock on the door that disturbs Anne's contemplation. Josh glances down the hall at the front door with a puzzled expression. Anne looks at her wristwatch. It's barely past seven a.m. 'Who could it be this early?' she asks.

'I don't know, babe, but you go ahead and finish your breakfast, and I'll go shoo them away.' Josh turns to his small daughter. 'Maybe after breakfast, you and I can watch this favourite movie of yours together, huh?'

'Yay,' says Suzie excitedly. 'Yes, okay!' She gets herself down from her chair at the table and scurries off to the lounge room. 'I'll get it ready, Daddy!'

Josh scruffs his boy's hair as he gets up and leaves the table. 'Dad!' complains Lucas, who immediately begins trying to repair the damage his father caused. Josh opens the door of his home to find two uniformed police officers on his threshold. There is a man and a woman. The woman has blonde hair tied up underneath her police cap. She stands half a foot shorter than Josh. She possesses a blunt nose, a lower lip double the size of her upper, and intense, narrowed eyes, lending her a scrupulous expression. Ironic, for a cop, thinks Josh.

'Good morning,' says the lady officer. 'My name is Senior Sergeant Price. This is Constable Rogers,' she gestures to the box-chested, square-faced brute at her side who stares at Josh with a pensive expression. 'Are you Joshua Dempsey?'

'Yes?' Josh's preposition carried a note of uncertainty. He looks back down the passage of his hallway and shelters the police from the view of his family with the front door. 'What's this about?'

'We're from the Missing Person's Unit. We would like to speak with you regarding Miss Rachael Wright. She was reported missing yesterday. Sergeant Price referenced a small notepad with illegible scribble scrawled over the pages. 'We were told that you had been with Rachael at her apartment on Friday afternoon. Can you confirm this?'

'Um,' fumbled Josh.

Anne noticed Josh close over the door to conceal what was going on. She strode down the hall. 'Is everything all right?' she asked, appearing at her husband's side.

'It's fine, babe,' he said coolly. 'Go back inside and finish your brekky.'

Anne ignored Josh. She directed her question to the female officer. 'What's this about?'

'We're following up on some leads regarding a notice we received concerning a missing person. Are you Mr Dempsey's wife?'

Josh held his forearm in front of his wife, preventing her from getting closer to the officers. 'I'm sorry, Officers, but I don't know anybody by that name. I'm afraid I can't help you.'

Josh attempted to close the door, but Constable Rogers pushed back, inserting himself upon the threshold. 'Mr Dempsey,' he said, 'might we have a moment with you in private?' He cast a cautious glance at Anne. Anne heard Suzanne's little footsteps approaching.

'Daddy, come watch Frozen with me!'

He put his hand on top of his daughter's head and turned her around. 'In a minute, darling.' Suzanne peered up at the officers outside her door. 'Hello, Mr Police Man,' she said to the Constable. The imposing Constable smiled and gave a little wave. Suzanne laughed shyly, covering her face in her hands and scurried off back to the lounge room. 'Hurry up, Daddy.'

Josh touched Anne gently on the arm. 'Anney, would you mind going with Suzie? I'll be there in a minute.' Josh stepped outside the door to avoid further interruptions and secure his privacy, closing it behind him.

Anne lingered for a second by the door, listening intently to what was being said on the other side. 'A friend of Miss Wright's was supposed to meet her for lunch yesterday, but Rachael did not show up,' said Sergeant Price. Anne heard the name. Rachael Wright. She hovered at the door for another few seconds, desperate to catch any more details as she eavesdropped on the conversation. Sergeant Price continued: 'Her family have looked for her at her apartment but did not find her there either. She has not contacted anyone since Friday. You are the last person known to have been with her before her family reported her missing yesterday. Do you have any idea where Rachael could be, Mr Dempsey?'

Oh my God, thinks Anne. Josh *wasn't* the last person she contacted. Anne looked at her email inbox on her phone. It was still there; Rachael Wright's email confession. It had been received to her inbox at 3.16 a.m Saturday morning. She had woken at six a.m and read it soon after waking. Now, she's missing? Anne wondered: could the guilt and shame of Rachael's conduct be so grave to her that she would just leave town without a word? Leave her job, her apartment, her family? Would she leave Josh behind without saying anything too?

Suzanne reappeared, taking her mother by the hand and leading her off to the lounge room. 'Come on, Mummy, we will wait for Daddy together.'

Anne followed her daughter into the living room. Josh's interaction with the police continued. 'I have no idea where she could be.'

'So, you *do* know her,' put in Constable Rogers.

Damn it, thinks Josh. 'What time were you with her Friday?' asked Sergeant Price. What should he say? Lying to his wife about his affair with Rachael was one thing, but the police? Was it a crime to lie to them?

'We were just working.'

'Oh, you're also a teacher?'

'No,' answered Josh. 'Not exactly.' He supposed financial education technically constituted being a *kind* of teacher. The same way a financial counsellor is a psychologist, he thought with self-deprecating sarcasm.

Officer Price frowned with disbelief. 'So, what kind of work were you doing together, at her apartment, on a Friday night?' Josh resents the mockery that results from her accentuation of each of the three points.

'I'm a financial advisor,' said Josh. 'I was giving her…'

'Financial advice?' Price's question practically drips with sarcasm. Senior Sergeant Price stepped close to Josh and spoke to him at a lower volume for the sake of discretion. 'I understand that this could be a *sensitive* matter for you, Mr Dempsey.' Her eyes glanced towards the door and his family contained therein. 'But if you're involved in a relationship with Miss Wright, and you have any information on where she could be located... Well, the nature of your relationship with Miss Wright is none of our business, Mr Dempsey. I just want to be able to do my job. I'm only interested in securing Miss Wright's whereabouts. Can you help me?'

Sensing Joshua's hesitancy, Officer Rogers interjected, 'Miss Wright's family has lodged an official missing person's report with us, Mr Dempsey.' Josh observed a nosy neighbour next door parting the curtain to spy on the scene unfolding. He shuffled uncomfortably on the spot.

'What Constable Rogers is trying to convey, Mr Dempsey, is that it is within our power to arrest you for questioning in this matter. Now, I would prefer that you aided us willingly. I'm sure you would prefer that than having us place you under arrest to bring you down to the station for questioning, wouldn't you agree?'

It was a threat being levelled against him, and it weighed heavy on Josh. Where the hell could Rachael have gotten to? He didn't need this kind of trouble. How was he going to explain this to Anne! 'Look, it's not entirely out of character for Rach to go off-grid. She's done it before. She always turns up a few days later. I'm sure she's fine, and she'll resurface soon.'

'I certainly hope so, Mr Dempsey. Be that as it may, I still need to take a statement from you. Can you come down to the station?'

'Now?' he looked at the door and then back at the cops. 'I was going to watch a movie with my daughter.'

'It'll still be there when you get home,' inserted Price flatly.

What other choice did he have? 'Um. Yeah. Okay. I'll take my own car, though.' Price nodded, signalling her agreement. 'Fine. Just let me get the keys and give me a sec to let my wife know what's happening.' He went back inside to an eerily quiet home. Clearly, Anne had done her best to listen in discreetly without making it obvious she was eavesdropping. He found her in the kitchen, tidying up the table. Lucas was still at the table, paying no attention to his surroundings, texting on his phone. 'Lucas, would you give your mother and I a moment, please? Go watch some TV for a minute.'

'What are the cops doing here, Dad?' the boy asked.

'Nothing mate, it's nothing. Give your mother and I a second, would you, son?'

Lucas shrugged and sulked off out of the room. Suzanne was already in the lounge room singing along to the TV while waiting for Josh to join her. 'Are you coming, Daddy?' her little voice calls out from the other room.

'In a second, sweetheart,' Josh called back. When he was alone with his wife, he spoke the first lie that came to his mind. 'Listen, Anne, the cops want to talk to me about a colleague from work who has gone missing. They want me to come down to the station to give a statement.' Josh's wife eyed her husband warily. She *knows* he's lying. How can he be so casual about it? Who is this man!

'I heard you tell the police you were giving this client financial advice on Friday night,' said Anne, preparing a snare for her husband.

'Yeah.'

'At her apartment?'

'Yep.' Anne wondered, how is he keeping a straight face? It only served to infuriate her. How he could be so cavalier about the whole thing? Smug bastard.

'Pretty unorthodox to be giving advice to a client, in their home, after hours, on a Friday, isn't it, Josh?' Josh stared at his wife, who leered at him. Neither said anything to the other. What felt like whole minutes went by. Anne finally broke the stalemate. 'I *know,* Josh,' she boasted, crossing her arms over her chest. 'The cops are showing up at *our* door to ask about some random, platonic client? C'mon. I wasn't born yesterday.' Josh stepped forward in an attempt to offer an apologetic hug. Anne retreated. 'Don't,' she said, holding her hand towards him like a shield. 'All these late nights. The distance that's been festering between us. This is the reason. You're having an affair, aren't you?'

'No!' Josh's protest was too defensive to legitimise his answer. He downcast his eyes shamefully. 'I mean, it's not like that. Look,' he said, rubbing his forehead, 'can we talk about this later? The police said if I didn't come willingly, they could arrest me for questioning. I don't want the kids to have to see that, not to mention the bloody neighbours. Mrs Benheim next door was peeping through the window while I was talking to the cops and had a good, long gawk, so you know she'll be stirring up trouble around the neighbourhood.' He attempted to touch his wife on the shoulder, a simple gesture of assurance, but she shrugged him off. 'I won't be long, all right? I'll come home soon. We can talk about everything then, okay?'

His wife appeared deaf to his words. She simply nodded with vacant, empty eyes. After reading Rachael's email, Anne wondered how her husband would react when confronted. She imagined a variance of reactions. She didn't anticipate that her own response to the knowledge of the affair and her husband would be identical. Both were in denial. Anne's was self-imposed, and Josh's was delusional. She had been too busy and tired to acknowledge it until she got the email from Rachael. She had delayed a confrontation with Josh about the changes in his behaviour and the obvious signs of neglect out of self-preservation. Nobody wants confirmation of infidelity in their marriage. The path of least resistance was voluntary ignorance, which is essentially no different from being in denial. 'We will talk about this when I come home,' promised Josh as he collected the car keys from the key rack and made his way to the garage. Anne stood motionless, like a stunned fish, and watched him go. It was all so real now. There was nowhere she could hide from this any more. Lucas, who had been listening to his parents argue from a safe distance, made his way back into the kitchen after his father left.

'Everything all right, Mum?' Anne's reverie was momentarily cut off. Her son's question gave her a poignant moment of lucidity.

'Yes, darling,' she lied with a convincing soothing tone packed with motherly tenderness. 'Everything is fine. Your dad just had to go out for a while. How about you and I go and watch Frozen with Suzie for a bit, eh?'

'Oh, c'mon, Mum,' complained Lucas. 'I'm too old for that crap.'

'So am I, Lucas,' teased Anne, 'but let's just do it for Suzie, okay?'

'Fine,' Lucas grunted with defeat.

'Good boy. Come on.' She placed her hand on her son's shoulder, and together they went to the lounge room where Suzie was already watching the latest episode of The Wiggles.

'Where's Daddy? He said we would watch Frozen,' complained Suzie.

'Daddy had to go talk to the policeman,' explained Anne.

'But he can watch it with you when he gets home.' Anne sits on the couch with her six-year-old daughter beside her. Suzie convinces Anne and Lucas to watch Monsters Inc for the fourteenth time this month. She watches Suzie's face light up when the animated characters come on screen. Joy is such a splendid thing to see in children. It comes easily for them. Were it only so for grown-ups. Suzie tries to quote the character's lines, having memorised some of the script, but her vocabulary remains too stilted to get it just right. Anne stares at the screen, the images and sounds nothing but white noise. Since she read Rachael's email, she had been protecting her emotional vulnerabilities inside a mental fortress of her own making. She constructed the walls of her castle from self-assurance. Every brick was bound to the next by the spirit of encouragement she preached to herself. She introduced the warmth of self-kindness with doubt-proof insulation in the ceilings. For a day, her inner castle had withstood the torrential rains of heartache and sheltered her from the harsh, bright light of truth. A question echoes through the halls of the crumbling castle, penetrating every chamber: Why was my best not good enough? The beckoning question torments. It is an invasive overture, the chords of which resound in every act of the play that is her life at this juncture. She stares with vacant, unblinking eyes at the TV screen, while inside, the hurt cascades like waves colliding with the rocky bluffs beneath her fortress with astonishing violence. The invaders, called Loss and Ruin, have arrived at her gates with the battering ram. *Crash, crash, crash.* How long can she hold out before the gates of her castle splinters and collapses under the relentless hammering of her impending doom? Her defences were not impenetrable, nor her fortress impregnable. The conquering of her stronghold had not come from enemies outside the gates but from within, betrayed by her King, of all people! And the trumpets on the parapets sounded the call that the castle is fallen. God save the Queen.

Chapter Six

Sunday, 12th December 2021 7:46 a.m

Senior Sergeant Price sat with Joshua Dempsey inside one of the quiet interview rooms in the South Brisbane Police Station. Mr Dempsey did not object to having their conversation recorded while conducting her interview. 'For the record,' began Officer Price, 'the time is 7:46 a.m on Sunday, 12th December 2021. Present is Mr Joshua Dempsey, who has consented to be interviewed concerning a Missing Person's notification received on Saturday, December 11th, 2021. The person identified in the notice is Miss Rachael Wright, aged forty-four, of Spring Hill. The notification was submitted by her mother, Mary-Lou Wright of Indooroopilly.' Price looked across the table at Josh. 'Mr Dempsey, please acknowledge for the record that you understand you are not under arrest at this time and that you have agreed to participate in this interview voluntarily.'

'Uh, yeah. I understand,' said Josh in an uncomfortably matter-of-fact manner.

'Could you please begin by describing the nature of your relationship with Miss Wright?' Josh hesitated. He stared at the recording device on the table like it was a venomous snake poised to strike. He gestured that he wanted the recording to be stopped. Price switched it off.

'So, just to get things straight, nobody will hear this, right? I mean, my wife won't learn about anything you record on this thing?' asked Josh.

'The only occasion that this recording would be heard by your wife is if it were to be presented as evidence in court.'

Josh bit at his lower lip and frowned. 'And, why would it appear in court?'

'Well, for instance, if evidence became available that linked you to Miss Wright's disappearance and you were charged with an indictable offence, this recording might be presented in court at a trial.' That sounded heavy-handed, thought Price. She tried to correct her course, being mindful the point wasn't to scare the guy but to get him to open up: 'Look, the bottom line is, if you had no involvement in Rachael's disappearance, then I can assure you that your wife will never learn of what you say here today.'

'Okay,' said Josh feeling reassured. 'Then let's get this over with.' Price switched on the recorder. Josh spoke. 'Rachael and I are friends.'

'Is that a platonic friendship, or are you involved in a romantic relationship?'

'Yes.'

'Sorry, Josh, just to be clear for the record, is that "yes" indicating your relationship is platonic or that you are romantically involved?'

'Oh, sorry,' said Josh, shifting uncomfortably in his chair. 'I meant that we're romantically involved.'

'Is there a sexual component to your relationship?'

Josh raised his brow disconcertingly. 'Is that relevant?'

'Yes.' But she wouldn't tell him why.

Josh shifted uncomfortably in his chair. 'Then, I suppose, yes: we're sexually involved.'

Sergeant Price scribbled a note on her notepad. 'How long have you been involved?'

'Well, we dated for a while, years ago. But we ran into each other back in July one night and kind of took up again then. So, like, five months or so.'

Price copied down the information on her pad. 'When was the last time you saw Miss Wright?'

'I was with her two days ago.'

'That would have been Friday, December 10th. Is that correct?'

'Yes.'

'Approximately how long were you together for that day, and what did you do while you were with Miss Wright?'

Price could see Josh was nervous. He wouldn't look her in the eye. 'Um, let me think.' He taps his fingers on the table. 'I was there from about fourish to sometime just before seven p.m. We were just, you know, hanging out.'

To Price's ear, he sounded almost defensive. 'Where do you mean when you say, "there" – 'Rachael's apartment?'

'That's right.'

'Your wife can verify you were home at seven p.m that night?'

'I thought we were leaving my wife out of this,' said Josh. His voice sounded spiteful. Price watched him closely. He folded his arms over and kept his whole body facing hers, a non-verbal and often involuntary reaction exhibited to signal intimidation when men feel threatened.

'There is nothing inherently suspicious about your wife being able to verify your whereabouts at a particular time, Mr Dempsey.'

The corner of his lip tightened and raised. 'I suppose not. Yes, Anne can verify I was home that night.' He tilted his head and pursed his lips before adding: 'If she had to.'

Price made notes on her pad. **Defensive. Antagonistic.** Addilyn Price didn't like Josh Dempsey very much. Cheating on his wife isn't a crime, but it *could* be a motive concerning Rachael's disappearance. Especially if his secret affair somehow threatened his marriage. 'When you were with Rachael, how did she seem?'

Josh's head was tilted slightly downward. He glanced up with a smug, half-smile. 'Aroused.'

Price added another note to her pad: **egotistical**. She observed Josh, who leaned back in his chair with an air of confidence as if this whole thing was beneath him. When he first came in, he had seemed frantic and uncomfortable. He had answered nervously, fidgeted in his seat and shown paranoia about the record of the conversation. Now, his whole demeanour had changed, and he gave off a very conceited, self-assured vibe. Was this macho act an attempt to hide something by smothering it with overly-masculine arrogance? Or was he just another arsehole who believes his own shit smells of roses? 'Let me rephrase the question. Was Rachael behaving strangely in any way that was uncharacteristic for her? Did she seem afraid? Anxious? Was she worried about anything?'

Josh shook his head. 'No, nothing like that. She was happy with me. Her pleasure was... evident.'

It took everything Price had to constrain her disgust. She found herself wishing she could wipe that smug smile off his face. This is a missing person they're talking about, and he's behaving as if the matter isn't even worth his time. 'What did you talk about?'

'You want me to go over every little thing we said to each other? I'd rather not.'

If Price pushed him just a little, would he reveal something?

'Oh, I get it. So, your relationship with Rachael is not a real relationship. I mean, you don't talk about the important stuff. You have sex and go your separate ways till next time the mood strikes. Is that it?'

'More or less,' said Josh with a slight shrug.

'So, it's just a fling between you, then?' says Price, dangling the bait. 'You're just her sex-toy. She calls you when she's horny, uses you, then sends you packing?'

Narrow lips, flaring nostrils, unblinking, slight squinted eyes glaring at her under a tense brow. It's plain for Price to see; resentment. 'You're wrong,' says Josh thickly. 'I'm more than that. *We* are more than that.' *Here we go*, thinks Price. All she has to do is keep quiet. He'll keep talking. He's betrayed by his own inflated ego, desperate to prove her wrong about how badly she needs him in her life. Inside the eye of his mind, Josh recalls the memory of Rachael presenting her arse to him and instructing him to perform cunnilingus upon her. That wicked smile, those beguiling eyes. 'I'm not just her fuckboy,' he protests. He wants to believe it, but even he isn't convinced. They don't go on traditional dates. They don't eat at restaurants or go to the movies or events around the City. But that's only because Josh is married and to be seen together in public is too risky… Isn't it?

Price goes on. 'If that's true, and you two are so close, why is it you can't tell me where she is?'

'I'm not her keeper,' said Josh harshly. 'I don't know what she does every minute of the day.'

Price decided to probe a little. 'Are you not concerned that she is missing?'

'Of course!' there was a fierceness to his exclamation, which hinted at his defensiveness. Eager to dispel the disposition his outburst framed him in, he went on to say: 'But this isn't the first time she's done something like this. It's like I said before. She drops off the radar for a few days from time to time. She always comes back, and she's always fine.'

'Is there anyone else that she might be seeing during these periods, another man, perhaps?'

'No,' said Josh. 'I'm the only guy she's seeing.'

Price could see the doubt in his eyes. He wasn't positive he was the only man in Rachael's life. 'Are you sure?'

No, thought Josh. 'Yes,' he said. This cop was making him doubt everything. Price could recognise the signals of uncertainty in his facial patterns. The body struggles to conceal the truth, generating observable signs when a lie is produced. Josh's earlier bravado now seemed mispla ced and petty. He is lying.

'Is there any place that she might regularly frequent during these absences?'

Her drug dealer's house, Josh thought, but he wasn't going to tell a cop that. 'No. Not that I'm aware of.'

'In the past, when she disappears, would she normally do so without alerting her friends and family? I mean, doesn't that strike you as a little strange?'

Not for a drug addict. 'Not for Rachael. As I said, she's been known to go rogue occasionally.' Right now, she's probably tucked away in some cosy Airbnb, smoking dope and snorting thick lines of MDMA, listening to her outrageous screamo music at a deafening volume. She hides her drug use from her family, acting like the mild-mannered primary school teacher with no rebellious or anti-establishment ideals. As for whether any of her friends know, he imagines it unlikely. Her very closest friends, maybe, but as far as he knows, there are only two people she has a close relationship with besides him, and one of them lives overseas. 'Rachael's a very private person. She'll show up in a couple of days, and all that will have happened is you wasted your time.'

Addilyn Price feels something niggling at her insides. Something doesn't quite feel right. Josh should appear mildly concerned about Rachael's disappearance as her lover. She adds another note to her pad: *Dempsey insistent on discontinuing search. Suggests he knows more than he is saying.*

'I'd like to go home now,' says Josh. 'I promised my kid I'd watch a movie with her before I came down here. I'd rather not be scolded by my six-year-old.' Once again, Josh's persona seemed to alter back to the version Price had interacted with when he first arrived at the station. The devoted father. Thoughtful, personable. Where has the smug creep gone to? *Four seasons in a day with this guy...* Despite his quirks, she has no reason to keep him.

'All right, Mr Dempsey. I have no more questions at this time.' Price notes the interview concludes at 8.06 a.m and switches off the recording device. 'Thank you for your time. She presents him with a form. 'If you could just jot down your details and contact info and sign at the bottom, you're fine to go.'

'What do you need that for?' asked Josh eyeing the form with uncertainty.

'Just in case I need to get in touch with you again.'

He pushed the form back towards Officer Price. 'I don't think that will be necessary.'

'Would you rather I come to speak with you again at your home or workplace?' ventured Price. Loathingly, Josh penned his information on the form. He handed it back to Price, then turned away without another word and left.

When her husband returned home a couple of hours later, Anne was waiting for him in the kitchen. 'Anney,' said Josh with warm affection as he came into the kitchen and spied his wife. 'What a bloody waste of time that was.' He popped his head into the lounge room, looking for the children. 'Where are the kids? Promised Suzie I'd watch this movie with her.'

Anne gestured to the empty seat beside her at the kitchen table. 'Why don't you take a seat? We need to talk.'

Josh was hesitant. He didn't want to have this talk. Not right now. Judging by how his wife looked at him, delaying this confrontation was out of the question. 'All right,' he said. The way he moved to seat himself at the table felt like the final footsteps of an inmate shuffling his way down the corridor of death row towards his inevitable demise.

Anne had her hands crossed over her chest. When her husband was seated, she asked, calmly: 'How long have you been seeing her?'

He did not meet his wife's eye when he answered. No getting around it. What's the point in lying? He confesses: 'About five months.'

'A teacher at your own son's school, Josh? Of the multitude of women you could have cheated with… I mean, did you even think about the indignity and shame this would cause me if this affair came to light? Half of Lucas' classmates attend his after-school activities and let me tell you, those mothers are a bunch of catty-bitches. If this came out, it would be hell for me.'

'Wait, how did you know—?'

'Why, Josh? That's the question I can't stop asking myself. I clean the house, cook the meals, help with the kids and suck your bloody cock when it's hard; what more could you want? We have a good life. I give you my best, and it's *still* not good enough? Why!'

'It's nothing you did or didn't do... It's her. I've just always been weak around her. We actually used to see each other, Rach and I—'

'Oh, it's *Rach,* now, is it?' interjected Anne.

'Rachael,' corrected Josh. 'Anyway, like I was saying, we used to date for a while years ago. Before you and I met. We ran into each other one night a few months back, and... I don't know. It just, kind of, happened.'

'"Just kind of happened", are you fucking kidding me, Josh? You screw another woman for five months, cheat on me and ruin our marriage, and your excuse for this incredible act of selfishness and stupidity on your part is, "it just kind of happened?"' She wanted to stand up and leave at this point. Not out of anger or spite, but resentment. 'Even now, after I confront you about your miserable deceit, you *still* can't be honest with me and give me a straight answer?'

'I'm sorry, Anney...' Her face flushed red, and she slammed a fist on the table.

'Don't call me *Anney,* Josh. I'm not your Anney. I'm the wife you screwed over.' She breathed a heavy sigh. The anger is subsiding, melting into depression. 'I mean, we have a good life, don't we?' She gestures to the walls. 'This lovely house. Two great kids. We're not unhappy in our marriage. I mean, it's not the same as being happy, but it's not worse either. Maybe if it had just been a one-time thing, you could have come to me, and we might have been able to fix this.' She looked her husband in the eye with a defeated expression. 'We could have at least tried.'

'I know, Anney. I'm so sorry, and I understand that you're angry, and frankly, you have every right to be...'

Anne raised a finger, indicating Josh should stop talking. 'That's the thing, Josh. I'm *not* angry.' All the colour drained from his wife's face. She looked pale and tired. 'I *should* be. I should be absolutely *furious*. But I'm just not. And I've been thinking about why that could be ever since I got this email from your mistress yesterday.' She slides her laptop over to him on the table.

'Email?' His sudden inquiry provoked such contempt from his wife that she could cut flesh with her stare.

'After giving it some thought, I came to realise the reason I'm not angry is that I've just been living as if the things I want, *my* needs, don't matter.' She stared bravely into her husband's eyes. 'I don't love you any more. I don't think I've been in love with you for a while. I've just been living as if our marriage dictates that loving each other is a given, but it's not. With the way our lives are, with work and the kids, I don't think either of us has really had the time to think it through. So, I guess, for what it's worth, I'm not blameless in this either. The difference is Josh, I didn't go and jump on some other bloke's cock because I was bored.'

Josh remained silent. There wasn't really anything he could think of to say. The damage was done. This business about an email had him curious, though. 'I don't know what to say, Anney. I fucked up. I can't take it back; I can't change it. All I can say is, I'm sorry. I wish I could go back and choose differently.' He wasn't sure that was entirely true, and he could see Anne wasn't fully convinced either. Much like other areas of his life, Josh had failed to make a choice between his wife and his mistress, and now, life had chosen for him.

She eyed her husband with suspicion. 'The thing is, I honestly don't know if you're telling the truth, and that bloody *scares* me, Josh. When did you become such a great liar? Five months you have been lying, and I was too blind to see it for what it was. The worst thing is, you didn't even tell me yourself. *She* did. It's humiliating, and it's devastating to learn you have such little respect for me after everything we have been through together. The fact you did this for so long, thinking you could keep fucking around with her, all the while sitting at *our* dining table, eating Sunday pancakes here with the kids and me as if you had done nothing wrong? I wonder: if Rachael hadn't emailed me, how long would you have continued with this charade?'

Josh snorted with exhaustion. 'I don't know what to say. I fucked up. Big time. I said I was sorry. I lost myself in it... I didn't realise until I ran into Rachael how unhappy I'd been with my life. It's just fucking work and the kids, and I felt like I didn't have any personal identity any more. For a while, she made me feel like myself again. That's it. I don't know what else to tell you.' Anne listened to Josh discharge these pathetic excuses as if they could somehow explain away the hurt he'd caused, the carnage he'd created. She could judge that this conversation would never go in a direction in which Josh expressed sincere remorse. She could see in his eyes; he wasn't sorry he did it; he was only sorry he got caught. Josh knew there was no right time to ask, so he just did: 'What's this email you keep going on about?'

Anne nodded at the laptop. 'See for yourself.'

Josh opened up the laptop and read the email that Rachael had composed to his wife. When he finished, he closed the laptop shut. The shift in his mood was so swift it was frightening. A bulging vein in his forehead indicated his anger. His fists were clenched so hard his knuckles were white. 'What the fuck was she thinking... That fucking *bitch.*' Anne was shocked by his reaction, but she studied her husband carefully. This was really him, the part of himself he took every precaution to conceal from the world. His agitation and aggression originated from pain. Inside, Josh is just an angry man, immature and selfish, a narcissist who fails to recognise his ruthless tendencies. He stood up so suddenly the chair he was sitting on fell to the floor. His outburst caused Anne to shudder with fright. 'What fucking right does she think she has!'

'I suppose she couldn't bear the weight of her guilty conscience,' said Anne with stoicism. Then, with just a hint of her own spite, she said: 'That's more than I can say of you, sadly.' Josh looked at his wife with fury behind his eyes, inside a raging storm that he struggled to keep at bay. Some part of her husband's prefrontal cortex competed well enough with the amygdala to overcome the emotional instinct. Exercising what discretion remained, Josh refrained from lashing out at Anne. After all, he wasn't the victim in this scenario, and there was no use in pretending otherwise. 'Looks like she found God or something. Wanted my forgiveness, as you read,' said Anne.

'Picked a strange time to find religion,' he said through clenched teeth. 'Did you happen to notice the time-stamp on that email? It was sent at 3.16 yesterday morning. What's more likely than a religious epiphany is that she got shit-faced on pills. Then, somewhere in her drug-addled stupor, she figured it was better to besmirch me and make me the villain so she could relieve herself of her own guilt.'

In all their years of marriage, Anne had never once witnessed this side to her husband. Had it always been there? The bitterness, the anger, the nasty bite of his maliciousness? 'Maybe,' said Anne. 'But now, according to the cops, she's missing.' She bravely met her husband's eye. 'Do you know anything about that?'

Josh seized his wife with a callous glare. 'What are you

getting at? Do you think I had something to do with her disappearance?'

'Did you?'

'No,' he said scathingly. 'How the fuck should I know where she is. Probably sleeping off one of her benders in the bed of some other bloke like the addict scum she is.'

'Maybe.' If Josh was pining for sympathy, he chose poorly. 'Or, maybe she gave you a clue about how guilty she was feeling, maybe she mentioned she was thinking about reaching out to me, and you convinced her to piss off for a while.'

'How could you even say that? What, you reckon I threatened her, got her to leave her home, her family, her job? You might as well be accusing me of killing her! Is that the passive-aggressive message you're trying to communicate right now?'

Anne shrugged. 'I honestly don't know what you are capable of any more, Josh. The last couple of days has revealed so much about you I couldn't have imagined to be true in my wildest dreams. I don't know who the hell you are. I'll tell you this much right now, though: I don't want you in this house a second longer. Pack a bag and find somewhere else to stay. I think it's appropriate we have some space from each other for a while.'

Whether Josh's anger had subsided or he had just found a way of pressing it down inside himself until it was no longer evident, it was the calmness he presented now that made Anne feel more fearful than when he had overtly expressed his rage. 'Fine.' His lips were so stiff, his mouth barely moved when he spoke. 'What about the kids? What are you going to tell them?'

'I'll tell them the truth, Josh. Unlike you, I won't lie to the people I love. I want a divorce. Our marriage is kaput. I think you can agree; there's no coming back from this for us. Even if there was, honestly, I don't want it.'

His contempt made another appearance: pursed lips, a furrowed brow, and narrowed eyes. 'So, you're going to make *me* the villain?'

Anne was dismayed by the depths of her husband's narcissism. That he was so blind to the degree of his own self-interest caused a sadness in her she worried she would never reconcile. 'The fact that you could imagine yourself as anything other, Josh, is precisely what *makes* you the bad guy.'

Chapter Seven

Sunday, 12th December 2021 8:10 a.m

After Josh's departure, Sergeant Price approached one of the Administration Officers at the station. Even aged in his mid-twenties, Jeremiah had such a youthful face it would be easy to mistake him for a teenager. 'You mind transcribing this for me, please?' she asked, handing him the recording device. 'When you finish, upload it to QPrime under the name R. Wright.'

'Can do,' he said with the same enthusiasm of someone who had too much to drink the night before and wasn't thrilled about working on a Sunday morning.

'Send me an email when it's done,' she said.

'Copy that.' Jeremiah saluted.

Returning to her desk across the station, Price observed a man in plain clothes waiting by her desk. He wore grey trousers that were slightly too large for him and a plain, sky blue collared shirt with a cheap blue necktie strung loosely around his collar. The stranger hadn't shaved in a few days, so his face was covered in thick, black bristles. He wasn't a civilian; that much was plain. The gun holstered at his hip indicated he was a cop. He stood hovered over her desk, rifling through papers with a calm disposition. Price judged him to be aged in his forties, his sun-kissed skin showing signs of ageing around the eyes. His forehead bore noticeable crease lines. His unkempt black hair had whispers of grey on his sideburns. 'Excuse me,' she said to get his attention as she approached her desk. 'Can I help you?' She cast her eye at the papers on her desk. 'It's not very considerate to go through someone's things, you know. Poor etiquette.'

The man looked up, levelling his gaze on her. There was an intensity to his brown eyes that was harshly contradicted by his casual body language. He rested his rear on her desk and folded his arms across his chest. 'Senior Sergeant Price, I presume?'

'That's right. Who might you be?'

He ignored her question. 'Four years with the Queensland Police Service. A year at the Beat. Three years at Missing Persons come March next year. You put in an application to join Special Operations two months ago.'

'Yes…' Where is this going, she wondered. He had this way of looking at her that made her feel as though anything that happens to fall under the scrutiny of his attention is deserving of the most extreme measure of observation. She tried to ignore the unsettling knot that it caused to creep up her throat.

'You're currently investigating a missing persons notification received regarding Miss Rachael Wright, lodged by her parents just yesterday. Correct?'

'I'm afraid I can't discuss specifics of cases with unauthorised persons,' she said assertively.

He reached inside his pants pocket and withdrew a Detective's badge. 'Detective Coltsworth; Special Operations. Is that authority enough?'

'Sorry… Sir,' she said, almost bowing apologetically. She cleared her throat. 'What can I do for you?'

'Well, Senior Sergeant Price, I have some good news and some bad news for you. The good news is that I'm here to inform you that your application to transfer to Special Operations has been approved.'

The feeling of elation was immediate. A promotion! She had worked so hard for this. She maintained her composure, determined not to let her excitement show until she was alone. 'That's fantastic news, sir. I'm very pleased. But, uh, isn't this the kind of thing usually communicated by email? I had expected to get a notice from HR.'

'You will, and yes, *ordinarily,* that's how this appointment would be communicated, but, unfortunately, these aren't ordinary circumstances.'

'Sir?'

'Well, that brings me to the bad news. I found your missing person.' He took out his mobile phone and swiped his finger over the screen, then presented the screen to Price. On it was an image of a naked, pale corpse lying on the edge of a dirty, brown body of water. A creek or river, likely. Coltsworth studied Price's reaction while she looked at the image. She didn't flinch seeing the macabre sight. That was good. 'Rachael Wright is dead. I just got confirmation from the Coroner's Office that she was murdered. I'm here to officially welcome you to Special Operations. As of this moment, you will be assigned to the Homicide Division. I want you to help me apprehend whoever is responsible for murdering Rachael Wright.'

Price had hoped there would be an opportunity to quietly celebrate her new promotion, but the actuality of Rachael Wright's death had come as such a shock it spoiled any satisfaction she would have derived from rejoicing. Detective Coltsworth and Senior Sergeant Price walked together outside to the back of the station where the marked and unmarked police cars were parked. 'We are going straight to the Coroner's Office while they conduct an external examination of the body,' explained Detective Coltsworth as he unlocked a nearby navy blue Toyota. 'It's a bit of a drive, so you can fill me in on the details of your missing person's investigation along the way.'

'Okay,' agreed Price as she entered the front passenger side of the vehicle. 'There isn't much to tell. The Missing Person's notification was lodged yesterday by Miss Wright's mother, Mary-Lou Wright. I accumulated a list of Rachael's known associates. Family, friends, co-workers. One of Rachael's friends, assisting Rachael's mother, advised us that Rachael had been seeing a man named Joshua Dempsey. I literally just concluded interviewing him before I ran into you.'

'That's a shame,' commented Detective Coltsworth as he steered the car out of the station.

'Sir?'

'The tactics employed by homicide investigators during interrogation will vary from those you're familiar with in Missing Persons. If Josh Dempsey was the one who killed her, that first encounter with police can be critical when it comes under the scrutiny of the courts. How did he present during the interview?'

'Honestly, it was a bit of a mixed bag with him. When he first came down to the station, he seemed quite meek. He was paranoid about the interview being recorded, hesitant to answer questions. I put it down to the fact that he's married and doesn't want his dirty laundry aired. As the interview progressed, he became confrontational, arrogant, even antagonistic.'

'Hmm,' mused Detective Coltsworth. 'You and I will revisit that recording when we get the chance.'

'You think there's something there?'

'Could be. If he killed her, and it wasn't planned, you probably took him by surprise. Having caught him off guard, he couldn't figure how to play it during the interview, so he improvised. That would explain the change in his constitution.'

'I see, sir.'

'Colt. Around the bullpen, that's what they call me.'

'Oh, I'm sorry.'

'Apology not necessary. Listen, Price. Special Ops can be a bit of a boys club. Pro tip: don't apologise unless it's warranted. It'll be tougher to garner the respect of the veteran investigators if you do.'

She almost repeated it – sorry – by beginning to enunciate the word, then stopped herself. 'Thanks for the heads up.'

'So, why homicide?' asked Colt as he navigated onto the highway.

'It's simple, really. Last year in Australia, fifty-one thousand people were reported missing – that's a hundred and forty individuals on every day of the year. Nationwide, 98% of those reported missing are located alive and well. But what the statistics omit is, of that 2% which constitute long-term missing persons, those cases are either unresolved because the person is never found, or they're found dead. When cases like Rachael's come up, they take the case from my desk and drop it down on yours.' She gazed out the window at the trees flashing by. 'I figured it was time to stop working for the 98% and start doing what I can for the 2%.'

Graham Coltsworth sucked his teeth. 'Well said. In fact, it's why I prefer to work with people like you than the clock-watchers and the yes-men.'

'People like me?' *What does he mean by that?*

'As you probably know, a QPS Officer has to have been in service for five years before qualifying to be recommended for Detective. Human Resources have recently granted Senior Detectives some discretion in the selection process. I looked over your application personally. You recorded your marital status as single on the forms, and you have no dependents. You also indicated your ambition to become a Detective. As far as becoming a Detective goes, having no spouse or kids is a good start. You've been doing this long enough to know that being a Detective is nothing like it is in the made-for-tv dramas. The work is hard. The hours are long, and you'll be on call. To top it off, the pay is abysmal. But, I trust people like you with this kind of work. The people who care about the 2%. There are plenty of desk jobs in QPS for clever, hard-workers like you. Jobs with more flexible work arrangements, better pay and a loftier title to go with it. Suppose your concern for the 2% of unresolved cases is sufficient to motivate you to join homicide? In that case, I'll gladly have you at my side down here in the trenches.'

Price stared out the passenger window for a moment in quiet, watching the world unfurl outside her window. She attempted to suppress her guilt that Rachael's tragic death had created such good fortune for her career. For a few minutes, she contemplated the irony. 'What about you?' said Price after some silent deliberation.

'What about me?'

'Do you have a family? Wife, husband? Kids?'

'Sometimes I bloody wish I was born gay,' he mused. 'Might have had better luck with blokes than I have had with women. Divorced; twice, actually. No kids of my own.' Price didn't quite know what to say. Colt observed her silence and volunteered: 'I know what you're thinking. No family, no life beyond the work – kinda *does* sound like the paperback sleuths.' He appeared mildly amused. 'I am partial to a good scotch, though, so I guess some of those lifetime-movie detective clichés hold up.'

'You don't strike me as the scotch-swilling womanizer type,' she snickered, smiling craftily. 'But then again, I don't know you very well.' The corner of his mouth lifted a fraction before his stoicism resumed. Price would come to recognise that, as far as Graham Coltsworth was concerned, a fractional, momentary corner-lip smile was as close as an ear to ear grin as he gave.

They had arrived at the Coroner's Office, a red-bricked building on the north side of Brisbane. Colt parked the car. 'This is your first homicide case. Naturally, I understand if you might be feeling a little nervous but just remember that I selected you because I've studied your work. You've got good intuition. Your skills are what is going to help solve this, so don't hold back. Okay?'

'Yes, s-, I mean, Colt.'

The State Coroner's Office employs many people, as Price found when the pair of officers made their way through reception in the lobby down to the morgue in the first basement level of the building. Colt checked his watch in the elevator. 'The pathologist should have finished the autopsy by now.' Addilyn Price had never witnessed an actual post-mortem before, but it wasn't her first time seeing a corpse. She had that misfortune throughout her policing career; the first appearance of a dead body came only a month into her first year as a Beat Cop. An elderly man had died in his bathtub and soaked there for three days before the body was found. She was one of the Officers sent to the man's house for a welfare check. He was more goo than man by the time they got him out of the tub. As the elevator doors parted and Detective Colt led Sergeant Price into the underbelly of the building, Price's curiosity was piqued.

'So, where did you find the body?'

'A couple walking their dog found her on the banks of the Enoggera Creek.' Thinking on this information, Price was bemused. It was an odd place to dispose of a body. Very open, close to the City and populated areas. The possibility of the act being witnessed was high. Lugging around a dead body isn't a very innocuous thing to be doing. 'She wasn't killed at the creek,' Colt announced. 'Someone deposited the body there *after* she was killed.' They were welcomed to the mortuary by the Medical Examiner, a forensic pathologist named Nancy. Her grey hair was tied into a tight bun. She was dressed casually in a blue blouse and black pants with a white lab coat over her clothes. Blue latex gloves covered her hands. 'Nancy, it's good to see you,' said Colt as the two entered the room. 'This is Senior Sergeant Price. She'll be aiding me in the investigation.'

'I wish we were meeting under better circumstances,' said Price.

'I agree,' acknowledged Nancy with a slight nod of her head. 'All right then, Graham, let me show you what I found.' All the attention in the room turned then to the pale, cold body on the steel trolley in the centre of the room. Rachael's lips possessed a slight bluish colour. Her eyes were milky and expressionless. Upon witnessing Rachael's dead body, a mix of heartfelt emotions wrestled for Price's attention. She had to concentrate on maintaining her focus. Maybe it was the absence of colour or the lack of animation, but whenever Addilyn was in the presence of a dead body, she could understand why some people imagine human beings possess the thing termed a soul. Looking at Rachael's body evoked a feeling. The body seems *empty.* The only word she felt was truly fitting for a lifeless corpse is precisely how Rachael appears – soulless. 'I estimate the victim died sometime in the early hours of Saturday morning.' Nancy pointed a gloved finger at Rachael's neck, marked with heavy bruising. 'Contusion around the throat indicates the cause of death was strangulation. And here.' She gestured to stitching on Rachael's left side. 'A long knife, which penetrated the lower left lung. The peculiar thing about this wound was that it was inflicted after the victim had already died. The x-ray revealed that whoever administered it did so with great precision. The blade made no impact on the rib cage before injuring the lung. Whoever stabbed her did so very deliberately and with acute precision. I suspect it may have been a purposeful act to ensure that the victim could not recover from the strangulation.'

'A failsafe?' inquired Colt.

'Sounds strange, but I think so, yes. The wound itself is too precise for me to conclude that it was administered out of mere curiosity or some frenzied, fleeting rapture. It was done deliberately, likely to make sure the victim stayed dead.' Nancy moved to the side of the gurney. 'There is one more thing I found during an external examination. And it is quite troubling.' She lifts Rachael's forearm and turns it over. Price inspected the wound closely, as did Colt. 'It isn't a burn mark as you might expect from this kind of brand. And, do you see this slight bruising on the skin around it? Here, look at this.' Nancy invited the two officers to consult a computer screen. On it was a photographic image of the wound but magnified significantly. 'The edges of the pattern are so precise that there is no digression from the initial impression whatsoever. The killer imprinted what can only be called a stencil of the shape using some sort of razor-edged implement, like a specially shaped cookie-cutter. Once the impression of the shape was complete, afterwards, they took the time to flay the skin using what I suspect must have been tweezers and a scalpel to create this marking.'

'How long would something like that take?' asked Colt eyeing the strange shape made from the presence and absence of skin.

'I cannot say for sure. But, if you asked me to estimate how long it might take *me* to reproduce this to the same degree of accuracy, I would estimate a few hours at the very least.'

Colt inspected the mark with eyes of detached indifference. With the layers peeled away in symbiosis with the skin that remained, the pattern appeared to form a line that rounded off into a spiral at both ends. It looked like two giant, dizzying eyes. Circles within circles. 'A signature? Maybe some sort of ritualistic symbol?'

'Whatever it is, the time and dedication the killer administered to apply it suggests they were unconcerned about any time restraints and definitely not afraid of being interrupted. This was delicate handiwork; it would have taken a practised hand. The killer wasn't clumsy. This stab wound; they knew where to strike and what level of force was appropriate to get the job done with as little effort as possible. Additionally, discarding the body in such a well-populated area so close to the City... well, it's bold, to say the least. This kind of inclination for risk and low regard for the likelihood of capture suggests a confidence characteristic of someone who might have done this before.' Nancy walked around the table, her watchful eyes taking in the abhorrent violence that resulted in this woman being deprived of her life. 'The attention to detail, the meticulousness of care the killer took doing this suggest to me that they were deeply invested in the killing.'

Colt began speculating. 'Strangulation is a very intimate method of murder. It's up close. Personal. On the other hand, the post-mortem stabbing and the forming of this mark have been carried out so carefully, and with such time and care, I can't help but think it requires a certain degree of detachment to do this with such meticulous attention to detail. It's surgical, methodical.'

While Colt spoke aloud his thoughts, Price had been searching on her phone, looking for information on the mark. She presented her phone to Colt when she discovered a website that listed ancient pagan symbols and their meaning. 'Killing with passion, mutilating the body with detached indifference. That's no coincidence. Look.' Price presented her phone to Colt and Nancy. 'The symbol is called a Double Spiral. Supposedly, it was used in ancient cultures to represent the balance between opposing forces. Creation and destruction, birth and death. It says here that the Double Spiral is mainly symbolic of the immutable connection between the physical and spiritual realms.'

Colt considered the new information. 'So, it could be a cult symbol. A ritual killing, maybe.' Price saw Colt's eyes glaze over absent-mindedly as he entered deep thought. He stared at the mark on Rachael's arm like it was telling him a story. 'Whatever his motive, the mark is significant to him. It is not without some personal attachment, meaning that to us probably seems obtuse but is pertinent to him.' He faced Price. He hid his emotions well, but Price had studied non-verbal language long enough to recognise the subtle signs of his excitement. 'Right,' he said resolutely. 'We have the where, when, and how. Now we just need the who and why.'

Chapter Eight

Sunday, 12th December 2021 10:19 a.m

The Special Operations division of Brisbane's Queensland Police service has headquarters on the North and South of the Brisbane River. Detective Colt gave Price a brief tour of the northern facility, introducing her to various members of Special Operations. Organised Crime, State Intelligence, the Drug and Serious Crime Group – these squads recruit the finest officers the State has to offer. Walking around the office, Price was humbled. This is the big leagues. The homicide squad working out of Brisbane North possessed fewer officers than Price imagined. As Colt explained: 'The Brisbane North Detectives are spread thin across the Crime, Counter-Terrorism and Special Operations division. Many are presently working in partnerships with the feds on various Task Forces across the Special Ops sub-divisions.' They passed two rows of empty desks. 'That was part of the reason Human Resources sought to appoint more staff to Special Ops, to fill in some of the gaps.' They arrived at the place in the office where homicide worked from. Price counted seven officers working cases out of the North Brisbane office. Four of them, including Colt, are Detectives. The remaining three, including Price, are uniformed officers sharing her rank. She wondered if her fellow uniformed officers would become friends, competitors for the Detective shield, or both? Colt offered a brief introduction to the team but was called away by Superintendent

Lisa La Pila, the officer in charge of the Brisbane Region. 'Graham, could I see you in my office a moment?'

Colt signalled La Pila with a wave, casting a glance at Price. 'Come on, meet your new boss.'

La Pila's office was a private, cavernous space that occupied the entire corner quadrant of the first floor. At first, Price suspected it might have been merely a temporary space assigned to the big-wigs whenever they came around. It had to be some sort of meeting room or multipurpose room. Anything but an office. But, once she was ushered through the door by Colt, she came to know that it was anything but shared space. La Pila's diplomas hung in ornate frames on the walls behind her egregiously large desk. Medals were showcased on a bookshelf, nestled among a row of cacti and bonsai trees. A photograph of La Pila accepting some sort of certificate from the Commissioner hung in a prominent central position on the wall to her right as she entered the room like a prized trophy. La Pila remained seated behind her desk as the two officers entered. She had a thin, hooked nose with almond coloured skin. Her eyes were so disproportionately small they looked as if they had been pencilled into her face by a cartoon illustrator. 'Superintendent La Pila, this is Senior Sergeant Addilyn Price, our newest recruit to homicide.'

La Pila didn't even stand from her chair to greet Price, who had to overextend herself awkwardly over the huge desk between them just to shake her boss's hand. 'Hmm,' sounded La Pila. 'Firm handshake.' Price noted that La Pila's was marginally firmer than her own.

'Well, ma'am, my father was a cop, and he always said that the first step to earning an officer's respect is with a hardy handshake.'

La Pila presented a tired smile as if it were an anecdote she'd heard her whole life. 'It's good advice. Welcome aboard, Price. Please, take a seat.' She gestured to the empty chairs across from her. When Price and Colt sat down, Price noted that she felt distinctly lower than La Pila so that she actually had to raise her head to look up at her boss. La Pila turned her beady eyes upon Colt. 'What did the Medical Examiner have to say?'

'The vic was strangled. The killer punctured one of her lungs post-mortem and took the time out to carve a marking into her flesh before dumping the body on the creekbed.'

One of La Pila's thin eyebrows rose sharply. 'A marking?'

'A Double Spiral, ma'am,' disclosed Price as she presented a photograph of the symbol on her phone. 'Supposedly, the symbol represents opposing forces. Life and death, destruction and creation, and so on.'

La Pila glanced at the image and then leaned back in her chair. She ran her fingers through her hair, crossed her legs and looked at Colt. 'You think this could have been religiously motivated? Some sort of ritual killing? A Satanic thing, maybe?'

'Could be,' said Colt. 'Too early yet to say. Forensics find anything at the vic's apartment?'

'You would know already if they had,' quipped La Pila icily. 'I'll leave you to it, Graham. I expect to be updated the second you have new information. This one is going to get a lot of attention from the media. A forty-four-year-old Caucasian teacher from the inner-city suburbs. Rachael Wright is the kind of woman that paints a target on this department. She can all too quickly become the poster child for departmental incompetence the longer the case remains unsolved. We need a win on this one, and we needed it yesterday. You're excused.' Colt stood up to leave. It seemed to Price the invitation to depart couldn't have come sooner. Price had nothing nice to say about Lisa La Pila as far as first impressions go. Price moved to join him. La Pila raised her hand, 'Senior Sergeant, a moment please?' Price gave Colt a nod as he left the office, closing the door behind him. 'I wanted a minute to speak with you privately,' began the silver-tongued Superintendent. 'It can take a while for a newbie to learn who's who in the zoo, so I wanted to give you a heads up about Graham. He's a good detective, scrupulous, attentive, detail-oriented – but he's not a very good team player. There have been…' She paused to select her word carefully. '*Incidents,* in the past. My superiors are inclined to turn a blind eye when he goes rogue because of his solve-rate, but there's a reason he sought you out for this appointment. Believe me when I tell you it's got less to do with your skills as an investigator – which, don't get me wrong, I'm confident are very admirable – and more to do with the fact that you're fresh blood.' La Pila's watchful eyes looked Price up and down. 'You're the perfect kind of partner for him: inexperienced, eager to please, ambitions to become a Detective… You can't step on his toes, so to speak. If you don't believe me, you should know that I tried to partner him with another Detective for the Wright case and, for the first time since it was introduced four years ago, he chose to exercise the discretion HR issues Senior Detectives to recommend candidates for appointment to Special Operations.'

Price did her best to display neutral body language. She didn't want to appease La Pila but wasn't keen to offend her either. New job, new role, first impressions; it's all a game. 'I appreciate your candour, ma'am, but I'm curious as to why you're telling me this.'

'I tried to partner him with another Detective, and he exercised a discretion he hasn't bothered with since it was conceived. Consider why he might do that. The program requires the Detective who submits the recommendation to partner with whichever candidate they put forward for the first four weeks of their appointment so that the successful candidates can shadow the Detective and become acquainted with the role. They call it the Buddy-system. It was the ace he kept up his sleeve to get around my duty roster.' Could this be true, wondered Price? Was she just a pawn in some silly political game, a tit-for-tat between Commissioned Officers? La Pila opened a folder on her desk. 'I've looked over your application myself. Pulled up your record. You've done fine work with QPS. You're clearly very smart. You're articulate and hard-working. Overall, I think you show great promise. There could be a bright future for you in Special Ops if you play your cards right, Addilyn.' La Pila's face was hard to read. She had one of those photogenic smiles that could be replicated at a moment's notice. The kind of beaming grin that could be photographed a thousand times and never once appear any different. It seemed to be sincere but not natural. However, her small, vindictive eyes maintained a silent maliciousness that no smile could disguise. 'Just be mindful of him. You would be wise to keep Colt at arms-length where his reputation can't infringe on yours before you've even had a chance to make a name for yourself.'

Price wasn't sure what to say. She didn't want to ruffle any feathers, so she remarked only: 'Well, I appreciate the heads up, ma'am.'

'I'm glad we could have this talk,' said La Pila duplicitously with an accompanying shooing gesture. 'Good to have you aboard. You're dismissed.'

Colt looked up from his computer when Price returned. He had headphones on. Price observed that the desk directly across from Colt's was empty, as were the two behind his. Empty space all around him. Was it the other officers who kept their distance, or Colt who preferred to be separated from the others as La Pila had hinted? 'This one taken?' asked Price as she rolled the chair out to take a seat across from Colt.

He removed the headphones from his ears. 'All yours. And listen – whatever La Pila had to say to you in there is between you and her, but I would caution you about her. She's ruthless. She's had it out for me ever since I knocked back the offer for her job. Keep that in mind and take whatever she says to you about me with a grain of salt.' Price nodded in acknowledgement. Day one and already things were becoming more challenging than she anticipated. Lines were being drawn in the sand, and so far, it seemed that the feud between La Pila and Colt could be the central divider.

'You really declined it, the Superintendent job?' It was a big deal. The Superintendent of the greater Brisbane region would have positioned him to work towards a role in State Command.

Colt shrugged dismissively. 'It's like we talked about earlier. Those who care more about the 98% like to decorate their big comfy offices with ribbons and medals. Have no doubt; it is the work of the investigators focused on the 2% that *put* the plaques on those walls. You can either do the work or climb the ladder. You'll find it's rare the two interests share much common ground.'

Price nodded in appreciation. 'It's not my first rodeo, Colt. I know it's all game theory here, just like anywhere else.'

Colt smirked. 'Not *quite* like anywhere else. But you'll see that for yourself soon enough. Everybody does at some point. Look around' —he gestures to the empty desks with a nod— 'easy to become ostracised if you don't show any interest in playing the game.' Colt indicated towards the headphones he had been wearing until a minute ago. 'Anyway, that's enough of politics for one day. I just finished listening to the interview you conducted with Joshua Dempsey. As we learned from Nancy, Rachael was killed in the early hours of November 11th. That puts Josh Dempsey at Rachael's apartment approximately eight hours before she died there. You know what that means?'

'Yeah,' said Price.

'Josh was one of the last people to see her alive before she was found on the banks of the Enoggera Creek.'

'He was having an affair with Rachael. Maybe he was worried his wife would find out, so he killed Rachael to keep her from spilling the beans.'

Price reflected on her interview with Josh. She had reason to believe he could be capable of violence. He was quick to anger, proud, boastful. It was the marking, the double spiral symbol, that bothered her. Her impression of Josh just didn't align with that kind of callousness. 'If Josh Dempsey is our guy, your interview will have spooked him. If that's the case, he'll get rid of any physical evidence that might be in his possession as soon as he's able. I've already submitted an application to get a warrant to the Magistrate's Court. La Pila will fast-track it. We need to sweep the Dempsey house.'

Chapter Nine

Monday, 13th December 2021 6:52 a.m

Obtaining a warrant to search Josh Dempsey's house took almost twenty-four hours. Colt understood from his previous experience in these cases that the earliest intervention of an investigation often startles the guilty causing them to take action by seeking to destroy or remove evidence. If Josh is guilty of this murder and Price's interview hadn't put the wind up him, he was either stupid or very confident. Fortunately, the element of surprise still remains on the side of the law. Unless Josh somehow has insider departmental knowledge, he can't yet know that Rachael Wright is dead. As long as he believes that the police are still treating it as a Missing Person's investigation, he's unlikely to have the foresight to dispose of any evidence linking him to the crime.

Anne Dempsey, Josh's wife, answered the door when Colt knocked. The forensic investigators waited inside their vehicles parked on the street so as not to make their presence known until it was absolutely vital. 'Good morning, Mrs Dempsey, I presume? My name is Detective Inspector Graham Coltsworth with the Special Operations Unit of Queensland Police Service. I am here to serve you a warrant that permits Queensland Police to enter and inspect your property and household contents for evidence relating to a crime.' He handed Anne a copy of the search warrant and stepped foot inside, radioing the forensic team to follow. He could hear the clinking of metal spoons on ceramic bowls down the hall as the children of the house finished their breakfast. 'Mrs Dempsey, can you please tell me; besides yourself, who else is home right now?' Anne was still trying to read over the warrant, shocked and a little frightened by the sudden entry of a police officer and forensic team into her home. Men and women clad in blue coloured hazardous material suits covering their bodies filtered through her front door, marching past, ignoring her presence altogether.

'Uh, just myself and my two kids.'

Colt surveyed the living room that broke away from the front door of the Dempsey home. 'Where is your husband?'

Anne shrunk away. 'He's… er, not here at the moment.'

'I beg your pardon, Mrs Dempsey, but that isn't what I asked.'

The way Colt spoke, his direct manner, was very off-putting. It made Anne very uncomfortable. 'He is staying at a hotel. He could be there, or he could be at work already. I don't know. You would have to ask him yourself.'

'Thank you, Mrs Dempsey. I'll be sure to do that. May I ask which hotel he's at?'

'Essence Suites, over in Taringa.' She referred again to the search warrant, reading aloud: 'Um… I'm sorry, Detective? It says here a Magistrate has granted rights to the Police to conduct a search of the premises and personal effects therein under provisions of the Police Powers and Responsibilities Act for the purposes of seeking evidence in relation to a homicide…?'

'Yes?'

'And it has my husband's name here, at the top of the order…'

Colt issued directions to the forensic investigators to begin coordinating their search of the home one room at a time. He'd done this on so many previous occasions and dealt with the confusion of occupants that Anne Dempsey's voice was virtually white noise while he focused on the task at hand. 'That's right.'

Anne turned over the warrant in her hands. 'I'm sorry, I'm confused. What is going on?'

Colt concentrated on the features of his face in an attempt to convey the most sympathetic expression he could muster. 'I'm sorry to have to tell you this, Mrs Dempsey, but your husband is being investigated as a person of interest for murder.'

Her body stiffened, her mind quietened. The people around her just seemed to fade into the background. 'Murder? Who has been murdered?'

'A woman by the name of Rachael Wright.'

Without thinking, Anne's unadulterated reaction burst forth: 'She's *dead*!?' She covered her mouth in shock. 'Oh, my God…'

Colt rounded on Anne Dempsey. 'You knew her?'

'No… No…' stammered Anne, realising too late her mistake. 'I mean… not really.'

'Not really?' Anne's mind sharpened just in time to correct her blunder. 'She is a teacher at my son's school. Teaches English. I've met her a couple of times at parent-teacher interviews.' Colt observed the shock wear off a lot quicker than it ordinarily would under the circumstances. Something was askew here. At a certain point in a detective's career, they develop a keen sense for this sort of thing. Right now, Colt's intuition was warning him that Anne Dempsey knew more than she was letting on. He would have to tread carefully… 'Wait, so, you think that *Josh* could have done it?' murmured Anne.

'I don't know yet; that's why I'm here.' Anne avoided eye contact, using the warrant in her hands as an excuse to keep her attention elsewhere. She was clearly very distraught, and that was understandable given the circumstances, but Colt sensed there was something else going on just beneath the surface. When he looked her in the eyes, he could see the wheels turning. Did she know about her husband's affair? He couldn't rule out that it might have been Anne Dempsey who was responsible for Rachael's death, and while it was unlikely she killed Rachael with her own hands, it was plausible that she might have arranged someone else to commit the murder on her behalf. A jilted wife arranging the execution of her husband's mistress, it wasn't beyond the realm of belief. 'Mrs Dempsey, I'll need the kids to remain together and not touch anything while we conduct a search of the premises. Would you mind bringing them into the lounge room here?'

'Oh, yes, of course.' She scurried off down the hall to retrieve the children. During her brief absence, Colt took a stroll around the room. It was an immaculate home; even the picture frames didn't seem to harbour any dust. Was it Josh or Anne who kept such a clean home? Family photos hung on the wall. Smiling, happy memories framed for all to see. The picture-perfect suburban family. He glanced at one of the pictures in which Josh Dempsey smiled with his two kids hanging on either side of him at the beach. He wondered, could this happy, family man throttle a woman to death and carefully carve a pagan symbol into her skin? Anne returned shortly later with her kids, who asked questions about what was happening. Colt recognised the hopeless expression on Anne Dempsey's face. He'd seen it plenty of times before. She had not the slightest clue what to tell them. The children's presence represented an opportunity for Colt. While adults were typically more mindful of what they said to a police officer, kids – with the exception of the occasional street thugs – were educated to trust the police. That, coupled with their lack of knowledge of the law, made them prime candidates for total transparency.

'The police are just having a quick look around the house,' he said to the children. Addressing the boy, he asked: 'What's your name, mate?'

'Lucas,' answered the blonde-haired youth sheepishly.

'I have a son about your age, Lucas,' lied Colt, hoping to build some rapport with the boy. 'He goes to school over at East Brisbane. He hates math. He's always complaining about his math homework.' Colt produced a convincing fake laugh. 'What about you, Lucas? You got a favourite subject at school?'

Lucas grinned cheekily. 'PE, sir.'

Colt almost smiled. The kid had gusto. He was clever and possessed a quick wit. He wondered, was it a case of like-father-like-son? 'Are kids still playing bullrush these days?'

'Occasionally, but the teachers hate it. Tried to ban any rough games, but we still get around it from time to time. Miss Wright almost gave me detention for it once but let me off with a warning.'

'Oh, yeah?' The mention of Rachael's name caught Anne's attention, soliciting a baleful glare directed at Colt from Lucas' mother. 'What do you think of her, Miss Wright?'

'She's all right,' said Lucas. 'She let us watch the movie of Romeo and Juliet instead of having to read the play. Leonardo DiCaprio is in it, and it has guns and stuff, so it's not as boring as the original.'

'Sounds like times have changed since I was at school,' said Colt casually. 'Let's hope they save you having to read Jane Austen. If you think Shakespeare's boring, I don't reckon you'll be too fond of Austen's books.'

'Actually,' said Anne Dempsey with protective self-righteousness, 'I happen to think her books are classics. Pride and Prejudice is a masterpiece.'

'That it is, Mrs Dempsey. In fact, I would go a step further and say that the qualities of Pride and Prejudice are as relevant in society today are they were for Elizabeth and Mr Darcy in Victorian England, wouldn't you agree?' His quip didn't go unnoticed by Anne. She ushered the kids away to the television on the other side of the room to put them out of Colt's inquisitive reach. 'Mrs Dempsey, if you could collect all the electronic devices in the home for us, I would greatly appreciate it. Laptops, phones, tablets and the like.'

'Oh,' mumbled Anne. 'You're searching our computers?'

To Colt, Anne's concern was suspicious. 'Yes. Is there a problem?'

Anne sheepishly averted her gaze. 'Well...'

'Mrs Dempsey?'

'Stay here with Suzie for a second, Lucas. Okay?' She touched her son on the shoulders with motherly tenderness. 'I just need a minute with the Detective. I'll be right back.' Anne indicated she wanted Colt to follow her, and the two proceeded to the kitchen. On the kitchen table, Anne opened up her laptop. 'I suppose if you plan on going through our computers, you would have found this sooner or later. I'm sure that in your job, spouses are typically combative, but I don't want to be a hindrance, so if this helps, you might as well have a look at it now.' Anne opened up her email application and navigated to the email confession she received from Rachael Wright. Colt read it over carefully.

When he finished, he asked Anne: 'Are you a religious family, Mrs Dempsey?'

'Not particularly. I mean, we baptised the kids, but that's just more out of tradition than anything else.'

'Your husband, Josh; does he ever talk about spirituality?'

'Josh?' she cackled. 'He's more of a hedonist than spiritualist.'

Colt read over the email one more time. It was heavy on the religious stuff. It was the hyperlink pasted into the body of the email that brought up a passage from the book of the Romans that really leapt from the page: **to set the mind on the flesh is death, but to set the mind on the spirit is life and peace**. To Colt, that sounds exactly like the kind of sentiment embodied by the way in which the meaning of the double spiral symbol is described. Dead flesh, living spirit. Natural opposites. Colt took a note down, observing the email was received to Anne's inbox at 3.16 a.m. That was inside the window of when the Medical Examiner estimated Rachael's time of death. Could this email really have been written by Rachael? The correlation between the contents of the email and the meaning of the double spiral felt almost too alike to be a coincidence. It *could* be that whoever killed Rachael used her computer to write this email, perhaps as a means of structuring a motive for Josh. In the realm of pure speculation, it was equally as likely that Josh might have killed Rachael if he had attended her apartment only to discover she had sent this to his wife. Perhaps somewhere in this confession, there is some clue. Was Rachael trying to communicate something? Or, maybe these are the killer's words. Regardless of which is true, it couldn't be meaningless. There had to be a purpose to it; Colt just had to figure out what it was. He called to one of the forensic analysts. 'Bag up the laptop and get it over to Cyber immediately. Have them contact me the minute they find anything.' Returning his attention to Anne again, Colt said: 'I'm sorry, Mrs Dempsey.' He touched a hand on Anne's back with sympathetic gentleness.

'It must have been troubling – to say the least – reading this email.' First, he would sympathise with her. That would diffuse any inclination to avoid cooperating. Second, knowing she is alienated from the husband gives him a strategic advantage. Anne is less likely to protect him knowing he betrayed her. 'You did the right thing, showing me this. I know it's difficult, Mrs Dempsey –'

She flinched. 'Please, don't call me that right now. Just call me Anne.'

'Anne... Look, there's no easy way for me to approach this, so I'll just say it: do you have any reason to believe that Josh might have hurt Rachael? Has he been behaving differently, have there been any incidents of violence, anything unusual, or out of character for him?'

Anne recalled the moment Josh finished reading the email in the very chair the Detective now occupied just yesterday. He was so angry, so... bitter. It had taken her by surprise, seeing that side of him. He had never shown such rage before. Not in all the years she had known him. It frightened her, and her mind wandered... Could he have done it? He was hardly the man she thought she knew. Capable of incredible deception, he had proven in more ways than one that she knew less about the man she married than she could believe. But murder? Was he capable of that? 'I can't believe that Josh would hurt anyone, Detective. But if there's even a chance he has, I certainly won't defend him.' Looking utterly dejected, Anne shuffled back to the lounge room to be with her children. It was plain to see the toll this had taken on her. Colt recognised all the usual signs; he could tell that Anne was barely holding it together.

'Detective Colt!' Someone from upstairs was heralding him. He made his way to the second floor and came to the master bedroom, where a forensic officer was waiting. 'You need to see this,' he said, pointing to the large chest of drawers positioned against a wall beside the door that led into an ensuite bathroom. The forensic officer had withdrawn the bottom drawer to reveal the space between the underside of the bottom drawer and the floor beneath the dresser. A torch was shone into the dark hidey-hole. The light revealed a pair of women's black lace underwear stained with what appeared to be at first glance either a vaginal thrush stain or dried semen. When the forensic officer picked it up and examined it more closely, he discovered tiny specks of dried red upon the black lace. A quick on-the-spot chemical analysis by the forensic practitioner confirmed Colt's suspicions.

'Its blood.' There was no doubt in Colt's mind that the blood would match with Rachael Wright's once the two were compared later. The underwear was bagged and sealed, and marked appropriately. In addition to the underwear, two other items had attempted to be hidden beneath the drawers; a bloody knife and a journal.

Colt issued the order to the forensic team in the room. 'Bag it all up. Get it tested asap.' He withdrew a pair of rubber gloves from his pocket and used them to handle the journal. He leafed through it briefly, reading a few of the entries. The author recorded sexual encounters with Rachael Wright in graphic detail. The very last entry was dated just the previous day. It contained a string of profanity, referring to Rachael in the foulest language and harshest terms. The journal entry noted that Josh's wife confronted him about the affair. Josh blamed Rachael for ruining his marriage. Colt got on the phone to Price, who he had left back at the station to finish compiling a list of all the people they had intended to interview in Rachael's life. 'Price, it's Colt,' he said when she picked up the phone. 'I need you to head over to where Josh Dempsey works and see if he's there.'

'Uh, yeah, okay. I can do that.' Internally, Price began to fret. She worried she might have screwed up her previous interview. Was there something she left out, something she should have done differently? Was this the first sign that her partner and mentor didn't have faith in her ability to do her job to the standard of a detective? 'Can I ask why you want to talk to him again? Did you find something at his place?'

'*Something* doesn't even cut it, Price. We hit the veritable jackpot. We just found a blood-stained knife, a pair of underwear that presumably belonged to the victim containing blood and semen samples and a journal filled cover to cover with records of Josh's sexual encounters with Rachael. Some of which, upon a preliminary examination, appear to fetishise violence. If you find Josh at his workplace, arrest him on suspicion of murder.' Price couldn't believe what she was hearing. Having interviewed the man herself, she had felt assured that he wasn't capable of these heinous acts. A self-interested prick, she thought, sure. But not a killer. How could her instincts have been so wrong?

'Yes, sir. I'll get over there right away. What will you do?'

'He's not at the family home,' explained Colt. 'His wife said he's staying at a hotel over in Taringa. I'll head over to see if he's there. Either way, one of us is making that arrest today.'

On the drive over to the Hotel, Colt was bothered. Nothing about this case felt right. It was all over too easy. Never before in the history of his career had a murder case be so quickly resolved with the murder weapon and physical evidence so clumsily concealed at the suspect's home. Even murder-for-hire thugs aren't stupid enough to store a weapon used in the killing under their undies drawer. Surely the killer who branded Rachael so methodically couldn't be foolish enough to keep keystone pieces of incriminating evidence in his own bedroom. Could he? Maybe he was just mad. Delusional, detached from reality, and didn't consider the risks of saving keepsakes from the killing. It seemed unlikely. It troubled him deeply, having never seen a case so open and shut. This case was practically made for law textbooks insofar as how easily it demonstrated that compelling physical evidence could convict a suspect in court. That was precisely why he had such reservations. Every Detective's dream is to have such damning evidence come to light this early in an investigation. But Colt isn't in the business of dreaming, and his gut says it can't be this easy. He considered the email Rachael sent Anne Dempsey. If Colt presumed Josh Dempsey innocent, the email was a clever move by whoever really killed Rachael. It creates a motive for Josh killing Rachael that prosecutors can easily present in court to a Jury as a convincing narrative: Josh, the scorned lover, seeking to silence his mistress before she spills the beans and screws everything up for him. The unknown subject responsible for the killing directs blame for the crime elsewhere and gets to flaunt his superior intellect by taunting investigators with the insertion of a subtle clue concerning the nature of his motive for killing Rachael. The level of planning and time required to frame someone else for this crime resonates more closely with the impression of the man who killed Rachael Colt has in his mind. Clever, patient, ruthless. Then, there's the email. In and of itself, there was nothing overtly strange about the contents of Rachael's email. Anyone who read it could believe that having had a change of heart, she sought to relieve herself of her guilt by confessing the truth to Anne. Plenty of people would have felt compelled to do the same, and lots of people probably *have* done similarly. However, those words take on a new meaning when scrutinised collaboratively in conjunction with the double spiral symbol. The polarity of opposite forces. That passage from the book of Romans that Rachael was supposedly contemplating when she composed the email. **To set the mind on the flesh is death, but to set the mind on the spirit is peace and life.** It is plausible that Rachael might have been feeling guilty, and in the depths of despair, she could have come to resent the lust that bound her to Josh. It's a nice thought, imagining the nobility of denying the body's impulses while seeking purification by focusing on the holiness of the inner, spiritual self. It could also be a message from the killer. Something that explains his agenda. Opposite forces, life and death, flesh and spirit… Perhaps he believes that the two cannot exist mutually? That one cannot exist while the other endures and that for the soul to live, the body must first perish? These were questions for another time. Colt's real problem if Dempsey was innocent is that very few could believe it. With the emergence of this evidence, the department would consider any expenditure of resources into alternate theories counter-productive. Once the forensic lab analysis linked Dempsey to the evidence – and Colt was certain it would – the department would push for a conviction. Superintendent La Pila had already warned Price and Colt that there was an urgency to close this case during their meeting. And if the media learned about the double spiral brand left on Rachael, it would be a feeding frenzy. The public would go nuts. The internet would be ablaze with endless theories. La Pila wasn't wrong about the threat Rachael Wright's case represented to Queensland Police. It has all the potential to become a national media story. For the police service, that's terrible news. The court of public opinion has a lot of sway in state parliament, and that's the sort of thing that can affect grant requests for funding and has the potential to stifle prospects for career Commissioned Officers who like to keep an eye on opportunities to rise in the department. The case had to be solved in as timely a manner as practicable. The problem Colt faces as the lead detective is the conflict between competing priorities; solving the case quickly and apprehending the guilty party. The interrogation would end the debate. Colt would know once he could sit down with Josh and speak to the man face to face whether or not he was guilty of this crime. Graham begins to dread what he knows will be an uphill battle if he believes Josh is innocent. His reputation won't be enough to keep the waters of bureaucracy at bay for very long, even *if* he somehow managed to convince Superintendent La Pila to allow additional time and resources to be allocated to pursuing other leads. In that scenario, Josh could protest his innocence until the cows came home, but as long as the evidence is strong enough to secure a conviction in court, the department will crucify him for this, regardless of whether he is innocent or guilty. And, it could be that Josh deserves to go down for it. Maybe he *is* guilty. Colt can't rule it out. It's too soon to make a determination with any certainty. Right now, only one thing is absolute: in his twenty years of police work, Colt lived with a clear conscience. He never harboured a single doubt that every suspect he had apprehended throughout his career was guilty of their crimes. Spoiling that record was out of the question. Whether he had the department's support or not, Colt was determined he would find the person guilty of killing Rachael because, at day's end, he knows he cannot abide living with going after the wrong man.

The Essence Suites is a rundown, three-star roadside hotel with a neon sign at the front advertising vacancy and cable TV. The attendant at the hotel reception is a second-generation Chinese teenager who didn't show any enthusiasm for being stranded at his post at the reception desk. He treated Colt amicably until the detective produced his police ID and badge. Then, the kid became acutely attentive, and his discomfort was palpable. Colt could only imagine that the boy was raised on stories of the improper imbalance of power maintained by Chinese authority figures to the point where he would regard even an Australian police officer as a potential threat to his safety. He confirmed Josh's room number and avoided making eye contact with Colt for the remainder of their exchange. A couple of minutes later, Colt was knocking on Josh's door. It was approaching nine-thirty a.m, so Colt was a little surprised when Josh answered, having expected him to already be at work. 'Mr Dempsey?' asked Colt.

'Who's asking?' Josh looked dishevelled. Unshaven, his dark wavy hair uncombed, he had dark circles beneath his eyes, and it wasn't difficult to smell the liquor on his breath.

Colt produced his police badge and ID. 'Detective Coltsworth from Queensland Police. You're under arrest.'

'What!' Josh took a step back. 'For what?'

'On suspicion for the murder of Miss Rachael Wright.'

'She's dead?' Josh began backing away further from the door. 'No, no, no… You've got the wrong guy, man. I wouldn't do something like that.' His bulging, mad eyes took on a lucid panic.

'Mr Dempsey, it's not necessary that I handcuff you if you come with me willingly, but if you resist, then you leave me no alternative. Will you cooperate?'

'Fuck off, mate!' Just like that, Josh's rage burst forth once more. 'You're not arresting me for shit.' He was looking around the room in a panicked state like a cornered animal, searching for an escape route. Colt placed his hand upon his firearm, saddled to his hip.

'Mr Dempsey, refusing to obey my orders qualifies as resisting arrest. If you continue to disobey my instructions, I am permitted to use the necessary force to detain you. I don't want to have to do that, Mr Dempsey, so I would appreciate it if you cooperate with me here.' Panicked and scared, Josh made for the bottle of scotch he had left on the table nearby. He took the bottle by the neck and raised it to strike Colt. Graham interpreted his movements. He saw Josh turn away, go for the bottle and pick it up. As Josh thuggishly swiped the bottle in a long arc from above his head downwards towards Colt's face, Graham sidestepped the blow before the glass made contact. Having missed Colt with the bottle, Josh lost his balance, and the resulting momentum caused him to stumble forwards. While Josh was off-balance, Colt only had to shift his weight onto his left foot and sweep Josh's ankle to disarm him completely. Josh collapsed on the floor, front-side first. The bottle fell away from his hand. Colt applied his knee to Josh's back, pressing his weight into him. At the same time, he cuffed one of Josh's wrists, then forced Josh's other arm closer, and despite his writhing and protesting, Colt managed to secure both wrists in handcuffs. He hauled Josh Dempsey up to his feet and escorted him to his car.

'I'm telling you, man. If you think I murdered Rach, you have the wrong guy. I don't know what bloody drugs she was taking when she decided to email my wife about our affair, and yeah, I'm bloody pissed off about it, but I'm not a murderer!'

People can be so stupid sometimes, thought Colt. This guy could say nothing; for his own sake, he *should* say nothing, at least until he has a solicitor present, but they don't think things through in the heat of the moment. 'Shut your mouth, Josh. Keep in mind that whatever you say can be used as evidence against you in court.' Colt wasn't unreasonable, and he believed in the tenet of the presumption of innocence. Josh didn't seem to comprehend that revealing his knowledge of the email his wife had received from the victim constituted a motive for Rachael's death. After securing Josh in the backseat of the car, Colt prepared a text message to Price:

Got him. Meet me at the station. Time for your first homicide interrogation.

She replied immediately: **Promise to wait for me?**

Colt answered: **Naturally.**

Addilyn Price was proving to be a good pick, thought Colt. A hard-worker, tenacious, good attitude and not blind to the politics involved in policing. He hoped she would prove equally formidable once they were in the box with Josh Dempsey.

Back at the station, Colt left Josh in a room purposed for interrogations to stew a bit while he waited for Price to catch up. She showed up within forty-five minutes, brandishing Anne Dempsey's laptop. Under the terms of the Search Warrant, Anne Dempsey was required to surrender her password and login credentials. 'Take a look at the email Rachael Wright sent Anne,' ordered Colt as they powered up the laptop. Addilyn read the email. Colt pointed to the hyperlink, which redirected to the bible verse. 'Bring that up again for me, would you?' Price read it aloud: 'Romans 8:6: For to set the mind on the flesh is death, but to set the mind on the Spirit is life and peace.'

'Thoughts?'

'Perfectly encapsulates the symbolism of the double spiral symbol, doesn't it? Flesh and death, spirit and life. Both ends of the spectrum.'

'My thoughts exactly.'

Colt brooded for a while. 'Did you review Rachael's social

media activity while you were investigating this as a missing person's case?'

'Of course. All the big sites. Why?'

'Was there anything online that gave an impression she was practising religion?'

'No,' answered Price decisively. 'Not a thing.'

'Her profiles go back a few years, I presume?'

'Well over a decade.'

'Odd then, don't you think? Rachael never outwardly expressed any interest in the topic before. Out of the blue, she has this change of heart and simultaneously a crisis of faith. She calls the whole thing off with Josh by emailing his wife with all this Bible-babble.'

Price could sense that her partner was alluding to something. 'It's definitely not consistent with her personality. But people do strange things. Sometimes these obscure things stick with people, you know? Verses from poems, bible passages. While it is strangely coincidental that it sounds similar to the double spiral meaning, it could also just be referencing her desire to abandon what she came to believe was a sinful arrangement with Josh, built on bodily instinct, in favour of what she viewed as a more virtuous life.'

Uncanny, thought Colt. 'That is how I reasoned it too.' Although they were the only two people in the room, Colt spoke to Price at a low volume. 'Look, cases like this are a slam dunk for the department. Believe me when I tell you; that never happens. We have a suspect who has a motive for the killing with physical evidence at the suspect's home to link him to the crime. It's very convenient for us.'

'When you put it like that, I suppose it does sound nice and neat.'

'You could practically wrap it up and put it under La Pila's Christmas tree. I've worked a lot of cases, Price. I've been a cop for half my life, and I've never come across a homicide case that was *this* easy to solve.'

'So, what are you saying? Josh is being set up?'

'That's one possibility. It could be there's another unsub out there who has arranged it so Josh goes down for this. It's either he's being set up, or he's guilty. You and I need to determine which it is.'

It was her first homicide investigation, so Price was inclined to defer to Colt's judgement, but he had specifically instructed her to express her thoughts earlier, so she didn't do him the discourtesy now: 'It would be tough to pull off. The unsub would need access to the Dempsey residence to plant the evidence. They would have to be intimately familiar with the family's schedule, and they would have to know about Josh and Rachael. Even his own wife didn't know. Seems unlikely a stranger could be privy to that information.'

'You're not wrong. But, there is this…' He pointed to the email sitting in Anne's inbox. 'Look at the time-stamp. 3.16 a.m.'

It took a moment for the realisation to strike, but Price's energy was instantly elated when it did. 'Oh, shit! That's about the same time the Medical Examiner estimated the time of death.' The dots began to connect in her mind. 'If it wasn't Rachael who wrote this email, whoever killed her could have sent this email to Anne from her computer that night.'

'Or, Dempsey showed up that morning at Rachael's and found she had sent this to his wife. Kills her for it.'

'What do you think?' Colt's face was stern, the angles of his face sharp, lending a severe expression. 'Listen to me, Price, because this is important: the wheels of justice turn slow. Courts are backlogged. QPS is underfunded. The department won't entertain any theories about elaborate set-ups if the evidence backs an easy conviction. You and I are sworn officers of the Queensland Police Service. It's not our job to demonstrate Josh's innocence. The state pays us to administer justice by apprehending the guilty. It's an important distinction because if you and I can't show that Dempsey's potential innocence supersedes the conclusion drawn by the evidence – he's going down for this whether he did it or not. Do you understand?' Price was some fifteen years younger than Colt, and her youthfulness prevailed at this moment. He could see the weight of the stakes reflected in her eyes. The stress was beginning to pressure her. She was grinding her teeth and fidgeting with her hands. She was clenching her jaw, creating impressions at her temples. But it was good she was worried. It means she cares about getting it right. '*This,*' enunciated Colt, 'this, Price, is the real stuff. Before we enter that room together, you need to be sure to comprehend that the action we take has profound, long-term, real-world consequences on the lives of a lot of people. The ripples cast from cases like this spread far and wide, reaching through time, shaping events and impacting people's lives for years to come.' He put a reassuring hand on her shoulder. 'You've demonstrated resourcefulness and diligence in this case, Price. I trust that, like me, you're the kind of cop who makes a clear distinction between closing a case and serving justice. Don't doubt for a second there will be pressures on us to close this, even if we personally doubt that this man didn't commit the murder. Our opinions, our suspicions; they count for nothing. All that matters is what we can prove.'

    Price nodded. She took a deep breath and steadied herself. 'All right. Let's do this.'

As it happened, Colt learned that Josh wasn't a total moron. The second they got back to the precinct, he requested to see a solicitor. Therefore, the police delayed interrogating Josh until a lawyer could be arranged to be present, as was his right. La Pila demanded that everything was done to the highest degree of professionalism. She would not permit any opportunity for a defence barrister to later poke holes in the case by allowing her detectives to speak with the suspect without the presence of a lawyer. Colt was fine with the delay because in the two hours it took for a lawyer to come down, the forensic lab acquired the test results from analysing the evidence. As Colt predicted, the underwear belonged to Rachael and contained stains of Josh's semen. The blood found on both the underwear and the knife belonged to Rachael. The Medical Examiner confirmed that the bloody knife matched the wound pattern found on Rachael's torso. The knife's handle had a partial fingerprint, a tentative match for Josh Dempsey. There was no disputing that the knife they found in Josh's home was the same implement used to puncture Rachael's lung after being strangled to death. So, there it was. Evidence, motive, now all that was needed to close this case was a confession. Even if Josh Dempsey maintained that he was innocent, police prosecutors would sink him at trial. Price followed Colt into the interrogation room with a sense of purposefulness and duty she never really felt a day in her policing career before. She had always been a hunter in the police, but in Missing Persons, she hunted innocents; now, she hunted predators. Sitting down across the table from Joshua Dempsey for the second time this week, Price wondered as she looked upon this intimidated man whether he could be one, a monster camouflaged so reliably as an innocent that she could not detect his darkness even at close range. Josh's lawyer entered the room.

'Kimberley Glib,' she said, shaking Josh's hand. As a Detective, Colt had become familiar with some of the defence lawyers around town. Kim Glib is good at what she does. They wouldn't send her for just anyone. It could be that the firm has an idea that this case has the potential to blow up, especially when media get wind of the Double Spiral mystery. It's not an easy case to defend, but often the defence firms don't care about whether or not their clients are innocent or guilty; they care only for the publicity and notoriety cases like this present as a public relations opportunity. Firms that can defend challenging cases gain a reputation among organised crime circles, and that's where there are opportunities for them to make serious money. Aged in her early fifties, Kim Glib had thoroughly plucked her eyebrows to the extent that almost no hair remained on her brow at all. She has a crooked smile that reminded Josh of a cartoon villain. She wears red lipstick and way too much blue eye shadow. 'I'll be recording the interview on my phone as well,' she said to Colt.

'No objections, Ms Glib,' replied Colt coolly as he set down his own police-issued iPhone and began recording. 'For the record, the date is December 13th, 2021, and the time is 11.48 a.m. I am Detective Graham Coltsworth. Here with me is Mr Joshua Dempsey with counsel, Ms Kimberley Glib of Russel & Barnes Law. Also present is Senior Sergeant Addilyn Price. Mr Dempsey, you have been conveyed here today to be questioned in relation to the death of Miss Rachael Wright. Before I ask you any questions, I must tell you that you have the right to remain silent. This means that you do not have to say anything, or answer any question, or make any statement unless you wish to do so. Do you understand?'

'Yes,' said Josh weakly.

'Has any threat or promise been held out to you to get you

to take part in this interview?'

Josh shook his head. 'No, I have not been threatened.'

'Let's proceed. Mr Dempsey, you previously volunteered to be interviewed by my colleague, Senior Sergeant Price, when this case was being treated as a Missing Persons investigation. During that interview, you volunteered that you were with Rachael Wright at her apartment the afternoon of December 10th from four pm to seven pm that night. Is that accurate?' Josh looked to his solicitor with the wide-eyed innocence of a man terrified of saying anything that could put him in jeopardy. Where had that same fear been when he was arrested, Colt thought? Drowned by the early-morning booze, probably.

'That's correct,' he said meekly.

'What were you doing?' asked Price.

'You asked me that last time, and I told you: we were just hanging out at her apartment.'

'Did you have intercourse with Rachael that day?' asked Colt. Again, Josh looked to his lawyer. 'It's fine. It's not a crime to cheat on your wife, Mr Dempsey; just remember that everything you say can be used as evidence against you.'

'Yes. We had sex.'

'Once?' inserted Price.

'A few times.'

'How many times is a few?' asked Colt.

'I don't know,' mumbled Josh. 'Twice, maybe three times?'

Colt asked: 'How would you describe your relationship to Miss Wright?'

'Good. It was... You know, good. We enjoyed each other's company. We got along great. We had a real connection. It wasn't just sex, you know. We dated for a while back in the day, so there was history between us.'

'History, eh? Would you care to elaborate?'

Josh looked to his lawyer. 'Wouldn't it be better not to say anything?'

Ms Glib leaned over to Josh and offered her counsel. 'That is your right. But, if you want my advice, a refusal to cooperate with police can sometimes be interpreted at court as a sign of guilt.' She cast a stern glance at the officers across the table. 'I'll be sure to interject on your behalf if the police appear to be trying to entrap you.'

Josh looked up, his head hanging heavy. 'We had a fling years ago when we were in our late twenties, early thirties. Just for a few months, but at that time, we were both unemployed, so we talked all day, every day. It got too intense, as these things do. In the end, I wanted a commitment, she wasn't into it, and we broke up. I didn't see her again until I ran into her a few months back, and things just kind of picked up where they left off.'

This is interesting, thought Colt. A history between them. It could serve to bolster the narrative that prosecutors could build to mould the idea of an obsessive, jealous maniac who murdered his lover because she threatened his marriage and wouldn't commit to him. Colt had witnessed enough cases at trial that he could easily predict how the lawyers would build their case against defendants. Then again, his defence team could argue similarly that it was their long history and affection over time that was reason enough to doubt he could have hurt her this way. Colt chose this moment to produce the diary found in Mr Dempsey's bedroom. He slid it across the table inside the plastic evidence bag.

'Do you recognise this, Mr Dempsey?' asked Colt, carefully paying attention to every detail of Mr Dempsey's reaction.

'Uh, yeah,' he mumbled, barely audibly.

'Excuse me, Mr Dempsey? Speak up for the record, please.'

'Yes,' he said rather loudly. Then, a couple of decibels softer, he added: 'It's my journal.'

'This diary has been seized as evidence,' explained Colt. 'In it, there are months' worth of entries detailing very explicit sexual encounters between yourself and Miss Wright. Many of these records recount the acting out of violent sexual acts. In one of the final entries, you wrote that Miss Wright asked you to roleplay a sexual fantasy of her design, in which she is the victim of a violent sexual assault to be perpetrated by you.'

'My client has no comment on this subject,' spoke Ms Glib. Josh took the cue from his lawyer and remained silent.

Colt went on. 'You wrote that she asked you to pretend to break into her apartment late at night to commit a burglary, and then upon discovering she is home during the robbery, she wanted you to pretend to be an opportunistic predator and molest her.' Colt doubted whether even a world-class actor could conceal the shame Josh was feeling at this moment. He looked away from the diary sharply. 'I'm having trouble believing that Miss Wright would ask such a thing of you, Mr Dempsey.'

'She did, though,' said Josh defensively.

'Okay, for the sake of argument, let's say she did ask this of you. How did she expect you to break in as part of this fantasy?'

'I would advise not to answer that question, Mr Dempsey,' instructed Ms Glib. He cast a timid glance at his lawyer but was visibly agitated.

'No, you know what? I'm not going to be intimidated by them. I'm innocent. I have nothing to hide.' Kimberley Glib looked so exhausted by her client's foolishness she may as well have rolled her eyes and sighed with discontent. 'Rach gave me a key to her place,' offered Josh. 'She liked rough sex. It's not unusual.'

'In your previous interview with Sergeant Price, you mentioned that you left Rachael's apartment that day between six-thirty and seven p.m so you could get home to have dinner with your wife and kids, is that right?'

'Yes.'

'Did you go back to her apartment later that night, Josh? Perhaps an act of spontaneity to fulfil her sexual request?'

'No! I was at home all night. You can ask my wife.'

Price discreetly referred to the case file she kept in the manila folder on her lap. The Coroner's Office estimated Rachael Wright's time of death between one a.m and three a.m Thursday morning. Six hours after Josh claims to have left. *Did* he go back? She asked: 'Can your wife verify that you were home between one a.m, and three a.m that morning?'

'I don't know,' said Josh. 'She was most likely sleeping, as I was. You reckon whoever sleeps next to *you* could tell us if you were there in bed at one a.m last night?'

'So, that's a no, then?' Price insisted, noting that he avoided answering questions directly where possible. Was he just scared, or was there another reason for his lack of clarity? Colt was quiet for a moment while he also reviewed the case file. Price continued with her questioning. 'So, you were with Rachael hours before she was killed. By your own admission, you had a means of entering her apartment. We found a knife used to cause grievous bodily harm to Rachael as well as a pair of her underwear containing *her* blood and *your* semen at *your* house. Hidden with this diary, in fact. So, why should we believe that you didn't kill Rachael, Josh? You had the means and the motive.'

'What? What bloody motive, what are you talking about?

Why would I want to hurt Rach? I was in love with her!'

Then, Colt asked: 'To your knowledge, Mr Dempsey, was Rachael a religious woman?'

Josh raised a brow. It seemed a strange question. He couldn't fathom any reason it would have any relevance to the matter. 'I don't know, I don't think so. I mean, she never went to church or anything. You know, Rachael wasn't this picture-perfect, wide-eyed innocent teacher people think she is. She loves sex, drugs even more and loud music the best. She's not really a bible-beating type. You've been to her place. I'm sure you noticed the bong and probably found her stash of pills too; she didn't hide them very well.'

Both Price and Colt ignored Josh's assertions. It was important not to detract from the facts. 'What about you, Mr Dempsey?' asked Colt.

'What about me?' Josh's tone was laced with contempt.

'Are you a God-fearing man? A worshipper? Do you practise religion?'

For the first time, Josh relaxed; he even laughed. He leaned back in his seat and crossed his arms over his chest. 'Fuck no.'

Colt knew he was lying. The puffery, the false bravado, clear signs he was trying to conceal the truth. 'Would you describe yourself as a spiritual man, then?' asked Colt, setting the trap.

'I told you already, mate. *No*. I don't believe in any of that crap.'

'Interesting, because I've read your journal, cover to cover. In it, the word God appears hundreds of times. You quote bible verses, you talk a lot about the connection between divinity and the natural world. On one occasion, you wrote that while in the company of Miss Wright, you wished that you could preserve her at that moment so that you might possess her for yourself to the exclusion of all others forever. What did you mean by that? Were you thinking about killing her when you wrote that?'

Josh's confidence was dashed. He glanced at the table, his chest shrunk, and he slunk into his chair. 'So what if I wrote that? Is it a crime to contemplate the meaning of existence? Writing about God makes me a murderer, does it?'

'I wasn't suggesting it makes you a murderer, Mr Dempsey. However, the repetitive references to religious doctrine in the contents of your diary suggest not just an interest in the matter but an obsession with the subject. But you have just said, in your own words, you "don't believe in any of that crap", so you can see why I'm having some difficulty believing that you're being truthful, can't you?'

'He's calling you a liar,' said Price sharply. 'And if you're lying about your spiritual beliefs, it makes us wonder what else you might be lying about?'

Feeling he was being made a fool, his anger emerged. 'You fucking pigs, you're trying to set me up, aren't you?'

'Mr Dempsey, I urge you not to say anything else,' said Ms Glib with a convincingly stern tone.

Colt began to push a little harder. 'You seem angry, Josh. Does this happen often? Hm? You get angry a lot, Josh?'

'Remain calm, Mr Dempsey,' suggested Ms Glib. 'They're trying to rile you up to get a rise out of you. They're looking for an in-road by targeting your emotions. Don't give them one.' She looked at the police officers scornfully. 'It's *indecent*, officers.' She spoke vindictively. 'I suggest you avoid lowering yourselves to such tactics moving forward.'

Colt raised his palms up to those opposite. 'We've been warned.'

Price decided to pivot and try another tactic. 'What do you

know about trials at court, Josh?'

Josh shrugged. 'Not a lot. Why?'

'They're long, for one thing. In some cases, they can be dragged out for months. But you have to get there first. All the proceedings beforehand, the backlog at the courts, this stuff can occupy years of your life.'

'Your point being?' inquired Josh sourly.

'You must know about the email Rachael sent your wife. The one in which she confesses to the affair and basically ruins your marriage?'

'Yeah, but there's no way Rach would have written it. She wouldn't do that to me—'

Price cut him off. 'That's motive, Josh. The bloody knife and underwear hid in your bedroom? That's physical evidence. The journal detailing your obsession with Rachael and infatuation with spiritual topics, well, it all adds up to make a pretty strong case against you.'

Colt could see the fear in Josh's eyes as the reality of his situation truly gripped him. 'So, why not just save yourself the trouble of wasting what could potentially be years of your life, not to mention the effects it will have on your family, and just tell us what happened. Tell us the truth.'

Josh's lawyer went to speak, but Josh ignored her and spoke over her. 'I didn't do this,' he said. 'I'm being set up. I would never hurt Rachael.'

'Why would anyone want to set you up, Josh? Can't you see how hard it is to believe that someone is setting you up when it all points to you?'

He struck the table with his fists. 'It all points to me *because* I'm being set up! I didn't do it!'

'Here's what I think happened, Josh,' said Price. 'You

returned to her apartment that night to surprise her and indulge this fantasy she asked you to facilitate. You found her just after she sent an email to your wife, confessing to the affair you'd been having. You got angry. In your anger, you forced yourself on her, just like she asked you to. After all, she betrayed you. Fucked up your marriage, screwed your life up, just because she had a change of heart. You rape her, and your semen gets on her underwear. She doesn't want it. Doesn't want you. She changed her mind, wanted out, so maybe she resists you, so you choke her into submission. You probably figured that you could fix things with Anne if she disappeared. It was her word against yours, after all. Now, she's dead, but you can't be *sure* that she's dead, so, you poke her, right here' —Price gestures to her ribcage— 'with a knife, just to be sure. It's early in the morning. The sun will be up soon, and people will be about. There's no time to take the body out of town to bury it in the sticks, so you go to the nearest spot you think is safest to dump her and leave her at the creek, only a couple of minutes' drive from her apartment in Spring Hill.'

Josh listened attentively, never interjecting, never protesting until Price finished her summation. He looked hurt as if her words had caused him physical pain. A tear rolled down his cheek. 'There's no way. No way I did any of that. I swear to God.'

'Funny,' said Price. 'I thought you said you didn't believe in God, Josh.'

Colt listened to Senior Sergeant Price with great interest as she summarised the case against Josh. A partially matched fingerprint on the bloody knife that penetrated Rachael's dead body was found in his bedroom. Combined with the underwear containing samples of his DNA, these two pieces of incriminating evidence vilify Josh. To add fuel to the fire, his diary recounted multiple occasions during which he boasted about savage sexual encounters with the victim, alluding to the possibility that he could be the sort of man capable of extreme violence. His diary also contained themes nearly identical to the sentiment found in the meaning of the pagan double spiral symbol suggesting an obsession with the symbolism contained therein. There were no signs of forced entry at Rachael's apartment, meaning whoever killed her either expertly broke in, had a key to enter the dwelling, or was invited inside by the victim. Given the time her death is estimated to have occurred, breaking in or gaining entry by key were the two likeliest outcomes. To that point, according to his diary, the victim gave Josh a key to her place and invited him to roleplay a break in which was likely why there were no signs of a struggle inside the apartment. Poor Rachael was *expecting* a mock-burglary in which the intruder – whom she believed to be Josh – was allegedly asked to force her into a sexual encounter. As Price put it, when Josh arrived at her apartment and discovered that she had just published an email to his wife revealing the truth about their affair, he lost it, and consequently, killed her. It all stacked up. Price's summation pointedly inferred Josh's guilt when framed in this light. Even Colt could reasonably doubt his innocence. As far as his character goes, Colt deduced that Josh Dempsey was a sociopathic narcissist prone to jealousy with potent anger issues and who was clearly obsessed with the victim. He could conceal his negative emotions very well, demonstrating an aptitude for deception characteristic of a sociopath, except when something substantially provokes his anger. His journal entries indicated a fixation with possession. In his journal, he wrote about wishing to preserve his time with Rachael, indicating that, at least to some extent, he maintained some level of insecurity about Rachael's reluctance to commit to him exclusively. A jealous man, prone to fits of rage, with a capacity for violence and an obsession with theology betrayed by his lover, takes advantage of her trust, kills her and then goes on to brand her with a mark that symbolises the polarity between his love for her and her abuse of that love. Maybe that's all there is to it. A revenge killing. A crime of passion by a petty, selfish man. That all fits the profile. The one thing that didn't add up, though… In his mind, he could see the image of the double spiral formed by cutting away pieces of Rachael's skin. The surgical precision, the cold, meticulous hand that wielded the scalpel; the fact nagged at Colt's instincts like an incessant splinter. It was the single weak point in the case against Josh. The making of that mark had been administered with such precision, requiring the steadiest of hands. Josh had already proven quick to anger. But anger was counter-productive to producing the double spiral marking. It was believable enough that an angered Josh could have choked his mistress to death in the heat of the moment, but there was nothing to persuade Colt into believing he could have then dedicated hours of his time afterwards to cutting pieces off her. What happened next would be telling. 'This is your chance, Josh. Tell us about the mark. It's obviously very meaningful to you. So, what's it about?'

When Josh answered Colt, it was as though they were the only two people in the room. Colt stared into Josh's eyes and held them. Josh glared back at him helplessly like a deer in headlights. 'I don't know what you're talking about.'

Undoubtedly, Colt believed him.

Chapter Ten

Tuesday, 14th December 2021 9:30 a.m

An emergency meeting had been arranged at Claremont College by the school Principal, Elaine Gallagher. In the seven years that Elise taught at the school, she could not recall any occasion when the teachers had convened together during the holidays. These were exceptional circumstances. On the six o'clock news this morning, the media announced a fact which Elise and Rachael's mother had been dreading since they lodged the Missing Person's notice with Queensland Police. Rachael Wright had been murdered. Her body had been located on the banks of the Enoggera Creek. The media reported that Queensland Police had apprehended someone they suspected guilty of the crime, Rachael's lover, Joshua Dempsey. 'I'm so grateful that you have all been able to attend personally today,' began Principal Gallagher sounding appropriately sympathetic. 'Rachael is known to all of you. I'm sure the weight of this tragedy is felt keenly by us all. I asked you all here so that together, we could have a private opportunity to acknowledge the tragedy that has befallen one of our own. Rachael was a wonderful, warm woman, as I'm sure all of you can attest. I want you to know that I have been in communication with Queensland Police concerning the matter, and while they are unable to share details of the investigation, they assured me that they are working tirelessly, around the clock, to ensure that Rachael receives the justice she deserves.

'They reported on the news that a man has been charged with the murder,' said Dale Bellringer, the school science teacher seated beside Elise.

'That's true,' said Principal Gallagher. 'We have all heard the same reports. A Brisbane man confirmed to have been involved in a romantic relationship with Rachael has been charged with her murder.'

Josh, thought Elise. She remembered talking to Rachael just days ago about him. *Why did he do this?* It didn't make any sense to Elise. Was it because Rachael finally figured out what she wanted and decided she didn't want to commit to him after all? Did he kill and mutilate her best friend for something as arbitrary as rejecting him? Elise watched Principal Gallagher's mouth moving, but the sound of her voice was drowned out by the deafening silence in her own mind. Her world felt to be falling apart. The situation did not *feel* real. How could she have been so intimately connected to another person for so many years and not sense that she was in trouble? She looked at her hands folded on the table in front of her. How many times had she eaten lunch with Rachael at this very table? For her best friend to be so suddenly and violently snatched out of existence felt like being engrossed in an enthralling film but being denied the pleasure of ever seeing how it ends. Naturally, being aged in her mid-forties, Elise had known a few in her time who had died. Grandparents, friends once removed from friends, but she had never personally known anyone to have been murdered. The carnage of murder leaves a different impression on those left behind. It is a whole other order of grief. Rachael didn't have the misfortune of becoming gravely ill or befalling a tragic accident. Her life was intentionally cut short by another person. Nothing could prepare those who loved Rachael for that. Elise had never met Josh, but she had seen plenty of pictures of him taken by Rachael. She felt she knew the man by how her friend spoke of him. He was thoughtful, generous, a little obsessive but harmless, or so she thought. The media told of how it happened. Rachael was strangled to death. According to the news, poor Rachael was also stabbed, and her body was dumped on the banks of the Enoggera Creek like she was a piece of trash. She tried to picture Josh Dempsey doing it. Hard as she tried, she couldn't imagine it. In her imagination, trying to cast Josh as Rachael's killer was like envisaging a poorly cast villain. Someone who doesn't look or feel the part. Josh is too ordinary. Josh should possess a dark, brooding temperament and have fixed, dangerous expressions to make it credible. His eyes should convey his inner darkness. There should be some evidently visible outward sign of his evil intent. Something other than human. A clue that hints at the demonic force hiding inside a man's skin. 'It's just so sad,' muttered Darika Patel, who sat to Elise's left. Darika's voice broke the spell of Elise's reverie. Her Indian accent lent Darika's voice a warm affection that comforted Elise in a way she couldn't describe.

Principal Gallagher gestured to the school chaplain, who stood with her in front of the teachers gathered around the staff room tables. 'Shane is a trained grief counsellor, and of course, he is at your service if anyone feels they need to talk about this matter.'

Shane, the hulking brown-skinned New Zealander and emissary of God in this room, stepped forward to make it known: 'I'm here for all of you.' Despite his hulking mass, there was a humility in the way he spoke. 'Anytime. Inside and outside school hours. If anyone feels they want to talk about this issue, or for that matter, anything else at all that might be bothering you, my door is always open to you. I'm not just here for the kids; I'm here for you all as well.' Shane withdrew, allowing Principal Gallagher to resume her address to the group. Elise wasn't paying attention. She sat in silence, hardly able to absorb a word anybody was saying. She was just waiting for it to be over so she could go home and sleep. That's all she felt like doing since she learned about Rachael from the news this morning. She didn't care about how these people were feeling. None of them really knew Rachael. They knew Rachael-the-teacher, not Rachael-the-human. Those were two very different people. She thought about how Rachael's mother must be getting on. She wondered whether she should go round and see her. Rachael's mother was very ill, and Rachael had feared she might pass away for months. Could news of her daughter's sudden demise be her reason to quit fighting? How could she comfort anyone else when she could hardly do the same for herself?

'How are you, Elise?' asked Darika when the meeting was concluded. Having lived with a diagnosis of depression for half her life, Elise *hated* this question more than anything else because the socially acceptable response for her during her depressive episodes – which occurred often – was always a lie. *I'm good, I'm fine, I'm okay.* Variants of the same sentiment. Essentially, people asked that question to be polite, but nobody really cared to hear the truthful answer. Not the girl working the cash register at the grocery store, not the customer service representative on the other end of the phone, and certainly not the people she worked with when the school urged teachers and students to probe those they care about on R U OK Day – a ludicrously shameful hallmark holiday for those living with supposedly healthy minds to pity those living with mental health disorders if ever there was one. Society would have her believe there is no shame or stigma in talking openly about mental health. Ask anyone who lives with it, and they'll tell you that's utter bullshit. At this moment, Elise didn't care about answering according to the unwritten rules of social convention. What did she have to lose that could hurt her any more than she already was?

'Honestly, Darika, it feels like some deranged surgeon has taken a scalpel, sliced me up the middle and stuffed my insides with a bunch of rocks and then stitched me back up. There is a burning feeling in my throat that won't go away, and it feels as though my brain is swollen to the point it's pressed against my skull, searching for a way to crack the bone and leak out of my ears. This pressure in my chest makes it feel like it's hard to breathe. My brain feels like it's engrossed in a fog so thick I can't think straight. I just… can't believe it's real. Rachael's gone.' She touched the smooth surface of the table with her fingertips. 'She will never sit here and eat lunch with us again. I will never hear her laugh or get annoyed because she had a song stuck in her head all day, and her refusal to stop singing the melody got it stuck in mine too. I'll never see her again. Her life, all the things that she could have done and the versions of herself that might have just been plucked out of existence. I just can't believe it.' Hearing her response to Darika's question, Dale, who sits on Elise's other side, stifles a laugh. Elise rounded her gaze upon him as if she could eject fireballs from her eyes. 'Did I say something funny?'

'No,' he said, smoothing out his grin for a more appropriate sentimental expression. He speaks quietly enough that it doesn't interrupt the discussion between Principal Gallagher and the other teachers – just like how the kids they teach annoyingly whisper among themselves while they try to conduct classes. 'It's just, it's kind of healthy, being that honest, isn't it? I mean, really, how often do we just tell people what they want to hear when they ask us how we're doing? It's like an automation thing, you know? We're all just made to believe it's perfectly normal to just politely go about ignoring how we and those around us are really feeling and just pretend like everything is okay all of the time. As fucked up as it is, tragedies like this shed people's inhibitions. Makes people more honest because we're less inclined to care about what others think of us when we speak our truth. Honestly, Elise, hearing you talk about how you *really* feel is invigorating.'

'I suppose that's true,' said Darika. 'Sometimes, I have found myself wishing I could be more honest about what I'm feeling during those times the world feels like it's just a crappy place to be.'

'Well, I'm glad that there is something positive to come out of my shitty mood,' said Elise.

'Hey, do you two want to meet for a drink tonight? We can trade stories about Rachael and just blow off a little steam,' proposed Dale. Elise turned her attention to the angular-jawed science teacher beside her. Surely he knew that Darika has a family and doesn't drink. There's no way she could go out for a drink on a weeknight, especially during school holidays.

'That actually sounds really good,' said Darika. *Here it comes: "but..."* thinks Elise. Darika offers her most apologetic look to her two colleagues. 'But I can't tonight. Family commitments. Raincheck?'

Dale turns to Elise. 'How about you, El?'

It would be a little awkward to say no after Darika has already bowed out, thought Elise. Drinking with a colleague sounded like a better proposition than crying herself to sleep at home. 'Sure. I could go for a drink.'

'Great,' said Dale. 'I'll see who else I can round up.'

Principal Gallagher concluded, 'Thank you all for coming in today. Obviously, I will address the issue with our students when school returns next year. Until then, be safe, all of you. Happy holidays.'

Dale got up and approached some of the other staff members. Elise supposed he was inquiring about who else might join them later for a few drinks. 'Well, I better be off,' said Darika as she checked the time on her wristwatch. It was then that Elise noticed that a man was speaking with Principal Gallagher at the door of the staffroom, someone she didn't recognise.

'Okay. Well, be safe and enjoy your holidays. I'll see you next year.' Darika hugged Elise. Principal Gallagher looked around the room until she located Elise and gestured, waving her over. Elise tried to muster some enthusiasm, saying to Darika: 'I hope you have a good Christmas.'

'It doesn't quite compare to Diwali, but it's got a certain charm,' teased Darika. 'Take care of yourself. Don't hesitate to reach out if you ever want to talk. Shane's a great guy, but let's face it, I don't think being told this is all a part of God's plan is really going to cut it right now.' After taking a stab at the school chaplain, Darika left, and Elise walked across the room where Elaine was still speaking with the mystery man.

'Elise,' said Principal Gallagher, 'this is Detective Graham Coltsworth. I invited him here because he wanted to speak with Rachael's colleagues about her. I hope you don't mind, but I was just telling him that of all the staff at Claremont, you were closest with her.'

'Would you mind if I asked you some questions, Miss…?'

'Arnott. And it's *Ms,* actually. I'm divorced, but I still have the bastard's name.'

Principal Gallagher frowned disapprovingly but wouldn't go so far as to comment on Elise's transgression, given the circumstances. 'Well, I'll leave you to it.'

Much to her dismay, the detective who introduced himself as Graham Coltsworth didn't look anything like how Elise imagined a real-life Detective would. He was slightly taller than her with a stocky build and clearly had minimal regard for his personal appearance. She expected someone clean-cut, dressed tastefully, who was warm and personable. Graham Coltsworth was about as far opposite to her expectations as could be. His hair was unstyled, a mess of black and grey curly tangles. His facial hair was untrimmed and made him look scruffy. He didn't even bother to close the loop on his necktie, leaving it hanging loosely beneath his collar. He had a humourless expression and detached, discerning eyes. The only thing that met her expectations of what a detective should be was that he took notes on a little paper pad as they talked. His first question: 'How well would you say you know Miss Wright?'

'She was my best friend. I've known her for over ten years. I've worked at this school for seven, and she was the one who actually recommended me for the job here originally. She was kind of a living legend around here. That's why Elaine called us all together today; I think if this had happened to anyone else among our ranks people would have felt less inclined to come in like this during holidays.' Elise became pensive for a moment. It felt strange to hear herself say she had known Rachael for more than a decade. Sometimes, the way time compresses the memory of experiences doesn't quite register properly. Things that happened just yesterday can feel like they occurred months ago, and memories from years past can feel much more recent.

'I'm very sorry for your loss,' said the detective sounding a little insincere. She tried not to take offence. That statement for him is likely as overused as when she tells people she's *fine* and *good* and *okay*. After a while, it's hard to say those words and still sound candid. The Detective began flipping through pages on his notepad. When he found what he was looking for, he presented the page to her, showing a ten digit number. 'Do you recognise this phone number?'

'Of course, answered Elise, squinting to read the writing on the page. 'It's mine.'

Colt noted it. 'Your number was the last one Rachael's mobile service provider registered in the logs before her time of death. According to the telecommunications record, you spoke with her on December 10th. Do you remember what you talked about?'

'Like it was yesterday. She had been with... *him* that night. I called her before we went to bed. She told me that Josh had been over at her place and expressed a desire to define the terms of their relationship. Rachael was having second thoughts about whether or not she wanted a commitment.'

'Did she mention whether or not they fought?'

'No, in fact, I'm sure they didn't.'

'How can you be sure?'

'Because Rachael told me she didn't give him an answer. If she had rejected him, they would have argued. She wouldn't have felt any confusion if she had told him she wanted to be with him. Ergo, no fight. She said she needed more time to figure things out.' Elise broke off and covered her mouth, visibly upset. After a moment, she gathered her composure. 'It was really him? He actually did it?'

'I'm sorry, I'm not permitted to talk about matters relating to an open investigation.'

'That sounds like the company line,' rebutted Elise. 'He has been charged with the crime. The news says that QPS found evidence linking him to it at his house.'

'Again, Ms Arnott, I'm sorry—'

'What are you doing here, then? I mean, if you have already arrested him for it?'

'We're just covering all bases,' said Colt without alluding to anything more. 'You mentioned that Rachael was having doubts about her relationship with Mr Dempsey. Do you recall what she said, exactly?'

Elise thought for a minute. She remembered teasing Rachael about being a commitment-phobe. The pain rose in her chest when she realised that was the last thing she ever said to her best friend. She felt her throat tighten, and she answered, choking back tears: 'Sorry,' she spluttered, trying to stop herself from crying. 'I just realised that was the last conversation I had with her. I teased her about being afraid of commitment. I even defended *him*. Why did I do that…? Rachael told me she wasn't sure what she wanted with Josh, that she liked things the way they were and didn't want that to change. She was worried about the impact that taking the next step with Josh could have on his wife and kids… I know she felt guilty about being *the other woman*. She loved kids, and they loved her. Kids were her whole life. Ask any student at this school, and they will tell you that she was loved by the people here.' Colt thought about his brief interaction with Josh and Anne's son, Lucas, who attended this school and spoke fondly of Rachael, even revering her for treating him mercifully when he was caught breaking the rules. Elise explained, 'the affair was a secret, but if they went public with their relationship, she knew it could impact Josh's wife and their children, and she was worried about that. she wasn't sure whether being with Josh was worth risking that kind of harm. Especially for Josh's kids. She actually said that she had concerns about how a divorce could impact his kids.'

This had Colt wondering… Why would a woman who was so concerned about the impact of committing to Josh go and email his wife about their affair? If what Elise Arnott says is true, it seems out of character for her. Then again, how well did Elise really know Rachael? There were drugs found at Rachael's apartment. Maybe she was high and not thinking straight when she did it. Or, perhaps she didn't send that email at all… Elise blinked, and two heavy teardrops fell from her eyes, rolling down her cheek. Kindly, the Detective offered a handkerchief he drew from his pocket. 'Thanks,' she said, wiping her face.

'I can see this is very difficult, Ms Arnott. We can stop if you like; it's just imperative to getting justice for Rachael that I gather this information for the case.'

'No, it's okay, we can keep going. What else did you want to know?'

'You mentioned she was debating whether she wanted a commitment with Mr Dempsey.'

'Yeah.'

'Did she say she wanted to end things with Mr Dempsey? What about other men; did she ever mention any other lovers?'

'I don't know if she wanted to dump Josh, per se. All she said was that she needed time to figure out what *she* wanted. Rach was always the kind of woman who enjoyed being single, you know? Like, I mean, she actually preferred it. Most people are desperate to be in a relationship because loneliness is such a killer, but Rachael was a really independent person. She could be happy on her own as much as she could being with someone. To know I'm right, all you have to do is look at her life choices. She was forty-five. She chose not to marry or have any kids. It's not so much that she was afraid of commitment; it's just that she preferred the freedoms of being single. As far as other men go, no, not that she mentioned to me anyway. It was just Josh she was seeing.'

'And she would have mentioned it if she was seeing someone else?'

'Of course. I would have known. Definitely.'

The Detective looked around the staff room. People were beginning to head home. 'One last question, Ms Arnott. You have been accommodating, and I appreciate that. To your knowledge, was Rachael a religious woman? She ever talk about God or express a religious side?'

Elise smiled at the question. Rachael, religious, now *that* was funny. 'No,' she said spiritedly. 'I knew Rachael for a long time, and I can tell you definitively that she was an atheist. Why, what has that got to do with anything?'

'As I said, Ms Arnott...'

Elise raised her hand, motioning the Detective to stop. 'You can't talk about the case. Forgot. Sorry.' She dabbed her eyes with the handkerchief. 'I didn't know Josh personally; all I knew about him was what I heard told of him through Rachael. But I really didn't think he could be the type of person to do something like this. Something so *evil*.'

Privately, Colt agreed. Josh doesn't seem like the type. 'Thank you for your time, Ms Arnott.' Elise attempted to return the handkerchief, but Detective Colt politely declined. 'You can keep it.'

The two parted ways. Elise said her goodbyes to those who remained in the staff room and then went home. Until she talked with Detective Coltsworth, the pain of this loss had been something she had managed to keep at arms-length. But as she crashed onto her bed at home, she felt all of it. She thought about how she teased Rachael the last time they spoke. She thought about how she would never hear her voice again or see her at school. Rachael was gone, and it left a hole in her life, and it felt like nothing, and nobody could fill that space. Her grief swallowed her whole, enveloping her in body and mind. Now that she was alone and she didn't have to pretend she wasn't miserable, she allowed herself to feel it all, letting herself be swept away by the icy, frigid white-wash that was the raging waters of her loneliness and despair.

It was already dusk when Elise woke. The sun had set on another Summer's day, the approaching night heralding cooler temperatures. It took her an hour to shower and do her hair and makeup. Dale had texted her while she was asleep to let her know he organised for those he invited to drinks to meet at the Riverside Bar near the City at seven pm. Elise arrived at six forty-five. She purchased a drink from the bar and selected a table at the edge of the venue, staring at the dark waters and watching the ferries glide lazily along the river. She could just make out the silhouettes of the people being carried by the ferries. She wondered about them. Did one of them lose their job today? Did another get diagnosed with cancer? Maybe one of them lost their best friend too. She sipped her drink through a straw and observed the people at the bar. Smiling faces, the sound of laughter, and the overture of slightly drunk patrons all speaking at a volume that is just fractionally louder than their neighbour. And all of them inevitably living one minute at a time as they each approach their doom unknown. The stark, undeniable reality of one's mortality is never as apparent as it is until after enduring the loss of a loved one, she brooded. Yet, for Elise, who doesn't believe in reincarnation or any sort of afterlife, the frightening truth of mortality also provides holistic gratitude. While Rachael is not, to be here now is its own miracle. Sadly, that same gratitude sparked a guilty conscience. It felt wrong to celebrate life when someone she loved had theirs stolen. She sipped her vodka and cranberry juice and gazed at the patrons in the bar. They seemed to take very little notice of her, except for some of the men who ogled her with little regard for being caught doing it. Ordinarily, she would resent such attention. That was not the case tonight. Rachael's loss had triggered a depression quite unlike any that she had felt in many years. For just tonight, she desperately wanted to feel *anything* but sad. When Dale showed up, she was impressed. He wore a blue blazer with a white buttoned shirt underneath. The two buttons at the top were unfastened, hinting at the remarkably firm chest lying beneath. He was clean-shaven; his hair was combed and parted at the side. Even in her heels, she still stood an inch or two shorter than him. He kissed her cheek when they embraced, and she caught a whiff of his cologne, a heavenly scent, a masculine musk that made her feel aroused. 'You look great,' she said, admiring the effort he made. He never looked so attractive when he was at school. How had she never noticed before? She supposed it was the bland clothes he wore at school. Elise had always thought Dale to be timid, an assumption she assigned because he was quiet and reserved. Now, it was like seeing a new man. Bold colours, stylish hair, gentle and attentive blue eyes and a jaw so sharp she could cut cheese on it. 'Wow,' she gawked. 'You look so handsome.'

'You too,' he said, taking her in. She wore a black floral button-up mini dress that displayed her ample cleavage and highlighted her bronzed skin. Gold hooped earrings hung from her lobes, and she had her hair tied up in a bun at the back. 'Pretty, I mean. Not handsome. That would be weird.' He laughed casually, a musical sound. Dale scanned the bar, searching. 'So, is it just us?'

'So far, yeah. It looks like it.'

'Well, I should probably get a drink.' He indicated towards the glass in Elise's hand. 'You look like you could use a top-up. While we wait for the others, it will give us a chance to get to know each other a little better.' His smile was infectious; it drew hers out the second he flashed it her way. The two made their way through the bar, steering themselves around tables and chairs and poorly balanced patrons. The bartender acknowledged them with a nod.

'What can I get you?'

'I'll have a pint of Pure Blonde, please, mate,' said Dale to the bartender. He looked to Elise beside him. 'And you?'

'Vodka cranberry, please.' Elise kept her back to the bar while they waited for their drinks to arrive. They didn't speak. Elise watched a middle-aged man dancing lamely to the live musician strumming her guitar. She didn't mind the silence. When the drinks arrived, Elise tried to pay for hers, but Dale insisted on buying. She compromised. 'I'll get the next round then.'

'Come on,' said Dale as he handed Elise her drink. He led Elise to a less populated area towards the back, which was quieter. 'I, uh, have a confession to make,' said Dale shyly as the two sat down. 'I was secretly hoping that the others I invited tonight wouldn't show up.' He cast her a sideways glance, momentarily meeting her eye.

'Oh?' she nibbled at the straw in her glass. 'Why might that be?'

He took a long drink from his glass. 'I sometimes feel like I have trouble connecting with people. When I heard you speak so honestly to Darika today, I dunno; it kind of felt like you could potentially be one of my tribe, y'know? Maybe I'm not making any sense, and I'm sorry if that's too forward...' He scoffed at himself in jest. 'I think you should stop me; I'm rambling already.'

Elise giggled. It was nice to see him be so open. It made her feel at ease. 'No, I get it. I sometimes feel that way too. When you think about it, we never *know* people. You can learn everything there is to know about someone – all the stuff they like and hate, their personal histories – and yet, sometimes it just feels as though there is always something missing, some essence that people just can't share with each other, even if they want to.'

'Exactly!' he said with great enthusiasm. 'You're a lot more articulate than I am.'

'Well, vodka tends to have that effect on me. Besides, you teach Science, I teach Humanities. Your world is full of hypotheses, things that can be measured and proven and verified. Mine is not so definitive. There's room for...'

'Surprises?' He flashed a handsome smile. 'Well, if social studies teach us anything, it's that people can always surprise you.'

He laughed delightedly and took a sip from his beer. She liked the way the sound of his laughter made her feel. This was her theory in practice; she had underestimated this man who apparently was full of surprises. 'I propose a toast,' said Dale, raising his tall beer glass. 'In memory of our friend, Rachael, may tonight only bring good surprises.'

'To pleasant surprises,' she said, clinking her glass against his. 'And to finding one's tribe.' She smiled seductively and drank heartily from her glass until it was empty because the second the words had passed from her lips, her depression beckoned, reminding her it was always near.

It seemed her face didn't hide her feelings because Dale looked up concernedly and asked: 'Is everything okay?' Then, he slapped himself on the forehead with his palm. 'Idiot. Sorry, Elise. That was a stupid question…'

'No, no,' she stammered in a poor attempt at reassurance, 'I'm all right. I was just thinking about how I've lost a member of *my* tribe.' Attempting to be casual and flirty, she added: 'On the bright side, I suppose that means there is a vacancy and tonight you're the prime candidate. So, Mr Bellringer, what kind of special skills do you possess that could be of value to my tribe?'

'Well, not to toot my own horn, but my knowledge of science comes in handy. I possess a very thorough comprehension of the laws of thermodynamics, so, y'know; fire…'

'I'm no scientist, but I think you mean *heat.*'

'Heat, exactly. Warmth. Every tribe needs that, right? Not such a bad thing when those cold winter nights roll around.'

'Okay,' said Elise dismissively flicking her head sideways as if his answer wasn't absolutely perfect. 'That's a *start*. What else?'

'Well,' he said with tantalising intrigue, 'I may not look it, but I'm quite strong.' He displayed his bicep in a pretend show of brute strength.

'I'll be the judge of that,' said Elise. 'Come here. Let me feel.' Dale rose up and brought his chair around to the other side of the table to sit next to Elise. He offered up his arm, tensing his muscles for her. She wrapped her whole hand around one, then tenderly stroked the muscles in his upper arm, assessing them on their merits. 'Okay, you weren't lying. So, you're smart and strong. I guess there could be a place for you as a hunter amongst the tribe.'

'Oh, yeah?' He inched a little closer to her.

'Mm-hmm.'

'What am I hunting?'

Elise looked Dale in the eye with confident intensity. 'Tonight?' She put her fingers on his collar and whispered: 'Me.'

'And what happens if I catch my prey?' He was so near that his smell was intoxicating. She was getting tingly feelings between her legs.

'It's a surprise! After all, isn't that what tonight is all about?' She put her hand in his lap, stroking his leg, easing her way towards the middle. Then, pulled away… 'But there's one more trial you will have to pass if you want to ensure your place in my tribe. A final rite of passage.'

'I like the sound of that. What does the matriarch require of me?'

She offered him her hand. 'Come on. I'll show you.' He took her hand, and she led him to the dancefloor. The live musician played a rendition of Little Talks by Of Monsters and Men. She began swaying her hips and dancing to the melody of the music, and she was delighted when he was able to match her charisma. They danced foolishly, not caring who was watching. When the performer transitioned into a song by The Lumineers, Elise slowed her pace and extended her hand to Dale, who took it and drew her in close to him. They danced in a slow embrace, shuffling side-to-side on the spot.

'So, what do you think, do I pass the test?' he leaned close and asked in her ear.

She stepped back and took him in. Handsome, witty, funny. How had she never noticed these things about him before? 'You're certainly off to an excellent start.'

The end of the song called for another drink. Things were going well. Elise was glad she came out. It was nearly eight p.m, and none of the other teachers Dale supposedly invited had shown up yet. Elise began to suspect that he never actually invited anyone else. At first thought, she found it odd that the confident, suave man with her tonight could be too shy to ask her out on a date. If he did orchestrate this night out just to spend with her, she surmised it was a matter of him just trying to be polite. If he asked her out directly and she said no, it would have made things awkward for them both at school. It was admirable, really, how conscientious it was for him to be so considerate of her feelings given the circumstances. Even if his tactics were a little shady. His clever little ruse was okay with her if the ends justified the means. They collected their drinks from the bar and stood side by side at the edge of the venue that overlooked the river. 'It's a shitty consolation, but for what it's worth, I reckon Rach is in a better place now,' he said, showing a pensive side.

This was a different sort of surprise. Unexpected, as the best surprises are, but not necessarily *wanted* at this very moment. Elise knew too well that Rachael would always be in her thoughts, but tonight she just wanted a break from herself and the tormenting voice inside that was constantly chipping away at her sanity. She figured she might as well follow the thread. 'What do you mean? Like, as in, Heaven?'

'Maybe. Who can say? All I meant was that I believe the spirit endures even after the body perishes.'

'I didn't pick you for the religious type.'

'I wouldn't describe myself that way,' he said softly. 'More of a naturalist.'

'You're certainly full of surprises tonight! A naturalist? Doesn't biology kind of contradict the idea of a soul and all that spiritual stuff?'

'Au contraire, mademoiselle,' said Dale with the pageantry of a stage actor. 'People often seem to feel that science and religion are at odds with each other. I don't think so, personally. In fact, I think they are quite complementary. Chemistry, physics, biology: in my view, these things don't serve to disprove God or spirituality. If anything, they remind me of how extravagant and miraculous life is. Consider, for example, the Earth's proximity to our sun. If this planet were positioned just a little farther away, or a little closer, to that star, you and I wouldn't be standing here. Whenever I feel down about life, I remind myself of the harmony of all the forces of nature that make being here with you right now possible.' Dale drew close to Elise. 'The sun's gravitational pull.' He put his hands around her waist. 'The attraction of the Earth and Moon.' She touched his hands, guiding them down her waist onto her thighs. She could feel the cadence of her pulse rising. He held her against him, pressing his body into hers and whispered gently against her ear: 'The hot, fiery mass at the heart of the world.' She softly exhaled with anticipatory lust.

'You know, I get the feeling you never invited any of the others,' she said, pressing her backside into him, teasing him with her body.

'I suppose it was a little naughty of me,' he said into her ear. 'Well, you're a teacher, so you know all too well what happens to boys who misbehave.'

He smiled devilishly, and she kissed him. It was sexy, the tango of their kiss. His hands gripped her arse firmly, squeezing and urging her backwards till she was hard-pressed against the balcony's edge. While he ravished her with his hands, she touched his face with her hands and traced her fingers through his hair. She couldn't remember the last time she had felt so turned on. His touch was eager, his hands encouragingly spreading around her body. 'You, uh, you want to get out of here?' she asked tentatively.

'Yeah. Let's go back to your place.' There was a row of cabs waiting for pickups just outside the bar. They held hands as they got into the backseat of the first taxi in the rank. Elise gave the driver her home address. He had his hand on her leg in the backseat while she touched the back of his neck affectionately. They didn't say much for a few minutes. They just enjoyed each other's touch. Elise felt at ease, giddy from the drinks and horny from the company. She was ready to know Dale better. 'It's strange, the interconnectedness of things when you think about it sometimes.' His words felt out of place, certainly not on the same wavelength of her mood. She had talked enough philosophy for one night. Less talking, more fucking, that's all she wanted now.

But, people seldom speak their thoughts. Therefore, she probed: 'How do you mean?'

'I had a bit of a crush on Rachael once. I asked her out a while ago, but she knocked me back.'

'I didn't know that,' said Elise, the mood shifting a little unfavourably for her as she began to feel like some kind of consolation prize.

'I'm not surprised she didn't mention it,' he said brazenly. 'But kind of ironic, isn't it? If what happened to Rachael hadn't happened… You and I might not be here together right now. I hate to say it, but I'm almost grateful she's gone because now I get to be with you tonight.'

What the *hell,* thinks Elise. 'How could you say that!' Her objection is filled with protective defensiveness.

'I'm sorry, I didn't mean—'

'Stop the cab, now!' shouted Elise to the driver. She withdrew her touch from him and pushed his hand away. 'Just let me out here, please.' The driver pulled over to the side of the road.

'Elise, please, I didn't mean that I'm *glad* she's dead. Seriously, I was just making an observation. C'mon, we don't have to let this spoil a good time.' He reached to touch her again. Was it pleasure or assurance he hoped to provide? She slapped his hand away.

'Don't touch me, Dale. For fuck's sake. I can't believe you could be so insensitive. I'll find my own way home.' She opened the door of the cab and exited onto the street. After she was out of the car, she turned to Dale, who was still in the backseat, saying: 'Tonight was supposed to be about good surprises, but you know what's *not* a good surprise? Finding out the sweet, thoughtful guy you're about to go home with is just another smooth-talking arsehole.' She slammed the door shut. She had no clue where she was. Some random curbside in the City. Nothing looked familiar. She began walking; it didn't matter which direction she travelled; she just needed to move. She walked as fast as her legs could carry her in heels, which was not very fast at all, but all that mattered was that she put as much distance between herself and that cab as possible. 'I'm so sorry, Rach,' she said to herself. 'I miss you…' She felt the tears come and didn't make any effort to keep them at bay. This is precisely the kind of event she would have called Rachael about. Rachael would have told her that Dale is a dick and she's better off and probably would have made some crude joke that would have made her laugh. But Rachael was gone, and Elise was alone. As she made her way home, she thought about how much better this night could have been if Dale had just kept his stupid mouth shut about Rachael. If only he hadn't said anything, it all would have been fine. If only... By the time she arrived home to her apartment, she was ready to succumb to the depression that teetered at the edge of her consciousness. She slept alone, crying herself to sleep, swallowed by the shadow of her grief.

Chapter Eleven

Wednesday, 15th December 2021 6:17 a.m

How had it come to this?

It was the question Josh had repeatedly asked himself since Detective Coltsworth arrested him and he was charged with murder. The interrogation had been a shit-show. As long as the evidence produced a compelling conclusion, the cops weren't interested in any alternative. No matter how often or loudly he protested his innocence, nobody was listening. Ms Glib, his lawyer, had reviewed the evidence. He didn't like the way she looked at him after seeing the blood-stained knife, his journal, and the semen-stained underwear that belonged to Rachael the police found at his house. It was like she was questioning internally whether he really was guilty. At the Watch House, police presented him with the charge sheet. He stared at that paper for what felt like hours. Reading *murder* on that paper made it so surreal. It felt as though this was all happening to someone else, some other poor sod, and Josh was just another guy in the room watching these unfortunate events unfold. Josh was transported to the Magistrates Court, where he attended what his lawyer called: the first mention. There, he sat in silence as he listened to the Police Prosecutors present evidence to the court concerning his case. As his lawyer explained, the prosecution's case was strong in pure evidentiary terms. There were no witnesses to the crime, so none were referenced or presented at the first mention. However, there was physical evidence: the blood-stained underwear, the bloody knife and a journal with many personal accounts of violent sexual encounters with the victim. In his defence, Ms Glib highlighted what she explained to him were known as mitigating factors. The fact that Josh had no criminal history or prior convictions and until this matter had been an upstanding, tax-paying citizen that contributed positively to his community. Having surveyed the evidence and acknowledged Josh's wishes to omit a plea, the Magistrate adjourned the case to the Supreme Court. Despite the Police Prosecutor's best efforts to prevent it, the Magistrate approved Josh's bail. The Magistrate reasoned that he did not believe Josh represented a risk to the community, despite the egregious nature of the crimes he was being accused of, because of the absence of any prior criminal history. His bail conditions were set, and for now, he was free.

After the whirlwind of it all, Josh sat alone in his hotel room brooding on the matter. His lawyer had provided him with a fact sheet and leaflets of information to go through, which explained the particulars of his situation. He sat at the small table in his hotel room, staring at a pamphlet that explained that under the Queensland Criminal Code, the circumstances of his particular case could result in imprisonment for twenty years. Twenty years... His son Lucas would be thirty-two by the time he was released. His daughter would blossom into womanhood, and he would be absent for it all. He was already being vilified by Anne for his transgressions in their marriage, but if his trial went poorly, he could lose everything; even his children might grow to deny him. Worse still, somehow, his location had come to be known by the media, and there was a swarm of reporters set up in the driveway of the motel, like vultures waiting for him to make an appearance so they could feast on his flesh. They would stalk him wherever he went. He was shut up inside this room with the curtains drawn closed, alone and scared in the dark. Again, the question rang through his mind… How had it come to this?

Josh had just finished breakfast when he was visited by the last human being he would ever expect to show up at his door. He opened the door to Detective Coltsworth, inviting him inside the room more out of a desperation to be in contact with another person than anything else. 'Have you come here to gloat?' asked Josh as the Detective seated himself at the table in his hotel room. They had sparred, the two of them, and Josh had come off second best. Defeated and broken-hearted, what could this asshole possibly want from him now?

'Nothing like that, Mr Dempsey.'

'Stop with this "Mr Dempsey" thing, man. You're the cop who could see me serving twenty years behind bars for a crime I *didn't* commit. The least you can do is call me by my first name. So, why did you come here?'

Colt looked at Josh with those same intense eyes. Studying him. Colt removed a piece of paper from his pocket. He unfolded it and kneaded out the wrinkles before sliding it across the table to Josh. On the paper was an illustration of the Double Spiral symbol, the same Detective Colt brought up during his interrogation two days ago. 'This again,' sighed Josh with exhaustion. 'Nothing has changed between now and when we spoke at the Watch House. As I told you then, that symbol has *no* meaning to me, man. Before you showed it to me on Monday, I'd never seen it before in my life.'

'You know, Josh,' began Colt with the kind of tone of voice that made Josh feel as though Coltsworth thought he was stupid, 'I'm inclined to believe you about that.'

'*What?*' This was the last thing Josh had expected. Was it some kind of game? Was he a spy for the police prosecution, sent in to earn Josh's trust so he might reveal some critical component that will secure a guilty verdict? 'But, if you believe me, why is this happening to me? Why don't you do something to help me?'

'That's precisely what I'm here for, Josh.' The Detective spoke so dispassionately that it was difficult for Josh to get excited. But, this was good, right? Having the lead Detective of the case on his side, surely that counted for a lot?

'Drop the charges against me, then.'

'I wish it were that simple.'

'It's not?'

'Unfortunately, no. I came here today, Josh, to tell you that I think you are innocent. Having interrogated you personally and looked over all the evidence, I'm not convinced you killed Rachael Wright.'

To Josh, it was like he had been living in a hole after being swallowed by the Earth and Colt's admission was the geyser under his butt that breathed him back into the world above the surface. 'Well, what are you doing, then? Go tell your bosses that. Tell fucking everyone! Get me out of this!'

'I told you, it's not up to me. Believe me, I wish it were. The thing is, the case against you is strong. The evidence links you to the crime. You had a motive; you had access to her apartment.' The Detective touched a finger on the spiral image on the paper in front of him. 'But this – *this* – is what your defence team will rely on to refute the State's case against you. The prosecution has to convince a jury you're guilty of this beyond a reasonable doubt to secure a conviction. Is it reasonable to think you would have been angry about the email sent to your wife? Reasonable to suggest you might have caught Rachael having sent the email and killed her in a moment of madness? Sure. Reasonable to deduce you're guilty based on the incriminating evidence? Absolutely. But this thing, well, suffice to say that I think the doubts I have about you being able to carve this symbol into Rachael's arm, with this kind of efficacy, are *beyond* reasonable.'

'Well, that's *something*, I suppose.' Better to have some hope than none. Josh looked at the symbol. 'What is it, anyway? What *does* it mean?'

'It's called a Double Spiral. It's an old pagan symbol representing the duality of forces in existence, the opposites of nature – birth, death, destruction, and creation. So forth. Whoever killed Rachael Wright took the time to carve this into her arm after killing her. If this thing had never appeared on her body, I might have believed you capable of this. A crime of passion. Dickhead egotist like you in the heat of the moment; I've seen it happen plenty of times.'

'Hey—' Josh began to protest, but Colt cut him off.

'But the killer took the time to administer this to Rachael's body *after* he killed her. Probably took him hours. I don't yet fully understand why. It could be a signature of some sort, maybe some kind of branding. I'm here today, Josh, because I want your help. You knew Rachael better than most. Is there anyone in her life, anyone you can think of at all that might have wanted to hurt her?'

Josh remained quiet while he took it all in. He looked at the double spiral, trying to imagine it being superimposed on poor Rachael's dead flesh. The idea made him feel nauseous. 'No, I swear.'

'What about you, then?'

'What about me?'

'Any enemies? Anyone you can think of who might want to

set you up for this? Anyone who might have reason to pursue a vendetta against you?'

Josh scoffed. 'Come on, man. My life isn't a Netflix drama. No, I don't have any enemies, and I can't think of one person who would want to fuck me over. I'm just an ordinary guy.' Colt took the paper, folded it up and put it back in his pocket. He stood as he prepared to depart, buttoning his suit jacket. He looked down at Josh, a wretched creature beneath him, afraid and lonely. Josh asked: 'Where are you going? What are you going to do?'

'I'm going to help you, Josh.' Colt rose from the table with the conviction of a man who did not waver in the face of unfavourable odds. He fastened the button on his suit jacket, saying to Josh: 'Now, listen to me carefully. As far as you're concerned, this conversation never happened. I intend to find the person responsible for killing Rachael, but my superiors won't support me pursuing other leads in this case. If they learn I'm continuing with the investigation, they won't hesitate to pull me off this case and then you won't have *anybody* in your corner. So, it's in your best interest to keep your mouth shut. Don't say anything to anybody about me, not those reporters outside, not your wife or your lawyer or your mates. You got it?'

'Yes,' said Josh meekly. 'But, you still haven't told me what you're going to do?'

'I'm going to do exactly what you asked me to do: I'm going to give everyone a reason to doubt you did this.'

'You'll advocate for me? How?'

Colt gestured to the paper on the table, which he collected, folded, and put into his pocket. 'By giving the country something worthy of inciting reasonable doubts about your guilt. Buckle up, Josh. Things are about to get dicey.'

Detective Colt walked out of the hotel room. Josh watched

from the corner of the blinds on his windows as he walked down the driveway. He saw Detective Colt pull aside one of the reporters stationed at the very back of the crowd. He saw the Detective slip the reporter the piece of paper he had pocketed. Detective Coltsworth stood very close to the reporter. It looked as though they were engaged in a brief exchange. Afterwards, Detective Coltsworth left the scene. Whatever Coltsworth had said to the reporter must have been important. The woman was barely able to contain her excitement. She was smiling like she had just won the lottery. Whatever information Coltsworth gave them was something they deemed more valuable than an interview with Josh because immediately after speaking with Graham, the journalist and her camera crew resigned their post at Josh's door and were the first of the vultures to depart for greener pastures.

Chapter Twelve

Wednesday, 15th December 2021 8:15 a.m

Superintendent La Pila addressed her precinct. Forty-six officers were gathered together, but only a handful served on the homicide squad. The rest were various departmental Special Ops, and the remaining were administrative personnel. 'It is difficult for me to imagine that any one of you could be *stupid* enough to leak specifics of the Wright case to the press.' She paced up and down like a school prefect, looking for untucked shirts and other defects among her subordinates. 'Police prosecutions have made an appeal to the Judge to delay the trial start date until the media frenzy dies down. The whole country is talking about this Double Spiral symbol now. The Coroner's Office has received multiple Freedom of Information requests. Authorities have had no choice but to confirm that Rachael Wright was mutilated with this mark. The Ethical Standards Command will be shining a light up all of our arses while they investigate whether anyone here is responsible for the breach. Those of you who are innocent of any wrongdoing have *whoever did this* – she cut a glance right at Colt – to thank for that.' Her tiny, rage-filled eyes settled on Colt as her inner fury climaxed. Then, moved on, sweeping over every face, boldly meeting every eye. Price fought the urge to turn away when La Pila's gaze fell upon her. La Pila would have just killed half the precinct if looks could kill. 'Make yourselves available to ESC Officers if they request it. I expect full cooperation from all of you, as long as it doesn't immediately impact any of your casework. All right, everyone. Back to work. Homicide, meet me in the conference room for an update on the Wright case.'

Senior Sergeant Price knew better than to ask Colt if he was the one who leaked the intel about the killer's double spiral marking to the media, at least while they were at the office. Colt was getting the cold shoulder from more than a few of their peers. Price suspected that they blamed him, even if the Ethical Standards Command had nothing concrete to satisfactorily prove he was guilty of the breach. Six officers gathered in the conference room. 'Right,' said La Pila once everyone was seated. 'As I mentioned, in light of this spiral thing going public, our prosecutors have appealed to delay the start of Dempsey's trial, but the real problem they have now is that this spiral thing was always the weak point in the case against Dempsey. So, what I need from this team now is to go out and look for anything that might link Joshua Dempsey to this Double Spiral mark. A tattoo design he considered when he was a fluff-about teenager. A decade-old photo from his unused Pinterest board, I don't care if it's something he doodled on a notepad at work; just find something!'

Marcus Belmont, a moustachioed Detective ten years older than Colt, made the decidedly brave decision to question the direction. 'With all due respect, ma'am, should we not consider that there *is* no link between Dempsey and the mark? Perhaps we ought to consider that there could be another unsub out there who is responsible for this.' The uniformed officers in the room, Price included, were stunned to silence by this brazen attempt at reasoning with La Pila, who was clearly on the warpath this morning. The way Superintendent La Pila rounded her gaze onto Belmont felt like a cinematic moment, the kind where the music crescendos and red lasers burst from Superman's eyeballs to melt the bad guy.

What La Pila said next only confirmed what Colt revealed to Price before interrogating Josh Dempsey. 'Let's get something straight, right now, squad: Josh Dempsey is the person responsible for Rachael Wright's death. There was enough physical evidence found under Dempsey's chest of drawers to put him behind bars for twenty years. *That* is the only lead I expect any of you to be pursuing.' She pointed her finger at each officer, warning: 'If I get even a whisper that any of you are taking any action in contradiction to my orders, you'll find yourself in a world of hurt. Because of this case, this department is under the microscope. This case will make or break our careers. None of us will be exempt from the praise or condemnation that falls upon us, depending on how this all turns out. You should all keep that in mind while you're working on this case. Consider your future prospects, think about the impact a demotion or transfer might have on your family. We've all worked too hard to get to where we are to see that spoiled by some bottom-feeder. Josh Dempsey, the Double Spiral; *get it done.*' She turned her back to the squad. 'Dismissed.' The group gathered their things and made to depart the room. 'Senior Sergeant Price, a word please?' Price remained behind while the others vacated the room. Her boss closed the door casually and invited Price to take a seat. 'I know it's been a bit of a crazy transition, and you must feel like you've been thrown in the deep end a bit, and I apologise for that. Your integration to homicide was supposed to be smoother, but Colt insisted on having you work this case with him.'

'It's no trouble, ma'am. I'm learning a lot, and I enjoy the challenge.'

La Pila smiled that overused smirk. Price couldn't help but

feel she wanted to strike her boss in the face every time she saw it. It was an expression of pure condescension, poorly concealed under the guise of a pleasantry. 'Speaking of Detective Coltsworth… Is there anything that you would like to bring to my attention? If you recall, in our last conversation, I indicated that you should come to me if you perceived Colt was preparing to take any action that might compromise the precinct.'

'Oh, no. Ma'am, I don't have anything—' Price began to object but was cut off by La Pila.

'I'm not trying to make you a pariah. *Believe me,* Price, I know how tough it can be for a woman in this place to get a spot in the men's pissing contest.' Price resented her boss using the gender card as a means of securing her trust. '*Someone* leaked the double spiral intel to the press, and yesterday, Colt was seen visiting the hotel Josh Dempsey is staying at.'

'You're having him followed?' La Pila remained silent. Of course, she would never openly admit anything that would incriminate herself. 'There are a bunch of reporters all gathered together on the driveway of Josh's hotel. Did you know that? Colt could have leaked the double spiral intel to any of them on his way out.'

'I'm sorry, Superintendent, but I honestly don't know if Colt was the one who leaked it. As far as this investigation is concerned, I have not personally witnessed him doing anything that would constitute a breach in protocol.'

La Pila sat down, crossed her legs and folded her hands in her lap. 'Well, that's good to know, Sergeant. I would appreciate it if you would do me the courtesy of alerting me if that fact changes.'

Price felt this wasn't the last sit down she would have with Lisa La Pila. 'Yes, ma'am.'

When she got back to her desk, Colt was sitting in his chair in a relaxed position, leafing through case notes. 'I'm reluctant to say: *I told you so,* but judging by the look on your face, there is really no need.' It aggravated Price that he could be so casually smug about this. That didn't change the fact that he *was* right. La Pila truly was willing to go after Josh Dempsey at all costs. And for what? What could La Pila get out of this that was worth seeing an innocent man convicted of a crime he didn't commit, carrying a penalty of twenty years? Colt could see the ethical conundrum was taking its toll on Sergeant Price. She appeared utterly defeated. He felt sympathy for her. 'Listen, Price. La Pila is a shark. Ruthless, cut-throat. She doesn't care who she has to clamber over to rise another step up on that ladder. She also doesn't care about casualties or who gets caught in the crossfire.'

'Thanks, that helps,' she said with such sarcasm that she could have set up a stall and sold it.Colt smirked at the quip and continued: 'Let me give you some advice: there are two kinds of people who do this job. Two interests.' He held up two fingers. 'One group makes a career out of doing the work. Another group makes a career out of playing politics. You need to start thinking about your future and decide which group is more closely aligned with your reasons for being here. Let me tell you, those on one side of the fence rarely cross over. But irrelevant of which side of the fence you choose, it helps to have friends. Friends help you get things done, and they have your back when it's up against the wall. So, my advice is: choose your friends wisely. It doesn't matter which side you end up on, but it *does* matter who your friends are. Because if you're mates with the right people, making enemies of the wrong people becomes a lot easier to deal with.' Price wasn't even a fortnight in, and things in Special Ops were getting complicated already. She wasn't absolutely certain that she could trust Colt, but there was no doubting that what he wanted to get out of this was nobler than what Superintendent La Pila wanted. Right now, that was good enough. If what Colt says is true, indecision could prove fatal to her career. There was no escaping the reality of the dangers of self-interest and ego in the workplace. As the pressures of this case mount and the department comes under scrutiny from external sources, sides are forming, and she knows that if she finds herself on the wrong side when the chips start to fall, she could end up allowing others to control her choices, or limit them, or remove them altogether.

Price's contemplations were interrupted when her desk phone rang. 'North Brisbane, this is homicide.'

'G'day,' said the sweet-sounding voice of a woman on the other end of the line. 'This is Detective Sergeant Peters from the Toowoomba precinct. I'm trying to get in touch with the Detective in charge of the Rachael Wright case. Do you know who that might be? The switchboard operator just forwarded me to homicide.'

'Uh, yeah. Can I just confirm your badge number first, please?' Price did a search on QPrime and confirmed the Detective's identity. She waved at Colt to get his attention. Then mouthed that someone wanted to talk to him. Into the telephone, she said: 'I'll transfer you to the lead Detective, Graham Coltsworth, now.'

Colt picked up his phone, answering with his usual tone of gruff indifference. After a minute, his eyes widened just a fraction. Enough for Price to judge that whatever was being said got his attention. Price listened to a one-sided conversation. 'When did you say this happened?' A pause. He jotted down something on a pad. 'Did you have any suspects?' Another pause while Colt listened. Then: 'And, when you were investigating, did you find any other cases where it also appeared?' Silence. 'Yep. Mm-hmm. Yeah, I see. Okay. Can you send over the case files? Yeah, you can get my email off the address book. It's

Graham Coltsworth, C-O-L-T-S-WORTH.' Another brief pause. 'That's it. You got it. Listen, Detective, I'd appreciate it if you kept a lid on this for now. If it gets out, it'll disrupt the investigation, and we're under strict orders since the news started reporting on it. Could you sit on it for a couple of days? Give me a chance to look over your findings?' More silence. He nods as if he's agreeing. 'Great. That's fantastic, thank you. Yeah, I'll be in touch shortly. All right. Bye now.'

'Sounds intriguing,' said Price after he hung up the phone. 'What was that about?'

Colt looked over at his younger ward, looking reinvigorated. He made sure that they were out of ear-shot of the other officers before he answered. 'That was a Detective Caroline Peters from out at Toowoomba. She heard about the double spiral mark on the news this morning and alleges it's connected to another case she worked a few years ago.'

'Are you serious!?' Price felt the sudden burst of special energy that accompanies being privy to controversial information before anyone else knows what it's worth. 'What did she say?'

'She had four vics out there from 2016–2018. All women, aged twenty-five to forty-five, strangled to death, and the pathologist detected post-mortem knife wounds on all four vics.'

Price couldn't believe what she was hearing. An identical MO. She was almost afraid to ask. 'What about the mark?'

'Present on all four,' Colt confirmed. 'You know what that means, don't you?'

Unbelievable, Price thought. This could be big. Melbourne Gangland big, Ivan Milat big. She answered with harrowed breath: 'This could all be the work of a serial killer.'

Detective Peters out at Toowoomba didn't stuff around. The case files came through to Colt's inbox in minutes. Price, sitting beside Colt, waited for him to open the email, but he held off. He locked his computer screen so that nothing of the email would be visible. 'Time to make a choice, Price. Just minutes ago, you and I were given a direction by the head of this precinct to undertake an exhaustive search for any evidence that links Josh Dempsey to the double spiral symbol. Opening this email and any further action we take to investigate any potential links between the Toowoomba cold case and the Wright case goes directly against that initiative. Time to pick a side. You can either march into La Pila's office right now and report me for insubordination, or you and I can work this together and try to get justice for these women.'

Price didn't hesitate. The chain of command is critical and exists for a good reason. But when Addilyn joined QPS and was sworn in as an officer, she decided what kind of cop she wanted to be. More importantly, she knows what kind of person she is, and even when those two dimensions come into conflict, she can hold her head up proud, knowing that there is no better nourishment for the soul than choosing to do the right thing. It just happens that self-interest and the right thing are the same in this instance. 'Fuck the politics,' she said harshly. 'Screw La Pila. When I first interviewed Josh when this was still a missing person's case, my gut told me he isn't capable of murder. This new information only emboldens that feeling. I'm with you, all the way. Let's pull on this thread and see what unravels.'

Since he had first introduced himself, Price had come to learn that Colt was endlessly tenacious, a straight-shooter, humourless and hyper-focused on the job. Frankly, he was a little grim. Maybe it was why it felt so satisfying to see him actually smiling. He put his hand on her shoulder and gave her an approving shake. 'Glad to have you with me, partner.'

Chapter Thirteen

Wednesday, 15th December 2021 6:38 p.m

Senior Sergeant Price invited Colt into her home. As she opened the door, the pair were greeted by her energetic Beagle. 'Jasper!' she laughed in protest as the little dog bounced excitedly at her leg, balancing his front paws on her shins as she tried to get through the door. 'Down, you silly boy.' Once inside, she leaned over and gave his head a scratch. Jasper quickly moved his attention to Colt, who came in after Price, carrying the many folders that contained all the information Detective Peters had sent over from what she called the *Double Spiral Strangler* investigation. The Beagle ran circles around his ankles, sniffing wildly, collecting the specific scent of his master's human companion. Whatever specific traits were present in Colt's scent, Jasper quickly made up his canine mind that Colt was worthy of acceptance and consequently extended his affections to the new human who had entered his domain. Detective Colt let Jasper lick his hand. In return, he gave Jasper belly rubs, which were the closest embodiment to Heaven Jasper could know. 'So, can I get you a drink? Coffee, tea? Oh, wait!' She pressed her forefinger to her forehead. 'Don't remind me… I remember when we first met, you mentioned you enjoy drinking scotch. Me, I'm a whiskey girl, personally. Two things I love about the Irish, their accent and their whiskey.' She had a chuckle to herself. 'Let me see if there's any scotch in the old liquor cabinet.' Price dumped her bags down just inside her bedroom and closed her bedroom door.

'A whole *cabinet* for your liquor,' teased Colt, 'it must be good to be Queen!'

'Oh, yeah!' mocked Price as she made her way to the old family cabinet where she kept her liquor. 'Haven't I told you? When I'm away from Buckingham Palace, I like to holiday at my one-bedroom apartment in South Brisbane.' She raised her hands up and twirled on the spot, gesturing to the infrastructure of the apartment. 'Welcome to Castle Price, my liege.' She curtsied and bowed. Colt enjoyed the sarcastic display. Addilyn Price had a lot of charisma once she clocked off.

'You should bring some of that energy to the office. I like it. With that kind of gusto, you could gently bully your way into the Detective rank.'

'Oh, that's a relief,' she said, twisting bottles in her liquor cabinet to get a look at the labels. 'Before you said that, I was just planning on sleeping my way to the top.' Colt actually had to stifle a laugh. 'Ah-huh!' she exclaimed triumphantly, producing a bottle of Johnny Walker Blue Label. 'I knew there was a bottle around here somewhere.' She went to the fridge and frowned with disappointment when she did not find what she had hoped would be there. 'Well, Colt. How do you feel about embodying the whole kitten-caboodle of Detective clichés tonight? I have no cola to go with your scotch.' She rifled through some items to get a look into the back of her refrigerator shelves. 'Or any soda water, for that matter. Would you mind if it is served on the rocks?'

'Coke!' He shook his head, sucking his teeth. 'Price, my dear girl, your education in scotch begins here. Do you even know what you have there?' He collected the bottle from Price, handling it with great care. 'Johnny Walker Blue is the finest of the Walker labels. And while you say you enjoy the Irish Whiskeys, this little bottle will convert you. By the end of your first glass' —he pours two fingers into a glass and refuses the ice cubes— 'you'll prefer the Scotsman to the Irishman.' He lifted the glass to his nostrils, gave it a swirl and a sniff. 'This is the way it was meant to be tasted. Cheers.' He offered his glass, and Price clinked hers against his and took a sip. Immediately, she was impressed. Her eyebrows rose half an inch, and she withdrew the glass to observe the golden liquor inside as if it had been brewed by some practitioner of ancient alchemy.

'That is *smooth*.'

'Not unlike the bloke who poured it, eh?' Colt smirked.

'Oh, my God, was that the great, stoic Graham Coltsworth making a joke! Do my ears deceive me?' Price was grinning from ear to ear.

'I'm not a total enigma,' he said, proffering his glass in the proposal of a toast. 'Now, a drop like this shouldn't go without a proper toast.' He thought on it for a moment, then: 'To catching the Double Spiral Strangler.'

Price thought of Josh Dempsey and La Pila's vendetta against him for the easy win. She remembered what she told Colt about why she wanted to join homicide in the first place. 98% of solved missing persons cases elevate the status of the La Pilas within QPS, decorating their office walls with plaques and certificates. In comparison, folks like Colt and Price are ostracised for seeking justice for the 2% who get written off because all the attention is directed to the majority. 'To the 2%, and to doing the right thing,' offered Price. They both remained quiet for a moment, both out of respect to the sentiment of their mission but also so that each could contemplate the weight and meaning of what they were preparing to do. It would not be an easy undertaking. Neither were ignorant of that fact. They were both putting themselves at risk, personally and professionally. Yet, neither of them were deterred. 'You may be right,' said Price after tasting a sip, hoping to lighten the mood a little. 'This may just be good enough to convert me.'

'Mmm,' murmured Colt. 'It is *very* good. Not cheap though, so enjoy it while it lasts.'

Colt took a look around Addilyn's apartment. It was a distinctly feminine home. The walls were painted a soft violet. Coloured pillows decorated the couch. The furniture was tastefully appointed, and the whole place possessed a minimalist aesthetic. Everything in its place, no junk, no trinkets. A small jungle's worth of house plants could be seen thriving on her balcony. 'Well,' said Colt taking a seat on the couch and spreading out the folders across Price's coffee table, 'let's see what we have, shall we?' Jasper grew increasingly irritable as he desperately tried to manoeuvre around Colt's defending arms to reach the man's lap. Colt offered a truce with a belly rub, which Jasper graciously accepted, settling in on the other side of the couch, satisfying both parties for the time being.

'God, you'd think I never give him any attention, and he's starved for it!' laughed Price, looking judgementally at Jasper, who appeared to be smiling the way dogs do when they're utterly pleased with themselves. Colt had been working Price hard for the last couple of weeks, and now, it is Friday night, and she is at home with him with a plan to study old case files. He felt guilty. She has so much lighthearted energy outside of the office, and while she is young, she should be enjoying her free time while she has it. If – more like *when* – she makes detective, there will be less and less of it. The least he could do to repay her commitment to the cause was delay the work a little and make an effort to try and get to know her better.

'So, Addilyn Price…'

'That's me.'

'You're thirty-four years old. Good career. Nice home. A lovely little dog with a big personality. And, you're not *unattractive*.'

She half-scoffed, half-laughed. 'Gee, thanks!'

'There's nobody special in your life? Nobody you would rather be spending your Friday night with than this dusty old, scotch-swilling Detective?'

She smiled at the quip. 'Nope. I've had my fair share of failed courtships in my twenties.' She said it casually, but Colt could discern the presence of some old wounds that perhaps still have not fully mended. 'I just want to focus on my career. Jasper is the only male companion I need in my life right now. Besides, all the blokes I've met in the last couple of years turned out to be arseholes. Got no need of that.'

Colt shook his head in understanding. 'It's not just the fellas, let me assure you, there are plenty of bitches out there too.' He took a pensive sip of his drink.

Price lifted her glass in a mock toast. 'Well then, to all the bitches and the arseholes out there, may we be free from their drama a little while longer.'

Colt flashed his famous half-smile. 'I'll toast to that.' They both drank down the last swallow of their liquor. Price set her glass down on the coffee table and scooped up one of the folders containing the Toowoomba case files. 'So, are we going to sit around and talk about our feelings all night, or are we going to try and find a serial killer?' Colt collected one of the folders and began inspecting the contents.

Chapter Fourteen

Friday, 17th December 2021 7:13 p.m

During the day, Detective Colt and Senior Sergeant Price executed their duties as police officers in accordance with the commands of Superintendent Lisa La Pila. Like the other homicide officers working the case, they continued searching for clues that would link Josh Dempsey to the double spiral symbol. After it had been leaked to the media, the police intel about the strange spiral mark superimposed on Rachael Wright had circulated the news networks to completion. A string of amateur sleuth activity had also become hot on social media platforms. The community wanted answers. The police sought to connect the double spiral symbol and Josh Dempsey but failed in their attempts. Their best effort to find any correlation continually returned them to the contents of Josh Dempsey's personal journal. Among Josh's many musings, poems, and records of his raw, unfiltered thoughts were many references to spiritualism, ancient philosophy and religious doctrine, but not once was the double spiral itself mentioned explicitly, or for that matter, its historical meaning. The media and members of the public debating the topic online had no access to the diary and instead elected to comb through every impression Josh Dempsey had ever made on the internet, searching desperately for some reference to the mark or its meaning in the pages of Josh's personal history. None was found.

Price and Colt met at Price's apartment after their shift ended and continued to work on the Double Spiral Strangler case in secret. Price was an enthusiastic and willing partner who never complained about the long hours or the negative impacts of working two jobs while only receiving a wage for one. Colt often felt guilty occupying so much of her personal time. More than once, he entertained ideas about her youth and the associations that should accompany it, according to his own opinion. She should be out having fun after work, blowing off steam, meeting new people, spending time with friends and family, not stuck at home with a crusty old Detective who only works tirelessly because there is nothing else in his life worth tiring himself for.

'Before we get started tonight,' he said, 'I think we should get out and get some fresh air. We've been cooped up staring at case files for too long. Let's take Jasper for a walk; what do you say?' At the mere mention of the word walk, Jasper's little ears were perked up, and he was already bouncing around madly at the spot Price hung his lead next to the door.

'Well, it would be pretty tough for me to object now, wouldn't it? Look at him.' Jasper sat in front of his lead, staring at it, then looking back at Addilyn, then back at the lead. As soon as her feet touched the ground, the dog became erratic, spinning himself in circles, jumping up at the lead. 'You won't say no to two walkies in one day, will you, Jasp?'

Colt and Price walked from her apartment in South Brisbane into the South Bank parklands situated on the southern edge of the Brisbane River. The seasonal flowers bloomed on vines grown along the path, lending a lovely scent to the air. Teenagers skated by on their skateboards while office workers clad in business apparel shuffled past, making their way home from their office labours. Jasper always kept a close eye on the Ibis birds.

They seemed to him winged villains that he must bring to justice, but the scavenging birds are to Jasper what the Roadrunner is to the Wile E Coyote. No matter how often he tried to get at them, they were always *just* out of reach. He loved the rope around his neck because whenever his human attached it to his collar, it meant they were going outside, and Jasper *loved the* outdoors. But the wretched thing never permitted him to get farther from Addilyn than he would have preferred if he could run freely. Nevertheless, he was outside! And outside is a place full of strange smells and unfamiliar things warranting a sniff and a lick. 'Shame there are no dog parks around for him to run himself ragged,' said Colt as they passed through the winding passage that delivered them to a boardwalk beside the river. The Storey Bridge across the water was bathed in bedazzling green and purple neon. People glided by on bicycles and electric scooters. The dark waters of the Brisbane River passively ebbed beside them, hiding all manner of ominous secrets beneath the shadowy depths.

'You see that?' Price pointed to a very high metal frame atop a tall building marked with signage: **Mater Children's Hospital**.

'The kid's hospital?'

'Yeah. You would never have guessed it now, but I was admitted there for a couple of weeks when I was a teenager.' She sounded solemn. The memory is obviously a sad one.

'What were you admitted for?'

She glanced down at her feet. Usually, Price held her head high, always looked ahead, unafraid of whoever might meet her eye. 'Depression. Being admitted to the mental health ward of that hospital taught me the difference between *moving on* and *letting go.*'

'What do you mean?' Price looked up at the high glass

windows on the face of the hospital. 'My first night after being admitted, I was standing behind the window in my room, watching the people on the street below. There's wire inside the glass, and metal bars are bolted onto the outside of the windows, measures they take to prevent people from jumping out of them. But it sort of makes it feel like a prison. I was looking down at the street, just watching people walk on by, going about their lives. I remember thinking: there's a reason I'm in here, and they're out there. It's because there is something present in them that is absent in me. A fundamental piece of humanity missing from my soul means I'm not quite the same as the regular people who don't get locked up in mental hospitals. I know, it was very teenage angst. But, back then, that's how it really felt. To qualify to join QPS, I had to show that I was medication and symptom-free for two years before being sworn in. Even then, it wasn't easy. I had to provide pages of medical evidence. It was *hard* for me to join the police force, but I persisted because I knew it's what I was meant to do with my life.' She went quiet for some time, watching Jasper at her feet trot along the boardwalk, the little Beagle oblivious to the sentiment of their conversation, quite simply content in just being. 'I still feel that way, sometimes. When I see people on TV at a cricket game or footy match, and they're carrying on like mad, waving their signs and dancing. I'm just not like that. I'm too conscientious. Or, sometimes, when I'm walking out here with Jasper. I look at people's faces, and it still feels as though I'm that girl observing the world from behind that glass as if it is a place in which I don't belong. But then, I put on the uniform, and I feel very differently. I feel as though I know my place and that I belong to something bigger than myself, and the work itself helps to remind me that there is no such thing as *normal*.'

Colt listened, taking in the details of her story, imagining the teenage version of Price behind one of the windows high up on the building contemplating life's meaning. 'It's good that you have known what it is to feel that way.'

'It is?' the question was more of an accusation than a proposition.

'I'd wager the guy we're hunting has felt that way at least once in his life. In fact, I would go as far as to say that he feels that way with uncomfortable regularity.'

'Why do you say that?'

'Have you heard of the American serial killer, Gary Ridgeway?'

'That's the guy they called, The Green River Killer, right?'

'The same. Gary Ridgeway was charged with forty-nine murders. At his trial, a statement from his family was read in court. It said: "Be assured that we were shocked to hear that Gary could do the things he has admitted to doing." His family said they loved him, but they also said that the Gary America came to know as the Green River Killer is different from the person his family knew. They said: "Clearly, there were two Gary Ridgeways." You see, his actions as a killer were so depraved that even his own family could not reconcile the monster with the man. To comprehend it, to believe and accept his crimes, his family had to separate the man they knew from the terrible things he did. That's the thing; when people hear about these psycho killers, they want to be able to point at something and say, *see? That's why they did it.* There needs to be some clinically diagnosable evil in them that isn't in the rest of us, just like it felt for you when you were looking out that window. The fact is, there was no difference between the girl behind the window and the people down on the street. We all have skeletons in the closet, ghosts that haunt us and demons we do our finest to keep hidden from the world.'

'You really think that's true?' asked Price with a healthy dose of scepticism. She didn't share that view. She couldn't imagine the killer they were hunting as being ordinary in any way.

'It's a spectrum, I think. Feeling different, feeling at odds with the world and ones self. Some feel it more keenly than others. Some may never feel it at all. And a few serial killers like the guy we're looking for never feel anything else. Take Maury Travis, for example. He was the first serial killer to be tracked down using the internet. He committed suicide, and in the note, which he left to his mother, he wrote: "I've never felt normal or happy at any time in my life." Just for a second, try and empathise with that feeling. Suppose it were true, never experiencing a single moment of happiness or a life without a constant nagging urge to kill. Can you imagine how agitating it must be to perceive it – normalcy – in others but never experience it personally?'

'I can, I suppose. To a degree. It would be like living my whole life as the girl behind the window, but never being freed from the room or the feeling of being unlike everyone else in some important way.'

'Exactly my point,' remarked Colt. 'That gives you the necessary perspective to catch this killer because the Double Spiral Strangler has likely had to work his whole life to learn how to blend in with the people he resents because he isn't like them.'

'Have you ever felt that way, Colt?'

'Occasionally. I don't remember ever feeling it more than when my ex-wife miscarried.' He remembered the old hurt, like seeing a bee fly past and remembering the sensation of being stung. 'We had been trying for a while with no luck. It sort of felt like it just wasn't in the cards for us. Cassie started taking it pretty hard. Then, it just happened. She fell pregnant. It was the happiest I remember seeing her. When she lost it, it was like there had been something in her that wasn't in me. We started going to couples counselling. But it only made things worse. The therapist shone a light on some of the issues in our marriage. It was like, for the first time, Cassie noticed that there was something absolutely crucial to the survival of our relationship missing in me. Something she needed from me, something I didn't have to give.'

'What happened?' asked Price, giving an over-eager Jasper a slight tug on the leash as he tried to break from the path and pursue an Ibis who had clawed its way to the rim of a bin.

'Our relationship had been weak for a while. Everything that went down after the miscarriage, well, it was just the straw that broke the camel's back. She filed for divorce. Moved on with another bloke, had two kids. She's happy now.'

Price seemed pensive. 'I'm sorry. Is that why you work so much?'

Colt nodded with a reluctant sigh. 'I suppose it makes me feel useful.'

Price took one last look at the hospital building before it disappeared from view. 'It's why I became a cop in the first place, you know. I was inspired by the nurses who cared for me while admitted to the mental health ward. Man…' A wry smile crept over her face. 'There was this one nurse; I can't remember his name. This Mongolian guy. Anyway, he was this awesome pool-shark and would come into the pool room and play with us sometimes. One time, he caught this other girl and me out on the balcony having a sneaky cigarette after dinner.' She began laughing at the memory. 'He popped his head out the door and warned us not to throw it over the edge when we finished. Guess it was like a Taoist thing.'

'Or, maybe just a not-a-jerk thing,' interjected Colt.

'Ha! Yeah. Maybe. Anyway, he didn't punish us for doing the wrong thing. And he could have. He probably *should* have, but I remember later thinking it was the discretion he exercised in his position of authority that made his impact on me so memorable. It wasn't only that he didn't report us that made me respect him. It was that he *could* have but decided not to, and by doing so, spared us some misery.' The memories were streaming into her mind now. Strange, she thought, how sometimes, it's these abstract moments that keep a place in memory when others are lost. She continued telling her story to Colt: 'I remember this one time; it must have been around lunchtime on the ward. There was this girl in isolation; I think her name was Evelyn. She was being treated for anorexia and bulimia. She never ate. Never left her room. She was so weak and frail that her organs were beginning to shut down. They had the anorexic girls hooked up to these machines with tubes down their noses that fed them this chocolate milk stuff. Evelyn was so malnourished she'd become anaemic. Anyway, I remember seeing one of the nurses at Evelyn's bedside bargaining with her to eat something. The nurse managed to eventually convince her to join her in the lunchroom before anyone else was allowed in, and she must have sat with her for hours trying to get her to eat something. I watched them from another room. Eventually, Evelyn ate a few slices of an apple. I just remember admiring how that nurse never gave up. She persisted, and even when Evelyn got furious with her, she never lost her temper. Those nurses, they really helped us. They were kind and patient, and they'll never know it, but that experience with them changed me. I wanted to be like them in my own way. Help people, like they helped me. More than that,

I promised myself that when I eventually became a Police Officer, I would exercise discretion in my position of authority wherever possible, just like the Mongolian nurse. That's why I chose to do this with you. I don't care if it costs me my career; I won't support the Superintendent's agenda to convict an innocent man.'

'Especially if it means the one responsible remains free,' added Colt. He looked at Price, dressed in her denim skirt, Birkenstocks and white tank top. A beautiful young woman with blonde hair, a confident demeanour and an appetite for justice. Seeing her now, it was hard to imagine her as a depressed teenager who thought of herself as someone who didn't have a place in the world. He imagined himself as he is now, a grown man, standing beside a teenage Price at that window, both of them haunted by that feeling. In his imagination, a shadow of a man stands next to them – the killer they hunt – also staring out the window too.

'She's been keeping tabs on you, you know,' said Price.

'La Pila?' he scoffed derisively. 'It doesn't surprise me.'

'She seems to really have it out for you. All because you knocked back her job when it was offered to you?'

'Pretty much,' said Colt flatly. 'Some of her superiors are guys I came up with when I got out of the academy. They took the desk jobs when they came around; I kept pounding the pavement.' He shrugged. 'I'm just not a desk-jockey. The thing is that these high-ranking Commissioned Officers respect me and they're mates, so they look out for me from time to time. They're a roadblock on her climb up the ladder, so she's always looking for the nail in my coffin. It's why I've been so insistent that we conduct our investigation outside of hours. Detective Peters has agreed to keep things quiet for now, and she seems trustworthy.

She's as keen to see this through as we are, but if La Pila gets wind of it, it will give her the ammo she's looking for.'

'Sorry,' said Price. Her phone had been noisily sounding every few minutes, but Price had been enjoying her walk and the conversation with Colt, so she had ignored it. Finally, she withdrew it and read over all the messages that had been piling up. Price handed the lead to Colt. Graham gave the lead a soft tug. As happy as he seemed, little Jasper was beginning to show signs of tiring. He gave the lead a shake, and the reverb perked him up. Jasper turned his head and looked up at Colt with the canine equivalent of an amused expression. 'It's my sister. She's one of those people who sends fifteen individual texts instead of just taking the time to prepare one longer message. She's been hassling me for weeks to babysit because it's school holidays, and my nieces and nephews are driving her crazy.' She resumed texting her sister for a second, and then something occurred to Price, which caused her to stop suddenly while she mulled it over. She looked away from her phone, her scrupulous eyes squinting in deep concentration. 'Hang on… Could it be?' Her attention turned to her phone again.

'What is it?' Jasper was most displeased with the sudden interruption to his walk. Futilely, he strained his neck against the lead, but it would not budge against the immutable strength of the man who held it.

'Oh, my God. Colt. I think I just figured something out!'

'What is it?'

'Come on,' she tugged at his sleeve. 'We have to get back to my apartment; I need to see the case files again. I don't want to say anything before checking to see if my hunch is correct. Let's go!'

Back at Price's apartment, she collected the whiteboards that hosted all of the intelligence they had gathered on the case so far. Most of what was contained on the boards came from Detective Peters in Toowoomba. Her casework had been meticulous during the two-year investigation into the Double Spiral Strangler. Jasper never shied away from voicing his displeasure concerning the presence of the boards in his already cramped domain. Their presence was unwelcome, but chewing at their legs did not seem to persuade the humans to remove them on his behalf. For Jasper, the five whiteboards and their tripod stands felt as though his kingdom had come under occupation by invaders who could not be repelled no matter how ferociously he bit at their metal legs or barked at their flat, white faces. On the face of their whiteboards, Price and Colt had arranged all the case files so that every inch of their surface was covered in scrawled writing along with photocopies of Detective Peters' original notes and observations. Everything they knew about the Double Spiral killings was featured on these five boards. 'Okay,' breathed Price with an unsteady breath. 'Let's go over what we know one more time.' She began at the first whiteboard, which contained all that the Toowoomba Task Force uncovered about the first victim. 'Holly Belmaine.' She pointed at the picture of the victim. Fair skin, dark hair, brilliantly sharp, youth-filled caramel-coloured eyes. 'Twenty-nine years old. Married with one child. Employed at a Toowoomba Aged Care facility as an on-site nurse. Killed March 27th, 2016. Cause of death; strangulation. Additionally, she was stabbed three times. Based on the forensic analysis of the wounds, the Coroner's Office suggests that Holly initially lost consciousness after being strangled, recovered shortly after that and regained consciousness. So, Holly wakes up, the killer panics.' Price makes three swift gestures with her hand. 'The killer stabs her three times. The first strikes her in the chest, the second in the shoulder and the third punctures her lung. Now, all things considered, you and I speculate that Holly was his first victim.'

Colt nodded in agreement. 'He was inexperienced. He failed to strangle her to death.'

Adding to Colt's point, Price voiced her thoughts: 'All the other victims were only ever stabbed once, and each stabbing occurred post-mortem. It's as if he doesn't want a repeat of what happened with Holly.'

Colt nodded. 'He's making certain his victims don't recover after he strangles them.'

'He learned from his mistake.' Price pauses to consider the gravity of what she is saying. It felt surreal to speak these words about another human being. What he does is so difficult to imagine. He's a butcher who executes women with surgical precision and mutilates their flesh for his own fancy. It's sickening. She goes on: 'After Holly is dead, the killer uses some kind of implement with razor-edges and stamps the double spiral mark into her left thigh post-mortem. The skin inside the lines marked by his razor tool is carefully peeled and cutaway, essentially flaying the victim until all that remains is his mark.' Colt is relaxed on Price's couch, listening attentively, thinking. Price points to the second board. 'Maria Rodgerson, his second victim. Killed July 27th, 2016. Strangulation, puncture wound, double spiral.' She moved to the third board. 'Joanne Tyson-Smith. Killed on the 18th of June 2017. Third victim. Strangled, mutilated, marked.' Price, at the fourth board: 'Hannah Reese. Killed on the 20th of June, 2017. Reese is different. While she was definitely strangled, it isn't what killed her.' She pointed to photographs of the woman's body made by the Medical Examiner. 'He stabs her in the abdomen twice, then four times in the back. She dies of blood loss. The *imprint* of a double spiral is present on her back, but the mark is unfinished. Why would he begin and not finish? I get the feeling that besides the act of killing itself, the double spiral is the most important part of his ritual. Is there something about Hannah Reese that differs from the others? Was she unworthy of the mark, in his eyes? Only the outline?'

'Not likely,' said Colt after a long silence. 'These women all share the same profile; caucasian, aged between twenty-five and forty-five, intelligent, attractive, middle class. He's selective. He likely stalks them until he is familiar with their routines before making a play for them. He chose Hannah Reese like he *chose* the others. But something happened before he strangled her to death.' He looked closely at the photographs of Hannah Reese's wounds. Brutal, savage. Lacking the sophistication of his ordinarily methodical approach. 'Something happened. Maybe his ritual was interrupted, or she said something that provoked his rage. Whatever the reason, he couldn't finish what he started with the double spiral.'

'But, why?' Price strokes her chin thoughtfully.

'It's speculative, but it could just be a matter of simple biology. It requires a steady hand and lots of time to complete the mark. He's flummoxed after having to digress from his ritual. His blood is filled with adrenaline. He can't pull it off, and it's so important to him that he would rather not do it all than do a poor job. So, he dumps her, leaving his work unfinished.'

'Could be. Whatever the case, he goes off the radar, disappearing for three years.' At the fifth and final board representing the Double Spiral Killer's profile, Price comes to Rachael Wright. 'Then, he resurfaces and kills Rachael on the morning of December 11th, 2021. That's three years after Reese's body was discovered in Toowoomba. Do you think there are other victims during this period we just don't know about?'

'It's definitely a possibility. It's a long hiatus. There could be any number of reasons he stopped killing, but I suspect the most plausible is because he fumbled killing Hannah Reese. Look at the others. Once he had cut his mark into them, he always deposited the body somewhere out in the open, somewhere public, as if to say: "Ha! Ha! Look at me, look what I can do!"' Colt pointed to a picture of the shallow grave where the killer buried Hannah. 'He didn't want Hannah to be found. Unlike the others, he buried Hannah. This suggests that he was ashamed, maybe because he felt that this killing didn't meet his expectations because he couldn't complete the mark. So, he decides to lay low for a few years. Traditionally, a lot of serial killers are relieved when they're apprehended. It's not that they want to be caught, per se, but most are such narcissists they want their crimes to be acknowledged. Often, once their crimes become public knowledge, they fetishise their own infamy. Hannah Reese didn't go as planned, and I doubt he expected her to be found so soon after he buried her. For him, it's the equivalent of someone uncovering the only mistake in an otherwise flawless body of work. So maybe his absence is like a self-imposed exile.'

Now that Price had been able to correlate her hunch with the data, she was positive they had their first lead. She explained: 'I think it was what you said about La Pila that put two and two together for me.'

'What did I say?'

'About how she's always looking to get one over on you. The killer is doing the same thing. He dumps the bodies in places where they will easily be discovered. No witnesses, no evidence, no suspects… It's like everything he does is an effort to demonstrate how much smarter he is than the people looking for him. Let's suppose that you're right about Hannah Reese, and he considers her death a failure of his abilities. He wants to prove himself with the next mark, so he gets bolder. He murders Rachael Wright in her own bed, leaving behind no evidence at the scene, and finds a way to pin the whole thing on Josh Dempsey. The planning that must have gone into this, it's just phenomenal. There's one more way in which he managed to pull the wool over our eyes, and it's a doozy. I actually think he's done this so that eventually someone would catch on, and it would make the cat-and-mouse game all the more intriguing for him.' She pointed to the board at each victim in turn, confirming the details one last time while Colt observed. 'Holly, killed March 27th, 2016. Maria Rodgerson was killed on July 27th, 2016. Almost a year later, he killed Joanne Tyson-Smith on the 18th of June 2017, and two days later, on 20th June 2017, he killed Hannah Reese. Three years later, Rachael Wright was murdered on December 11th, 2021. What do these dates all have in common?'

It clicked for Colt. As the realisation dawned on him, he felt an immediate surge of self-contempt. How could three investigators, himself included, have overlooked a fact so blatantly obvious? 'He's only killing during the school holidays…' Colt got to his feet fast and came to scrutinise the boards personally while he undertook a search on his own phone to cross-reference the dates with the school calendar from those years. Between the two of them, they triple checked every date, confirming it to be accurate. 'You're right.' He patted her on the back, a sign of affection that was the Graham Coltsworth equivalent of a hug. 'All the killings occurred during Queensland school holidays. I'm damn proud of you, Price. You just found us our first lead.'

'He could be a member of faculty, or a student, or an administrator. I don't think it's coincidental he kills exclusively during school holidays. It's also such a dangerous thing for him to do I can only presume it's intentional. I think he wants us to know.'

'To see if we can use it to identify him. It very well could be true. I can't imagine a guy who is clever enough to last this long without raising any suspicions about himself could also be so stupid as to make an omission like this. His own bloody ego could be his undoing, thanks to you.'

Addilyn was elated. Giddy, almost. *Finally*, she thought, maybe we have a chance to actually catch this bastard.

Chapter Fifteen

Saturday, 18th December 2021 6:14 a.m

Detective Caroline Peters had never felt like this before. If her feelings were a cocktail, the ingredients were equal parts elation and relief, with a dash of guilt and a pinch of disappointment. A sweet mouthful with a sour aftertaste. Last night, Caroline learned that Senior Sergeant Price, working with Detective Coltsworth, had made a breakthrough on the Double Spiral Strangler case. Finally, after years of searching, there was a clue about the killer's identity. The fact that the clue had been uncovered made her happier than she could ever recall feeling in her fifty-two years of life, but the fact the clue had emerged from her own diligently collected records and had been overlooked by her all these years was as close to unforgivable as could be. This oversight wrought a pang of guilt and shame that she could not shake. The only consolation was that it wasn't Caroline alone who missed it. The entire Toowoomba Task Force set up to investigate these killings had been put to shame by a single Brisbane officer, and not even a Detective at that! Caroline should like to meet this Senior Sergeant. Price sounds like quite the investigator. The big clue: the Double Spiral Strangler committed his murders exclusively during the Queensland State School Holiday period. If it were anyone else, this fact might just be explained away as a coincidence, but Caroline knew better. She had spent two long years chasing this killer, and even though she didn't know his face or his name, she knew *him*. He wasn't killing according to this schedule by accident. He did it to issue a challenge to those who would seek to apprehend him. *Catch me if you can...* School holidays are always a busy time of year. There are more cars on the road. More people occupying public places. To be able to get away with murder and discard a corpse in an open, public space where anyone could find it *during* school holidays is the killer's way of taunting investigators with his superior prowess. He's parading himself, showing off. Caroline hoped it would be his undoing, not only for justice for the victims but for the satisfaction of having him know that her team beat him.

When he called her the previous evening, Detective Coltsworth – he insisted she call him Colt – explained that they were investigating the case in an unofficial capacity during their rostered time off. As Colt explained, his superior, Superintendent Lisa La Pila, was adamant that Joshua Dempsey was responsible for this. Caroline had heard about Josh Dempsey on the news, and later, when the media started reporting that the Double Spiral symbol had been imposed on the woman he was charged with murdering, Caroline knew the Strangler had returned. She looked over Josh Dempsey's arrest details and learned what she could about the man. Josh is a father and husband, works as a financial advisor and has active involvement in his community through his children's sporting activities. She could very well have been describing the Double Spiral Strangler. The *real* killer made an excellent choice selecting Josh Dempsey as his fall guy. The only evidence she had was circumstantial, and while the true killer remained unidentified, what Caroline had wouldn't be enough to acquit Josh. It was, however, plenty enough to satisfy Caroline, Colt and Price that Josh was *not* the man they were looking for.

For one, all the killings before Rachael Wright had occurred in the Toowoomba region, an hour and a half west of Brisbane, where Josh lives with his family, and not one of the four Toowoomba locals who were killed had any connection to Josh Dempsey whatsoever. The man responsible for the killings was a Toowoomba local, at least during the period in which the first four killings occurred. Josh had never lived at Toowoomba. The worst possible conclusion Caroline could draw from the evidence was Josh Dempsey is a copycat killer. He killed Rachael, imitating the original work of the actual killer. The best-case scenario is that Josh is innocent, which means he can be vindicated, and he's being made into the scapegoat by the killer. When she first contacted the Brisbane office to speak with the team investigating the Dempsey case, she had wanted to bring her cold case to the attention of the Brisbane higher-ups, get a new joint Task Force set up and really go after this guy. But, after having talked with Colt about the matter, she reluctantly chose to abstain from sharing any information with her Brisbane counterparts until her joint investigation with Price and Colt identified a person of interest. That was the deal she struck with Colt. Unfortunately for Detective Peters, it meant that she would have to carry the brunt of the load of paperwork because, for the time being, Colt and Price were unable to use QPrime or any official police resources as long as their investigation wasn't officially being sanctioned by the Brisbane bosses.

One of the Detectives at the Toowoomba Precinct, Brian Hughes, came by Caroline's desk with an offering. 'You're 'ere early, Car.' He presented a mug of coffee he had prepared for her. Brian's thick Scottish accent, coupled with his boorish appearance, gave him a thuggish reputation. Truthfully, he is sweet and thoughtful, not at all the barbarian people make him out to be.

'Just had some catching up to do,' she lied, accepting the coffee from her colleague. 'Now, don't go thinking that just because you made my coffee doesn't mean I'm going to agree to give you a hand with any of your casework. Technically, it's my day off.'

He held his hands up, pretending to surrender. 'All right, all right, right ye are, Caroline. I was jus' stoppin' by to say 'ello. What're ye doin' 'ere on ye' day off, anyhow?'

'Just looking into a couple of things, you know how it is.'

Brian tipped his mug. 'Aye. That I do. Well, er, I 'spose I'll leave ye' to it, then.'

She tipped her mug in return. 'Thanks for the coffee, mate.'

'Any time, Car, any time.'

Once Hughes was well out of range, Caroline reflected on her old case notes. The four victims slain in Toowoomba were killed between 2016 and 2018. All four of the bodies were ditched in publicly accessible places around the region. The botanical garden at Queens Park, a winery, a railway track and the Ravensbourne National Park. For this reason, Caroline had always believed that the killer lived in proximity to Toowoomba. That fact itself was always unsettling. Whenever she visited the grocery store or watched her boys at one of the local footy matches, she could not help but speculate as she eyed the people around her. One of them could be him. Any of them. Before this new lead came to light, they had nothing to go on to help identify the killer. He could be employed in any profession, camouflaged perfectly as a common nobody in the community. For two years, he lived and worked somewhere in the region, preying on local women, taking four lives while evading capture. What made it embarrassing when she and the other officers of the Task Force failed to produce a suspect during the initial investigation was that Caroline was convinced the Double Spiral Strangler had a kill site somewhere in or around the town. He never left evidence at the sites where he disposed of the bodies, which likely meant he was killing them elsewhere before dumping them. He had to have a controlled environment where he could kill his victims, confident that it wouldn't matter even if he did leave some evidentiary trace. Someplace remote, or perhaps underground. As far as remote places go, it practically encapsulates the entire town. Underground is less likely; the expensive nature of building infrastructure underground coupled with the low availability of contractors in the region who could undertake such a job made the likelihood less conceivable. There are plenty of farming and rural properties in the area, though, with hectares of land to themselves, and he could be operating from any one of them with impunity. There were no witnesses, no reports of unusual activity from people around town, even when everyone was on high alert. The distraught families and friends of the victims found this fact the most difficult to accept. How could someone repeatedly kidnap multiple people without ever once being observed? She arrived at the last page of her dossier. The only clue they ever found. The killer's modus operandi was always the same; strangulation, stabbing, mutilation. After he killed his victim, he took the time to clean their bodies, washing their hair and skin and tending to the knife wound at the ribcage. For reasons unknown, something different happened with his last victim, Hannah Reese. Her death was the strangest of the four by far. Not only did her death occur only two days after he claimed his third victim – which was a much narrower gap between his previous kills – he didn't clean her, and he didn't leave her body in a public space to be found by whichever poor soul happened upon it first. He *buried* Hannah Reese out in Ravensbourne National Park. Lastly, Hannah's body didn't display the completed Double Spiral marking, only the lines cut into the skin by whatever implement he used to form the outline. Beneath Hannah Reese's fingernails, the pathologist detected trace amounts of a white powder which testing revealed to be magnesium oxide. She could still remember with absolute clarity the elation she felt when this first and only clue came to light. Two years with no leads, and then finally, she had *something*. The killer had been uncharacteristically clumsy with Hannah Reese. It was the first and only time evidence was collected from a scene or from the body of one of the victims. Something happened with Hannah that differed from the others, and it gave investigators hope they might solve the case after all. Sadly, it was a heavy blow when the magnesium oxide lead failed to manifest a suspect. Caroline had located every place in town where magnesium oxide had a presence. All told, there were two factories and one farm. Caroline investigated them all but found nothing suspicious. Nothing even noteworthy. It was used in the factories as a dehydration agent, and on the farm, it was applied to soil in pre-plant crops. She identified and interviewed every person who had even the faintest association with the factories and the farm. Employees, owners, contractors, even temporary farmhands employed for seasonal jobs. Every single person had solid alibis during the time which the killings occurred. Every lead was exhaustively investigated by the Task Force until finally, they had to admit that nothing that could propel the investigation forwards eventuated from the magnesium oxide lead. After Hannah Reese's body was discovered half-buried at the National Park by hikers, the killings stopped, and soon after, the case went cold.

Then, Rachael Wright was murdered. When she learned that Rachael's body had been marked by the Double Spiral, it was all the proof Caroline needed to confirm that the Double Spiral Strangler was still out there. Perhaps, after Hannah Reese's body was discovered, something he clearly did not intend given that he attempted to bury her corpse, he got spooked and went into hiding. After three years, either he felt confident he had gotten away with the Toowoomba killings and was ready to make a comeback, or the urges that compelled him to do what he did were too great for him to resist any longer, and he was compelled to kill again. Likely, a combination of the two.

She set aside the old case file and turned her attention to her computer. It was time to add some new intel to these old folders. From her desktop computer at the Toowoomba Police Station, Caroline compiled a list of every school in the district. While separating the private schools from the public on her list, she received an email from Roderick Melaney, Principal of Toowoomba Grammar School, who agreed to meet with her this morning. Somewhere on this list, she hoped she would find a connection, another lead, something to carry the investigation forwards.

Detective Peters waited in the administration block of the prestigious Toowoomba Grammar private school. Of the schools on her list, ten of them were private schools that didn't fall under the umbrella of the authority of the Queensland Government's Department of Education, so she would have to make inquiries individually with each one instead of just being able to deal with a single contact in the State Government for all the public schools. At the private schools, the administrators wouldn't release records without a court order, but Detective Peters had found in her tenure as a Detective that people were generally willing to cooperate with an investigation informally by answering questions if she met with them face to face. In the age of keyboard warriors, Caroline found that people who were ordinarily combative behind the security of their computers could be much more reasonable if they were engaged in an actual human conversation. 'Ah, Detective Peters, so very good of you to wait,' said Principal Melaney as he came hurrying out from a door stationed beside the administration front desk. 'I'm sorry to have kept you waiting. Can I get you anything, water, tea?'

'No, thank you,' said Caroline. Principal Melaney had a habit of waving his hands around theatrically when he talked. He dressed in a colourful, floral suit, wore stylish red-rimmed glasses and spoke with the lilt of a medieval bard.

'Very well. If you follow me, we can talk in my office.' A narrow corridor delivered them to a spacious office located at the end of the hall. Caroline took a seat opposite Melaney's desk.

'I suddenly feel seventeen again,' said Caroline casually. 'As if I'm a kid being called into the Principal's office for disciplinary reasons.'

'Hard to imagine you as a delinquent, Detective,' said Principal Melaney wittily, flashing a sly smile.

She shrugged, grinning personably. 'We all have a past.'

He laughed, not the natural sound of genuine joy but the well-rehearsed sound of a career bureaucrat. 'So, Detective, to what do I owe the pleasure of your acquaintance?'

'Were you Principal here during the period 2016 to 2018?'

He was a small man seated in an overly large chair. He shuffled uncomfortably as if he were offended that she didn't already know the answer. 'I'm proud to declare this is my tenth year as Principal.' The awards and diplomas hung in ornate frames upon the wall behind his desk indicated he'd worked hard to elevate himself into this position. Basically, Melaney is a CEO, and this school is his multi-million dollar business. It's apparent humility isn't something he values. He's flamboyant, proud, prone to boasting.

'Ten years, wow... Congratulations, Mr Melaney. That's a fine achievement.' She would have to appeal to his ego if she hoped to get the information she needed from him without exercising formal procedure. 'Given your many years as head of this school, I imagine you're familiar with every staff member who has come through this place in the last decade, then?'

'Oh, yes. Our school is very selective when it comes to our choice of staff. We are very thorough in choosing the right people for the culture I've cultivated here.'

Good, thought Caroline. He's hands on. The Double Spiral Strangler likes sophisticated women, educated, beautiful, hardworking. He picks middle class women because he probably has a sense of classism, believing himself superior to his victims. Whatever his connection to the education system, he would likely be attracted to private institutions because they are revered amongst elitist groups. The wealthy, the well-connected, those with power and influence. 'Was there anyone employed at the school during the 2017 school year who didn't return in 2018? A faculty member, a groundskeeper, a substitute teacher, perhaps?'

Principal Melaney thought on the question for a moment, casting his memory back. 'No,' he said at last. 'I'm proud to say our attrition rate is very low.' He was looking down his nose at her as he said it. 'Most of the teachers who work for the school are employed on long-term, permanent contracts.' His pride was evident in his tone. He bragged a little by drawing a generalised conclusion: 'Between you and me, that's not a very common thing in the *public* system these days…' He waved his hand as if dismissing an invisible servant beside him. 'Unlike Government employees, staff are not so interchangeable here.'

It didn't come as a surprise that her first inquiries at the first school she visited proved a dead end. Although she was hopeful, Caroline was too pragmatic to allow herself to be convinced that Colt and Price's stroke of good fortune would be extended to her too so soon after their first break in the case. 'Might I be so bold as to ask about the nature of your inquiry, Detective? I must admit I am rather curious about why you have chosen to speak with me today. Not to say that I am displeased with your company, of course! But if there is some criminal matter that you are looking into, well, I can assure you that nobody at *my* school has a criminal record. We conduct comprehensive background searches into our personnel and interview multiple references before committing ourselves to a contracted position.'

Right, thought Peters cynically, *because references are the definitive model for reliability in ascertaining information about someone's character…* 'I can't reveal information about an open case, I'm sorry.'

Her response soured his mood. His flare and showmanship disappeared. Now that the honourable principal was sure there would not be any hot gossip made available to him despite his cooperation, he became standoffish. 'Then, is there anything else I might be able to help you with, Detective? I am quite busy.'

'One more thing, actually.' Melaney didn't look too happy about Caroline taking him up on an offer that was intended to be rhetorical. Caroline ignored his reaction and asked anyway: 'What can you tell me, if anything, about magnesium oxide?'

Principal Melaney looked perplexed. 'I don't know? What *can* I tell you?' He shrugged and turned his face away from her.

'It's a chemical compound.' She smiled warmly, hoping it would be enough to win back his favour. 'Sorry, Mr Melaney, what I really meant to ask is: would there be any use for it in a school environment?'

'Well,' he deliberated. 'Chemistry really isn't my area of expertise, I'm afraid. However, you're welcome to raise the matter with our science teacher, Mrs Matheson, if you like.' He checked his wristwatch. 'She's usually here by seven thirty. Let me see if she's around.' He picked up the phone on his desk and pressed one of the buttons. 'Hi, Lisa. Could you check the staff room and let me know if Mrs Matheson is in yet?' He raised a finger to Caroline while the two waited for a response. 'Oh, great. Thank you.' He hung up the phone. 'You're in luck. She just got in. Let me take you down.' He stood up and chauffeured Caroline down the hall again, taking two turns and opening up a door that revealed a teachers lounge, a room that was barely larger than the size of the Principal's office – something Caroline was inclined not to comment on. Several staff members were nursing steaming mugs of coffee like it was a sacred elixir. Principal Melaney approached a frizzy-haired young woman with heavy bags under her eyes. Her shirt was unironed. She sat alone, an outcast from her peers who were comparatively well-groomed and dressed in presentable attire. Whatever misfortune had befallen Mrs Matheson, it seemed her peers feared it could be infectious. This wasn't her finest day, clearly, judged Caroline. 'Good morning, Mrs Matheson,' said Principal Melaney.

The dishevelled teacher looked up from her coffee at the Principal with a disgruntled expression, forcing herself to smile at her boss. 'Morning, Roderick.'

Melaney looked slightly wounded by the lack of enthusiasm displayed by one of his subordinates after all the high praise and bragging he had been dumping on Caroline in his office but elected to ignore it so he could save face. 'Detective Peters here has some chemistry questions, and as you know, I'm worse than useless in your area of expertise, so I hoped you might be willing to help her out.' He turned to Caroline, saying, with an air of self-importance: 'Detective, I have to be moving on, but if you have any further need of me, I'll be happy to schedule some time again.' He left. Caroline watched him go. He walked with the kind of swagger of a high profile celebrity as if he expected that anybody who might cross his path should disperse to make way for his passing.

'God, I hate that prick,' said Mrs Matheson, quiet enough for only Detective Peters to hear.

'It's not hard to see why,' offered Caroline sympathetically.

'You notice how he asked me to do him a favour the same way an army general issues a command to a lowly grunt? Bloody flowery idiot. Anyway…' She took a sip from her mug. 'Not having the best start today, but I shouldn't make my problems yours. How can I help?'

'I am sorry to interrupt you, Mrs Matheson; I just hoped you might be able to provide some clarity on a matter for me.'

Mrs Matheson finished her coffee. When she was done, she set the mug down on the table, wiped her mouth on the back of her hand, breathed a sigh and said: 'All right, I'm ready now. Shoot.'

'Magnesium oxide.'

'Mm-hmm… what about it?'

'Would it be present in any of your science classes?'

The science teacher pondered the question briefly. 'Well, not exactly.'

'Sorry?'

The science teacher explained: 'As an independent chemical agent, the students would not be exposed to it. However, I conduct an experiment with my seventh-grade class to demonstrate the principles of energy by creating an exothermic reaction using magnesium ribbon and a bunsen burner.' Mrs Matheson stopped and looked at Caroline as if she expected that explanation to suffice. When Mrs Matheson caught on that Caroline needed further clarification, she explained: 'When the ribbon ignites under the high temperature of the flame, it casts a blinding illumination. What remains of the ribbon once it is burned away is a fine, powdery residue. Technically, that leftover powder from the ribbon is magnesium oxide.'

Peters made every conscious effort to contain her excitement. Another clue. During her research, when she initially searched for domestic and commercial uses for magnesium oxide, she never thought to consult the schools because she found no reference to the experiment in her research. It was a manufacturing and farming compound, but the fact it was also a chemical agent in the school system was the most promising lead she could have asked for. She thought to get more information from Mrs Matheson. 'So, when you conduct this experiment, are you wearing any personal protective equipment?'

'Goggles for the light, tongs to handle the ribbon, but as far as high school chem experiments go, it's really not that dangerous. It's fairly rudimentary.'

'So, theoretically, it could be possible for some of the magnesium oxide powder that comes from the burned ribbon to transfer to an article of your clothing or be deposited elsewhere on your person?'

'Hypothetically, sure. The powder is very fine.'

Caroline worked to contain her excitement. 'Thank you, Ms

Matheson,' said Detective Peters. 'You've been very helpful.'

When she was back at the police station, she took the time to communicate her findings to Detective Colt and Senior Sergeant Price. It was essential that she updated them with what she had discovered. An exclusive group-text had been created on an encrypted app to communicate sensitive information imperative to their private investigation. Caroline typed a message: **Magnesium oxide found on Hannah Reese could have been transferred to the vic from the killer's clothing after conducting a high school chemistry experiment. For the time being, we should narrow our search to accommodate science teachers and substitutes of that discipline who worked in the Toowoomba region from 2016–2018 and are now employed by schools in Brisbane and surrounding catchments.**

In less than a minute, Detective Colt replied:

Great work, Peters! We need a court order for Education Queensland to assess their payroll records. Can you arrange a subpoena? Price, in the meantime, you and I will gather a list of all private schools in Brisbane and South East Queensland more broadly. Are you okay to take Brisbane? I'll concentrate on Scenic Rim, Ipswich, Moreton Bay region etc.

Sergeant Price answered a short time later:

No problem! Will get started right away.

Even after the Toowoomba Task Force deemed the case unsolvable, Detective Peters never gave up. Every day, for the last three years, since the discovery of Hannah Reese's in Ravensbourne National Park, Caroline was haunted by the case of the Double Spiral Strangler. For three years, she had no closure. She and the other Officers of the Task Force were condemned by the community for being unable to bring the killer to justice. It affected her career as well as her personal life. She struggled with it. The community still mourned the loss of four of their own. Innocents, callously taken by a predator who walked among them. When the initial investigation lost its momentum, Caroline was tempted to give up, try to find some way of letting go and moving on with her life. But she never could. Now, she felt a renewed sense of purpose. She could sense that redemption was within reach. With Colt and Price's fresh set of eyes, Caroline's partnership with the pair from Brisbane had given her a rare second chance at catching a serial killer, and she swore to any God who could be listening that she wasn't going to blow it.

Chapter Sixteen

Sunday, 19th December 2021 9:18 a.m

It's always dark in the place he has Elise imprisoned. When he visits her, he comes into the room by descending a flight of stairs. There are no windows or doors elsewhere in the room. Therefore, Elise feels confident the space is underground. It must have once been a cellar. The room itself is very spacious, but he has her incarcerated inside the bars of a cage positioned in the centre of the room. When she is alone, it is always dark. There is only light when he is in the room with her. The floor underneath her cell is coarse and cold to the touch. Inside her cell, the only furnishings are a seatless toilet that does not flush and a worn, tired old cot like the kind used in camping and emergency relief shelters. There are no blankets, and there is always a chill. It is an unhospitable and tormenting place to be. She cannot remember how she came to be here… There is no day and night cycle. The only break in the perpetual darkness is the artificial light that shines from the overhead fluorescents he switches on when entering the room. Without any awareness of the rising and setting sun, Elise isn't sure how long she has been in the cage. The hunger and thirst, coupled with the perpetual fear and dread she experiences, have created conditions in which time has no relevance. It could be a day or a week; it makes no difference. There is no relief. There is only survival. She only thinks of enduring the hunger and the thirst and living through the next beating he issues and the next occasion he rapes her. She has learned the hard way that if she offers any resistance by seeking to defend herself or protect herself by attempting to repel him or withdraw, his savagery is boundless. She feebly tried to fend him off the last time he attempted to sexually assault her. He struck her in the head so hard with his fist she lost consciousness. When she came to, she found he was sodomising her. The next time he came into her cage to hurt her, she didn't try to fight back. He gifted her a small plastic bottle containing 300ml of water before departing the room when he finished. That is how she understood that he was conditioning her not to resist by rewarding her with food and water when she let him do what he wanted to her. She doesn't know his face or the sound of his voice. Whenever he comes downstairs, he is always wearing a mask. She thinks he might have made it himself. It's a creepy, white plaster mask with cracks in the resin around the eyes, brow and cheek. Did he insert the cracks to make the whole mask appear more intimidating? He never takes it off. He rarely speaks, but when he does, he filters his voice through some sort of electronic device that gives his voice a tinny resonance. He doesn't want her to know who he is, at least not yet, and for that, she is thankful. As long as she doesn't know his face or his voice, she holds out some hope that he might consider releasing her. She doesn't know how she has been able to tolerate the physical violence and sexual abuse. The only explanation she can think of is that she is compartmentalising her trauma out of self-preservation. The pain in her body is constant. She has suffered one long, persistent headache since he struck the blow that knocked her out. Her vagina aches, having been penetrated by him multiple times. There are dark bruises on her upper arms from where he grabs her, and a dull pain relentlessly throbs in the side of her abdomen from where he kicked her once. The violence he commits against her, while so terrifying it makes her freeze, doesn't typically last very long. What is most unsettling are the long periods that he sits outside her cell perked up in a chair, silently staring at her through the bars. She curls up on her cot and does her best to pretend he isn't there, but she can always feel his eyes upon her. It's a predatory feeling that radiates from him, and it scares her to her core. She gets this sensation that as he watches her, he is struggling to prevent himself from acting out his dark urges. It's as if he is waiting, holding out for some special occasion that is yet to arrive, but he's struggling to contain himself, so he forces himself to savour the anticipation while he waits. The eyeholes in his mask are covered by a black film, so she cannot see his eyes, but it makes it no less uncomfortable and intimidating just having the dark holes of his mask watching her while she cannot do anything to escape his gaze. She lies on her cot with her arms wrapped around herself, crying and self-soothing, waiting for him to leave. Sometimes, while he watches her, he speaks. He doesn't say much during those periods, but there is one phrase he commonly repeats. She can tell, even though his voice is filtered, that he speaks the words with great pride, almost reverently: "My Angels walk with me wherever I go." She hasn't the faintest idea what it means. It's the nonsense of a mad man. Does he believe himself to be some sort of God? She tries not to allow herself to attempt to interpret his meaning because every possible answer she devises only serves to compound her anxiety.

When she is in the dark, alone, she tries to remember how she came to be here. The last thing she remembers clearly was going to bed after arriving home feeling utterly miserable after an awful date with Dale. The following day when she woke up – at least, she *thinks* it was the next morning – she found herself trapped here in the dark, surrounded by the flat steel slats of this cell. She had never suffered a more tremendous shock. For what must have been hours, she searched desperately in the dark for a means of escaping. On her hands and knees, she crawled the perimeter of the cell, seeking a flaw in its design. She had some inkling about the kind of place she was trapped, but it wasn't until he came in for the first time dressed in his dark clothes and that mask and he lit up the room that she realised the true horror of her predicament. Every minute for an intolerably long time, she half-expected to wake up from this lucid, nightmare-to-end-all-nightmares. But every time she woke after she slept, she found herself in the same place. She could no longer deny that this was her reality. So, she tried desperately to cast her mind back, combing her memory for some clue about her location or the identity of her captor. But she remembers nothing. Maybe that's why he starves her. To keep her body weakened and her mind foggy, so she is less likely to recall how he managed to get her to this place without any awareness of the transition from the comfort of her own bed to this hellish cage. When the Masked Man wasn't around, she made lists in her head of all the things she loved. The best things about being alive. Frequently topping that list is her fluffy ginger cat, Mr Weasley, named so in honour of her favourite character from the Harry Potter books. Poor Mr Weasley. He must be so scared. He was probably crying at the door of her unit, whining about being unable to get out. He must be so hungry, and thirsty, and lonely. With sad amusement, she realises that she and Mr Weasley share an identical experience; both are trapped inside a place they cannot escape. She wondered if her cat was yearning for her the same as she was for him? She misses his soft purring, his comforting warm fur. Sometimes, when she slept, she dreamed he was here with her in the cell, but when she woke to find his presence was only a dream, the sense of loss and longing it imparted was its own brand of vicious torment. In addition to Mr Weasley, she thinks about all the food she would eat if she could have whatever she pleased. First, a hot, cheesy pizza with buttery garlic bread. A chocolate milkshake and a strawberry doughnut for dessert. The thought makes her mouth salivate. As she repositions herself on the astonishingly uncomfortable cot, she envisions herself sprawling her arms and legs on her spacious king-sized mattress at home, nestling into her soft, cashmere blankets. She thinks about the kids in her class at Claremont, even willingly acknowledging that she would do anything to listen to their chaotic voices carrying across the playground as they run around like mad things. She *never* thought she could miss that sound. But what she wouldn't do for it now, to break the deafening, harrowing silence. She is tired, so hungry that her body feels terribly weak. Every tiny movement feels like a herculean task. She tries to remember the most prolonged period she has ever lived without any food. It has been a privileged life, was there ever even one whole day?

The Masked Man is away for a long time. It is the longest absence she has registered since she woke to find herself here. She is grateful because every minute she is alone means she is safe. An egg-shaped lump protrudes from the spot his fist connected with her skull, and she fears she won't survive another beating. It is a miracle she isn't dead already. She is even thankful for the ever-present hunger because the cramping pains keep her alert and remind her that she is alive. As long as she is alive, hope remains. As long as she survives, there is a chance to get out of here, back home to Mr Weasley. She has developed a mantra which she repeats to herself when she tries to soothe and calm herself, seeking to assure herself and steel herself against the threat of the Masked Man. In the dark, she whispers under her breath: 'Survive, stay alive, survive...'

The next time he comes in, she is blinded by the lights, for she has been too long in the dark. It takes time for her eyes to adjust to the illumination. Her eyeballs weep, sending lines of salty tears down her cheeks. The brightness feels so uncomfortable that her body instinctually wants to keep her eyes closed, but she forces them open so she can check to see if he is entering her cell to perpetrate violence against her. She has to know if he's coming in or staying beyond the bars. She repeatedly blinks, expelling the saltwater from her eyes as her vision adjusts. She hears no sound that indicates the cell door is being unlocked. Perhaps he has come just to stare at her a while again. He speaks. 'You shall not have to wait much longer.' His strange, filtered voice echoes around the room. 'My preparations are almost complete. Soon, I shall introduce you to the altar, and there I will bring about your transformation.' Through wet, squinting eyes, she sees him affectionately touching the criss-cross steel pattern of her cell as if to imitate the tender caress of a lover's hand upon her cheek. Now, the energy she feels radiating from him is gentler, less aggressive, yet no less maniacal. Is this the calm before the storm? What he says, the way he stands and holds himself – all if it conveys a madness most disturbing. He communicates with a rationale that only he understands.

She dares to ask: 'What do you mean? What kind of transformation?'

He takes a seat in the chair outside her cell. He lifts his shirt to reveal his hairless chest. Across his front, between the two pectoral muscles, there is the shape of a dark tattoo. A slanted, horizontal line that curls into spirals around each of his nipples. 'Do you know what this is?' he asks. She shakes her head. 'It signifies balance and symmetry between opposing forces.' He touches the spiral on the left. 'Life.' Then, he touches the spiral on the right. 'Death.' He traces his finger along the line, joining them in the middle. 'And here, the transitionary space. This is where the transformation takes place.' He lowers his shirt. 'Upon the altar, I have prepared for you, your body will die, and your spirit shall be awoken so that you will live eternally, bound to me, forever.' Elise looked at her trembling hands. Her legs could not hold her weight. She lowered herself and sat helplessly on the hard floor. All she could think was: *I'm going to die, I'm going to die, I'm going to die...* Could this be real? Surely it was just some vivid nightmare. She would wake soon and find herself at home with Mr Weasley. Safe. It can't really be happening. This doesn't happen. Her heart beats frighteningly fast. Too fast. 'I was asleep once,' says the Man in the Mask. 'As you are now. My true self was dormant, suffocated and suppressed by the rules of society and norms of the culture. And then, the miracle happened. I met my first Angel. She showed me how to embrace my nature and taught me to accept my higher purpose. After that, I was free. In time, I crossed paths with more Angels. I loved them, so I cut their wings so they could not fly away. Now, my Angels walk with me wherever I go.'

'You're fucking crazy,' she sputtered as she began to cry. Even during the occasions he beat and raped her, she did not feel the potency of fear as she did now. Violence was about intimidation, and by extension, dominance and control. When he hurt her, he hissed foul, cruel things from behind his mask. He would tell her she is worthless, that she is less than nothing, garbage beneath his heel. When he hurt her this way, he was expressing very fallible emotion. Contempt, rage, and a desperate need to be superior which likely stemmed from an inferiority complex that took root in his psyche during his adolescence. He exercised violence to prove to himself that he was in control, that he was powerful. These episodes of violent outbursts made him recognisably human. Flawed, angry, hurt. Pathetically textbook stuff. He is reenacting unresolved trauma but reversing the direction of the traumatic events so that he is not the victim but the perpetrator. In this way, it satiates his pain by making him feel empowered. Having studied child psychology in her double degree, Elise diagnosed his violent tendencies early on during her imprisonment. But this lunatic monologue of murder and Angels and transformation is utterly mad. He is so radically delusional that his reasoning is incomprehensible to a sane mind. And that scares her more than any violent act or harsh word ever could. She had been relying on the assumption that her jailor could be reasoned with, that when it came down to it, her survival could hinge upon it. He is calm right now, and although what he says makes no sense, there is a lucidity and consistency to his behaviour that isn't so apparent during his fits of rage. Maybe if she built enough rapport with him, she could bargain with him for her release, or failing that, appeal to his madness and find a way to convince him to be merciful. 'That's all any of us want,' she began. 'To have a purpose. To believe our lives are meaningful. That we matter.' She raised herself up from the floor and stepped closer to the bars. Closer to *him.* As much of what she hoped to communicate would have to be transmitted non-verbally in addition to what she spoke aloud. The way his head tilted when she spoke, she interpreted to mean that, for now, she had piqued his interest and, for the time being, held his attention. 'As for your Angels, well, they're forgiving creatures, aren't they? Compassionate beings. I'm sure they don't want you to hurt anyone, especially yourself. We hurt ourselves most when we hurt others. I don't think they would want that for you.' He stands from his seat just beyond the metal barrier that separates them, breathing so steadily he is imperceptibly still. He says nothing. Maybe she's getting through to him. She keeps trying: 'It's not easy, the struggle between the two sides inside of us. I'm sure it can't have been easy for you.' She pressed her hand to the metal in a pretence to demonstrate her affection. He touched his palm to the other side. For the first time, she was thankful for the metal bars of this cage, if they were not stationed between their hands, she was positive that her ruse would fall apart if she had to touch him. 'It's not fair, is it? To have to deny our true self and pretend to be someone we aren't for the sake of others. Why should you have to make such a sacrifice? I get it. I've been there too. I've felt that way. God, there have been times when I've been so angry at myself for repeating the same mistakes over and over again it felt like I was never going to do better. I've felt so mad I could have burned the whole world down given half a chance. I've made mistakes, just like you. I've hurt people. Let them down. Betrayed them. *Used* them. But you know what?'

'Go on…' he said.

'The people I hurt were able to forgive me, and I promise you I can forgive you for all of this. You could just let me go, and we could pretend like this never happened. I haven't seen your face or heard your voice. I don't know who you really are. Please, I beg you: ask your Angel; I'm sure it will urge you to do the right thing.'

He approached the bars until there was very little space between his person and the criss-cross steel of the cage. It took every measure of self-control Elise could muster not to withdraw as he got nearer. 'Which Angel should I ask?' A tingle traversed her spine. She tried not to let him see her shudder. She had to ask because her only chance for this to work was to keep him talking, to gain his trust. She took a few seconds until she was sure she could ask the question without stuttering.

'How many Angels are there?'

He raised his forefinger to the bars as if to say, *just a moment*. He left the room, climbing the staircase. He returned a short while later, holding what appeared to be a series of printed photographs. 'Shall I come in and show you?'

'No, no,' said Elise trying as best she could to contain her fearfulness. 'I can see just fine from here.'

He held up one of the photographs, pressing it against the steel cage so Elise could inspect the image. A fair-skinned, dark-haired woman was pictured with beautifully rich, light brown eyes. He held the picture up for Elise to see for a few seconds, then turned it around to gaze at it himself. He lovingly stroked the photographed woman with the infatuation of someone sickeningly obsessed. 'Holly. That was what she was called when she was of the flesh. She was the first to join me after I orchestrated her transformation. It was my First Angel who helped me discover the importance of who I truly am.' Elise backed away from the cage. He wasn't speaking figuratively. The Angels weren't a manifestation of psychosis or schizophrenic apparitions – his Angels are people. People he *transformed* into spirits by murdering them.He displayed a second photograph. Pictured was another beautiful young woman with distinctive brown hair, olive skin and gleeful eyes. 'Maria. My second Angel.' He displayed the following photograph. Elise felt her knees go weak. 'Joanne.' Another woman, older than the first two by ten years at least but not likely any more aged than Elise is today. Joanne had a world-wearied smile and sad green eyes. 'Hannah,' he said, displaying the fourth photograph. Another beauty, mousy blonde hair, a toothy smile and chubby, glowing cheeks. 'The unintended. Sent from the heavens to test me. Her transformation didn't go according to plan, and the heavens wept when I clipped her wings. I put her body under the ground, but the rain flushed her back out. I never wanted to make Hannah one of my Angels, but as they say, the Lord works in mysterious ways. Now, she walks with me too.' Elise fell onto her cot, sobbing uncontrollably, no longer able or willing to control her impulses. He held up the last photograph. 'I know you must miss her, but there is no need. Not any more. The spirit triumphs where the flesh fails. Soon, Elise, you will be reunited with her when you too join my order of Angels.'

'Oh, God...' wailed Elise painfully as she stared with disbelief at the face in the final photograph. 'Rachael!'

Chapter Seventeen

Monday, 20th December 2021 12:17 p.m

Detective Peters shared the subpoena results of the Queensland Government Department of Education's payroll records with Senior Sergeant Price via email. The results had been compiled for them on a single data sheet containing thousands of entries. Granted that many teachers employed by the department are hired on short-term contracts, some as brief as a single semester only, it was unsurprising that there was a long list of teachers employed during the 2016–2018 school years in Toowoomba who also later had contracts at schools in Brisbane and the surrounding region. While Detective Peters and Detective Colt were busy inquiring with the private schools in the broader council districts around Brisbane and Toowoomba, Senior Sergeant Price worked diligently to filter the list of names Detective Peters sequestrated. She sat at her computer in front of a copy of the department's payroll records from 2016 to 2021, surveying thousands of data points. It was dangerous to be using Queensland Police equipment for their secret investigation. Price did not know who could be trusted within the precinct and who might be spying for La Pila among her peers. It was a good thing none of the other officers had desks anywhere near Graham, and consequently, Addilyn. It meant she had the privacy she needed to conduct her search in peace without having to worry about prying eyes. Her first act was to apply a filter to the spreadsheet that narrowed the results to only those teachers employed by schools to teach science. The list of names was reduced considerably. Then, she cross-referenced the remaining names with a second data filter which excluded teachers employed in regions across the state outside of Toowoomba and the surrounding council districts during the 2016 to 2018 semesters. That group numbered only forty-one. She applied one more filter, which removed all the female names. Price, Colt and Peters all agreed it was safe to presume the perpetrator of these crimes was a man. The forty-one suspects became nineteen. When Detective Peters had learned that the only physical evidence ever left behind by the killer could be linked to a high school science experiment, the three agreed to exclude Universities and Primary Schools from their search parameters. They verified that neither of these institutions conducted this experiment. For the primary schools, thermodynamics was too advanced, and for the Universities, the basis of the experiment was too rudimentary. Therefore, chances were that unless the killer was employed by a private school, one of the nineteen names remaining on her data sheet could be the identity of the Double Spiral Strangler. She perused the list and thought about when she interviewed Joshua Dempsey for the first time – before Rachael Wright had become a homicide case. She remembered being curious about whether she would be able to see it, the part of himself he tried to hide, the narcissist, the deceiver. She recalled wondering, if Rachael had met with foul play at Josh's hands, would she know it, sitting across from him? The same curiosity teased her now as she looked over the list of names. Would it leap from the page, calling to her, if one of them were the Double Spiral Strangler? Would her heart warn her she was reading the name of a deadly, violent killer? It seemed not. All she felt looking over the names was that they were ordinary. She had to foolishly remind herself that ordinary was precisely the point. In fact, as Colt said once, the killer they hunted probably had to work very hard to achieve ordinary because he was anything *but* a common man. He cannot have eluded capture and detection this long without learning to blend in. He had to fake it to make it. People who do what he has done aren't walking around with nefarious names dripping with evil intent. Just like those around them, they're people with jobs, friends, family, and often an ordinary, unassuming name.

Price looked over every row on her datasheet but could find no indication that revealed whether any of these nineteen names were actively employed by the State Government at this time. There was also an irregularity in the numbers. Two of the men listed had an identical payroll identification number, and Price couldn't figure out why without additional information. Unfortunately, it meant she would have to make some inquiries. So, Price telephoned the Department's payroll to speak with them directly. It didn't matter that Peters' name was on the warrant. Under the terms of the subpoena, any officer from QPS could make additional inquiries once the information had been released into Police custody. Price dialled the contact number and waited. A particularly chipper payroll employee named Grace answered the phone and politely introduced herself. 'Hi, Grace, my name is Senior Sergeant Price, and I'm calling from QPS about the data we recently subpoenaed from your payroll office.'

Grace, sounding all too cheerful for such a tedious job: 'Oh, hi! Okay, how can I help?'

'I was looking over the list of names, and I need some more information. There also appears to be an error in the data. I was hoping you could clarify why there is a duplicate in the records. I'm looking at men employed by the Department working as science teachers in High Schools who worked at Toowoomba between 2016 and 2018 and were later employed at schools in Brisbane and the surrounding catchments any time in the following years to date. I've applied these filters to a data sheet we received from your office, and I've got nineteen names. But I think something is wrong with the record because two names have the same payroll ID number. I just need to make sure that your office's information is accurate. Can you help me, please?'

'Okay, just bear with me a moment. First, I'll need the approval number on the subpoena, so I know you are an authorised person, and I can release the information to you.' Price recited the number for her. 'Great! All right, let me bring up what you have so I can see what you're seeing.' Through the phone, Price heard the sound of Grace's fingers clinking on the keys of her keyboard and the little clicking sound of her mouse. 'Okay. So, you said you filtered the results to show only men who taught science and worked at Toowoomba between 2016 and 2018 and later secured contracts in Brisbane and the surrounding areas…'

'That's right,' said Price.

More clicking, more keys being furiously tapped. 'Okay. Nineteen names. I'm with you. You mentioned a duplicate?'

'Yeah, if you look at Daniel Cassidy and Dale Bellringer, these two guys have the same payroll number. Why would that be?'

'Ummm,' sounded Grace as she looked over the list. 'Oh, yep. I see. Dale Bellringer and Daniel Cassidy. Same ID number. That *is* weird. Sometimes the schools input the wrong names when they register with Queensland Education payroll, and accidents like this happen where two teachers end up with the same payroll ID. Do you mind if I put you on a brief hold just so I can have a look and see what's going on?'

'Yeah, no problem.'

The hold music was awful. Price was tortured by the sound of a solo, screechy violin accompanied by what sounded like the least passionate orchestra ever comprised in classical music playing Christmas carols for twenty very long minutes. Grace ended the hold just as Price was ready to hang up and call back again just to save herself having to endure another second of the awful music. 'Hi, Sergeant Price, are you there?'

'Yeah, I'm here.'

'Thank you so much for your patience; I'm *so sorry* to have kept you waiting so long!' You should be sorry for putting me through that hell, thought Price cynically. Grace continued: 'It was a bit of a mystery, but I eventually figured it out! The identical payroll number *isn't* a mistake. They're the same number because those employees are actually the *same person.*'

'What do you mean?' Price pulled a pen out from a mug on her desk and prepared to take some notes. 'So, Daniel Cassidy was employed at Toowoomba State School from 2015 to 2018. Strangely, there is no record of any termination or any record of him giving written notice to the school. It appears that for reasons unknown, he just didn't return to teach the next year. Then, I scoured the records. I found that the next appearance of Daniel Cassidy's payroll ID popped up in the system when a man named Dale Bellringer received his first pay from Kedron State School at the start of Term 3 in 2020. At first, I couldn't figure out what was going on! Payroll IDs are a unique number to individual employees. They never get reassigned, so I was like: *what's happening?*' Oh, God, thought Price. Come on, girl. Get to the point! Grace continued rambling: 'So I looked back at Dale Bellringer's employment history. After finishing the two semesters at Kedron, he applied for multiple positions advertised by the department.'

'Why is that relevant?'

'When a teacher applies for a position advertised by the Department, they can provide consent on the application forms which allow us to complete a search with the Australian Taxation Office to electronically verify their identity with the records the Tax Office holds. It's pretty standard these days. Anyway, applicants are given two options on the application form under the section requiring verification of their identity. They can either select to give us consent to complete the electronic check on their behalf or submit certified copies of their ID to us manually. Most don't choose the second option because it's a hassle to get photocopies of their driver's license or passport, or whatever they choose to use to satisfy the hundred points of ID, and then have them certified by a Justice of the Peace. But on *every* application, Dale Bellringer selected this option and mailed certified copies of his ID. Except for one. He ticked the box giving consent for the electronic check on one application.'

'An oversight?' asked Price, taking explanatory notes as Grace explained.

'Possibly, it's impossible to say. Regardless of why he made this exception, once the results of the verification check came back to us here at payroll, the system registered Dale Bellringer's details inside an existing account.'

'Daniel Cassidy's account,' put in Price.

'Exactly.'

'But that still doesn't explain why?'

'I didn't get it at first either. This is why I had you on hold for so long. I was looking over all the records we have on Dale Bellringer. I looked at every one of his job applications individually. On all the photocopies of the ID he had certified and provided to us, none of his personal details matches the information we have on Daniel Cassidy. Obviously, his name is different, but so is the address, the medicare number, his bank details – everything. I could not figure out why the system merged these two accounts when everything suggested they're different people.'

'So, how did you?'

'Dale Bellringer's Tax File Number is the same as Daniel Cassidy's. That's why the payroll ID is the same because when he provided consent for the electronic verification to go ahead, the results matched Dale's TFN with Daniel Cassidy's. He didn't supply his TFN on the job applications because it is voluntary. It's just another method we can use to undertake a manual check with the ATO, but we can also use a person's name, address, email, date of birth… But, when he consented to the electronic check, the program always uses the Tax File Number as the primary identifier by default, so when it verified Dale Bellringer's identity, the results came back with Daniel Cassidy's TFN.'

'So, let me get this straight,' said Price trying to comprehend the situation. 'The reason Dale Bellringer and Daniel Cassidy have the same payroll ID is because after Daniel Cassidy inexplicably left his employer at Toowoomba, he changed his name to Dale Bellringer. Later, he applied for teaching jobs under his new name, always using manual forms and providing photocopies of his ID. On *one* occasion, he made the mistake of ticking a box that gave your department consent to verify his ID electronically, and the results of that confirmation revealed they share the same Tax File Number.'

'That's right,' said Grace. 'He must have changed his name after leaving Toowoomba. When he moved to Brisbane, he applied for jobs where all his personal information was different, so the system didn't recognise they were the same person until that electronic ID check occurred. And then, *voila!*'

Price covered the microphone on her telephone. 'Holy, *fuck,*' she breathed. This *has* to be him. Daniel Cassidy worked at Toowoomba, teaching science. He vanishes suddenly at the end of 2018, providing no notice to his employer at the same time as the Strangler's fourth victim, Hannah Reese, is discovered buried at Ravensbourne National Park. Daniel Cassidy assumes a new identity as Dale Bellringer and pops up in Brisbane years later, going to painful lengths to ensure no trace of his former identity is recorded when applying for new jobs. Being employed is essential to maintaining his camouflage, so he must keep a job. Then, one tiny mistake – an omission, a moment of forgetfulness, ignorance or distraction – and a record is created linking his former identity to his new, solving the mystery of Daniel Cassidy's sudden disappearance. A man doesn't go to these lengths to hide an old identity without reason. He must have been trying to cover his tracks. He couldn't erase his former identity, so he just sought to abandon it and carry on with his new while avoiding any triggers that could pair the two. Price felt a tingling in her spine. It felt as though the air in the room had suddenly decreased by twenty degrees. 'Grace,' said Price with tremendous trepidation. 'Are you able to tell me whether Dale Bellringer is currently employed?'

'Yeah, of course. Let me see.' She paused while she conducted a search. 'Umm, yep. Here we go. He signed a contract covering the period from the beginning to the end of this year.'

'Where, Grace? What school?'

'Claremont College.' *Gotcha!* It all came together for Price:

Daniel Cassidy's mysterious disappearance, the alteration of identity, the timeline correlation between these events and the Strangler activity. He's a teacher. He kills during school holidays to mock the police. Claremont College was the school Rachael taught at. This bastard got so brazen he actually targeted someone who worked at the same school. He thinks himself untouchable. Price hoped she was there to see his face when he was proven wrong. A chill rose through her body. It made her shiver. Dale Bellringer, formerly known as Daniel Cassidy, could be the Double Spiral Strangler. She felt it in her gut. It's him.

'Grace, I'm going to need you to email me copies of those records. It's critical that you include an explanation as to how you reasoned that Daniel Cassidy and Dale Bellringer are the same man. Just type it up in a letter if you have to. Can you do that for me?'

'Um, yeah, sure,' said Grace tentatively. 'It could take a few days, though. I've got a lot of work already waiting in the queue.'

'I need you to do this for me today, Grace. It's *imperative*.'

That cheery sounding voice changed, and Price could hear the concern in Grace's tone. 'Okay, I'll have it to you by this afternoon.' Grace confirmed Price's work email to ensure she sent the records to the right place. Before she hung up the phone, Price ended the conversation by saying: 'Grace, you should know that you did something wonderful today. I can't say why but believe me, this was no small thing. Thank you. I'm very grateful.'

The compliment gave Grace some relief. The bright, cheery voice returned: 'You're welcome, Sergeant Price. I'll get started on that letter for you right away. Have a great day! Bye.'

A great day indeed, Price thought.

Price felt the effects of time more keenly than she could ever recall while she and Colt waited out their shift at work so they could go home and continue with their private investigation. Every second felt elongated until disproportionate hours tormented her conscience. Every minute they were delayed was a minute advantaging the Double Spiral Strangler. He was out there somewhere, right now. He could be planning his next kill. This very minute, stalking his next victim. Dale Bellringer was the most promising subject ever produced across two separate investigations. Price hated having to sit around to save face with La Pila and her henchman until her shift was over and she could get on with the real work, the work that actually mattered.

At the end of her shift, as Price and Colt were readying to leave for the day, Price was called into La Pila's office at the last minute. 'I'll wait for you to join me at your place,' assured Colt before the two were separated. 'I've already communicated your findings to Peters. She's using QPrime to conduct searches on Cassidy and Bellringer. If there's anything to know, she'll find it.'

In La Pila's office, Price was asked to take a seat. Her boss closed the door leaving the two alone in the office while the officers on day shift were replaced by those rostered on for the evening. 'Still no leads on linking Mr Dempsey to the double spiral symbol, I see,' said Superintendent La Pila. Price was quick to guess she had an ulterior motive for arranging this impromptu meeting, and it didn't take a genius to guess this was really about Graham Coltsworth.

'No, ma'am. Nothing beyond the journal entries. Detective Belmont oversaw another sweep of Josh's house as per your instruction. They found nothing. We even inspected his cubicle at the financial advisory firm that employs him. Nothing there either. Extensive searches have been undertaken of his online history.'

'And found nothing...' finished La Pila.

'Yes, ma'am.'

Superintendent La Pila scrunched up her nose and snorted. Behind her outrageously large desk, she leaned back in her chair, relaxed. 'I understand that you have been spending a lot of time with Detective Coltsworth.'

Price nodded. 'That buddy-system you mentioned has proven beneficial for me. I'm learning a lot. I'm grateful to be able to shadow him.'

'I meant *outside* the station.' La Pila's words carried an accusatory tone.

Price shifted uncomfortably in her seat. 'I wasn't aware that was an issue, ma'am.'

'Only if you're engaged in a romantic relationship. He is your *superior* officer and a senior ranking member of this precinct. It would be highly inappropriate if that were the case.'

'I can assure you,' scoffed Price, 'that it is *not* the case.'

'Oh, but who would believe that? Consider the facts... You are appointed to homicide, taken under the wing of a senior Detective who insists that you partner with him on a high profile murder case.' She pauses for effect. 'Your *first* homicide case, mind you. Then, the two of you are sighted in the company of one another during the evenings, off the clock, at your residence.'

'You have me under surveillance?' Price's question carried its own accusatory tone.

La Pila ignored Price's question. Price could sense La Pila's agitation despite presenting herself comfortably relaxed using her body language. 'I tried to help you, didn't I, Addilyn? I told you to keep an eye on Graham and come to me if you learned that he was in breach of protocol.' This talk had suddenly become very serious. Price could feel the imbalance of power here. In a contest of wills, she had no hope of besting La Pila. 'I asked you to keep an eye on him. I instructed you to report to me if he was doing anything that could put the Dempsey case and, by extension, this precinct, in jeopardy.'

Price said assertively: 'I have not observed any breaches.'

La Pila was silent. It dawned on Price that she could be bluffing. It was a marvellous strategy; she had to give her boss credit. La Pila relied on the intimidation her position imposed to lure Price into admitting details of their secret investigation by catching her off guard. But Price can see it: La Pila has nothing. She doesn't know about the private investigation or their progress. She doesn't know about Detective Peters or the Toowoomba investigation. If she did, she would have already brought the hammer down on Colt. This is why she has had people following them, and this is why she is resorting to vague threats regarding assumptions people might make about her and Colt being involved romantically and the benefits that would produce for the advancement of her career. Because as her team continues to come up short regarding Josh Dempsey's case, she's looking for leverage. The buck stops with her, after all. She needs a bad guy, someone to blame, and she wants that person to be Colt more than anything. La Pila presented her rage-inducing smile. A sickening display of her undiagnosed superiority complex. 'Very well,' she said scornfully. 'I just wanted to bring you in to have a quick chat because I think you should tread very carefully. People notice how much time the two of you are spending together outside of work. You wouldn't want people to get the wrong idea. An attractive young woman like you, it could be easy for the men of this office to suspect your career progression can be attributed to qualities other than your merits as an investigator. That kind of reputation could be lethal to your career prospects...'

Price forced a polite, appropriately innocent smile. 'Thank you for your advice. I'll take it on board. If there is nothing else, ma'am, may I be excused?'

La Pila waved a hand dismissively. Price could see the disdain she was trying to conceal. 'Of course, Sergeant. Give some thought to what I've said.' Price rose and made her way to the door. 'Price? One more thing before you go... Around here, rumours are like oxygen, and to a bright spark like you, a rush of air could either extinguish you or build you up. There are a lot of empty chairs around Graham Coltsworth's desk and, funnily enough, a lot of rumours out there about him too. Some food for thought.' She gave one last cunning look at Price. 'Goodnight, Sergeant.'

Price took forty minutes in peak hour afternoon traffic to get back to her apartment. She went a different way home, intentionally selecting a lengthier route to ensure she wasn't being followed. Until she could see this investigation through, she would have to be extra cautious when it came to La Pila and her goons. Whoever they are. Colt warned her about La Pila's ruthlessness. Now, the Superintendent was getting desperate and was barking pretty loudly. Price wasn't keen to feel the bite once La Pila realised the bark wasn't enough. 'There's no way it *isn't* him, right?' said Price of Dale Bellringer once she was back with Detective Colt.

'It's still too early to say for certain,' said Colt. 'But were I a betting man, I'd be putting every dollar at my disposal on him. I'm still waiting to hear back from Caroline, but given the promising nature of this lead, I think we should see it through before we go back to speaking with the private schools. If he *is* our guy, we'll only be wasting our time with the other schools.'

As usual, Jasper awaited eagerly at the door of Price's apartment at the time ordained that his master ordinarily returned home. The dog had become quite fond of Colt. The gruff Detective, a man, not ordinarily *or* easily pleased, appeared to have developed an attachment to the dog, who relentlessly sought his attention from the moment he arrived in Price's tiny one-bedroom to the minute he left. 'Well, how about a drink while we wait?' offered Price.

'Only a fool says no to a free drink,' said Colt. A minute later, she had prepared a drink for them both. They relaxed on the couch, giving Jasper a pat while they sipped their dark liquor and waited to hear back from Peters. 'So, what did the she-devil want?' asked Colt.

'La Pila? Oh, no bother.' She waved her hand dismissively through the air, just as La Pila had done to her only a short while earlier. 'Turns out she has been surveilling me. She knows you have been spending time here but came up short as to why. She was trying to entrap me. Get me to fess up.'

'She must think you're stupid,' mocked Colt derisively. 'That's an interesting one for the history books, though. A cop trying to entrap another cop. Must say, I've never seen that one before.'

'She kind of threatened me.'

'Really!' Colt perked up. 'What did she say?'

'She insinuated that a sexual relationship with my superior officer possessed certain negative reputational connotations that could disrupt my career progress in Special Ops.'

If Colt was the kind of man who was easily shocked, his jaw might have dropped. But sadly, this was just another typical page from the Lisa La Pila political tactics book on career warfare. 'She must think pretty poorly of you if she thinks a beautiful young woman like you would have to settle for an old horse like me.' He smiled affectionately, a sarcastic twinkle in his eye.

'Well, you know what they say, old man. Better to trot along at a steady pace with an old stallion than getting tossed around by a young colt...' Price waited. She looked up at Colt expectingly. '...Get it? Old stallion, young *Colt*...'

He wouldn't give her the satisfaction of his full belly laugh, but the lame pun did hit the mark and made him chuckle. 'Yes, I get it.' He raised his glass praisingly. 'You're the master of puns.'

Since knowing Graham Coltsworth, Addilyn felt an intense attraction for her mentor for the first time. His whiskered, wiry beard needed a trim, and he could benefit from a haircut. Colt wasn't a handsome man, with his sun-damaged skin, heavy brow, brooding eyes and rugged unkempt exterior. Still, he was the kind of person that worked hard to be a good man. That is a rare thing. He was patient, conscientious, attentive, thoughtful and possessed the wisdom to know when it was worth doing the wrong thing to achieve the right outcome. What he had rallied her to do with this investigation was undoubtedly the right thing, even if it put both of their careers at risk. The fact he was willing to put it all on the line, his life, his job, his reputation, to see justice done was the kind of thing that inspired her to follow him along this path, wherever it was leading. The feeling of attraction quickly dissolved when he burped loudly and asked for a second scotch, but the glowing admiration she felt for the man remained undiminished.

Colt's phone rang as Price poured him a second glass. 'It's Peters,' he said as he answered the call and put it on loudspeaker.

'It took all day,' said Peters, 'but I found that Dale Bellringer is renting an apartment in Brisbane that he's leased since December 2018. Dale Bellringer, formerly known as Daniel Cassidy, has no criminal convictions, not even so much as a speeding ticket. Daniel Cassidy is clean too. The only record relating to Dale's former identity I could find anywhere is a listing on the Australian Business Register naming him as the Director of a Corporate Trustee. The trust owns several hectares of land at an estate in remote Buaraba.'

Price looked up the location on her phone. 'Holy shit, guys. According to census data from last year, Buaraba has a populace of only 191 people. And look' —she widened the map with two fingers— 'it's right next to Ravensbourne National Park, where they found Hannah Reese's body.'

'This must be where he kills his victims,' proposed Colt.

'Those were my thoughts exactly,' said Caroline. 'I've wondered where his damn kill site was for the last five years, and here it was this whole time, right in my own backyard.'

'You couldn't have known,' Price said, trying to offer some assurance. It did Caroline little good. She had been scorched by this case, and those burns were not likely to quickly heal. She was just ready for it to be over. This was the closest she had ever been to getting closure, and it was making her edgy. Price searched for directions on the GPS application on her phone. 'Caroline, Graham and I can be at Buaraba in an hour and a half. I think we should go pay this property a visit.'

'I think it's time to call in the cavalry,' inserted Peters. Colt and Price gave each other a contemplative look. There was no way La Pila would sanction this based on the circumstantial nature of the evidence. Not while she had hard DNA evidence against Josh Dempsey. Sensing their reluctance, Peters urged: 'Look, I know your crew over there aren't able to follow any other leads right now. Your hands are tied, I get that. But the officers out here who were part of the Task Force have been haunted by this case, just like I have. None of us has been able to move on since Daniel Cassidy disappeared all those years ago. They deserve to be included in this. It's been tough to keep my people out of the loop. We're like family out here. What do you say, Colt? You agreed from the start that if this little off-the-books investigation of ours presented a suspect, we would bring it through the official channels.'

'Let's just have a look at the property first,' countered Colt. 'We don't for certain know that Dale Bellringer is the Double Spiral Strangler. The circumstances are promising but not absolute. Let's go out there, and you have my word that if we find anything even *remotely* suspicious, we will bring everyone in. For now, Peters, you know we hold the advantage. If we start organising strike teams and the rest of it, we lose time, and we can't afford that right now. We need this chance.'

Caroline was quiet for a moment while she deliberated the proposal. 'All right,' she said after a time. It was clear she wasn't comfortable with the plan, but she couldn't refute that Colt was right. Enough time had been wasted already. 'There's an Ampol petrol station in Buaraba. Let's make that our rendezvous point. We'll go out to the property together from there.'

'We'll leave right away,' promised Colt.

'We'll see you soon,' said Price.

Chapter Eighteen

Tuesday, 21st December 2021 7:18 p.m

He sits outside the cell that houses Elise, with the key to her prison in hand, watching her, soaking in every detail while she remains alive. For him, these final hours before he transforms his chosen into an Angel is the most enticing part of the ritual. Once the ceremony is complete, she will never be of the flesh again. Inside the scope of eternity, her time with her body soon ends. Therefore, he must memorise all her details while she still occupies this form. Her raggedy light brown hair, sharp V-shaped jaw, and swan-like, delicate neck. Her milky white flesh, her smoky hazel eyes. Uniquely her, and once she is gone, there will never be another like her. He has had her locked in a cage for a week. In that time, the aroma of her sweet-smelling hair and skin had petrified from the alluring fragrances of her shampoo and perfume to a rank scent that originated from her sweat, blood and tears. The toilet inside her cell was half full of urine and faeces. The rancid smell of salt, metal, shit and piss infected the windowless farmhouse basement. While admittedly putrid, he breathed in the air, savouring the scent as well as the sight of her battered, broken body. Soon, once the ritual was complete, his only memories of her physical body would be preserved in this room, crystallising the time they shared together in this space. Until he took the time to clean the room and prepare it for whoever fate destines will occupy this space after Elise, he could come back here whenever he wanted to engross himself in her musk. Unfortunately, he would not exhibit Elise to the world once her transformation was complete. Joshua Dempsey would be credited with his handiwork. Queensland Police would see to it now that the public had learned of the Double Spiral. The people must have their villain. They cry out for it. A necessary sacrifice. The acclaim means nothing as long as the work can continue. Making Angels is his destiny. His only purpose. And this task only he can do, and it shall never be complete. Better to have the chance to continue with his work anonymously than be locked up. Notoriety is nothing if he cannot fulfil his destiny. Elise cowered on the far side of her cell. Ever since he showed her the pictures he kept of his Angels while they were still human, she refused to speak, withdrawing to her cot where she cradled herself with her arms, rocking and weeping. So pathetic. He pitied her. 'Tonight belongs to you, Elise,' he said, fondling the key to the cage that he had built with his own two hands. 'The altar is ready. Upon it, you shall be liberated of your body, and after, you shall know peace for all eternity, and we will walk together into oblivion.'

Elise had no tears left to cry, and it felt like there were no more cards left to play. She had tried everything in her repertoire to find a way of getting through to the Man in the Mask. She begged for mercy. She tried bargaining, promising him money and sex, whatever else he desired from her. When those failed, she threatened that the law would find him and he would suffer inside a tiny cell, as she did. She warned of the revenge her loved ones would take against him when they learned what he had done. It didn't matter. Nothing swayed him. He is utterly set on his course. Completely deranged. There is no reasoning with him, no deal that could be struck or threat that concerned him. He is an interplanetary object gliding through space along a single trajectory towards his goal, and nothing but some unforeseen outside force could contest his inertia. After he finished speaking, the Man in the Mask departed, leaving her once more alone in the dark. Perhaps, for the final time. The sound of his footsteps upon the stairs grew distant, a haunting omen of what was to come.

When he reached the top of the stairs, he made his way through the archways that separated the rooms of the old family farmhouse until he came to the living room. The spacious room had been specially prepared for the occasion. The floors were covered in plastic sheeting. All the furniture had been removed, and situated in the centre of the room was the wooden altar he had built himself. He had dedicated a lot of time to get the details just right, both aesthetically and in terms of utility. He had outfitted the top with plumbing so that when he pierced her with his ceremonial knife, her lifeblood would collect into a drain, pass through cylinders he had implanted inside the altar, then empty into a bucket he had placed below a drainage pipe at the base of the altar. This would make it far easier to inscribe the Double Spiral into her flesh without so much blood seeping from the skin when he cut it. Each corner of the altar was fitted with straps to restrain wrists and ankles. A thick leather strap had been secured across the middle to ensure her capability for any movement was minimal. Finally, it was finished with a coat of black paint. He touched the smooth surface of the altar's uppermost face, admiring his work. Upon this spot, Elise would undergo a transformation that discarded the impurities of her body in favour of the perfection of her ethereal self, where she would exist beyond the taint of sin and suffering.

He glimpsed the room. The light of the candles set around

the borders of the room cast a gloomy, yellow illumination and caused shadows to dance upon every surface. The double spirals he painted on the walls and ceiling and floor appeared to swirl to his eye, their never-ending circle-within-circles beating with the sound of eternity's drums. Everything was as it should be. The room is ready. Now, all that remains for him to do is ready himself. He sits by the altar briefly as he seeks to embrace the moment. They gather around him, his Angels, and he looks upon their luminescent faces – Holly, Maria, Joanne, Hannah, Rachael – so perfectly preserved, so gloriously radiant. 'You must stay and witness her ascent,' he said to the ghosts he had made. He gazed thoughtfully upon his Angels and accepted that the hunger which compelled him to extinguish their weak, mortal flames was a compounding urge and one that demanded more of him as time went on. To have selected two people for the transformation who were so close to the identity known as Dale Bellringer was untenable. Yet, nevertheless, as dangerous as it was to select two women in such close proximity to his persona for transformation, it was also a thrill the like of which is second to none. Nobody suspected Dale Bellringer, the mousy, well-behaved science teacher, to possess such power. Just as those pathetic Toowoomba cops were too stupid to realise that Daniel Cassidy had also exercised such power over life and death. A name, an identity; these are such temporary, fleeting things. Easily discarded, simple to replace. The essence of his power lies not in his name or his face but in his work. That is the measure of his legacy. The very essence of his being. He is as like God as any man ever was, for only he possesses the ability to transcend death and create life thereafter.

It was a small price to pay to be denied credibility in exchange for making Josh Dempsey the face of his own infamous deeds.

He makes his way upstairs and removes his clothing. He sets aside the dark clothes he has worn for the last few days, removes the mask and detaches the small microphone voice filter employed to disguise his sound. He kicks off the black heavy combat boots from his feet. He dons a white linen shirt and tortilla brown business pants especially pressed and ironed for the occasion. He puts on his socks and brown leather shoes. When he finishes tying the laces, he takes a moment to admire himself in the mirror, buttoning his shirt and straightening his collar. His Angels stand behind him like shimmering water-top reflections in the glass. 'Time for Elise to meet the *real* me.' His Angels smile approvingly.

He makes his way downstairs to the level below and then traverses the steps to the basement. He switches on the light as he enters. Reacting suddenly, Elise realises that her captor is no longer disguised and vainly attempts to shield her eyes with her forearm. 'It's okay!' she cries out. 'I didn't see your face. I swear, I still don't know who you are. Please, *please,* just let me go.' But she knows her words are meaningless. Before she covered her eyes, she noticed he was dressed differently. It's like it were Sunday morning, and he was dressed for church. He hasn't changed clothes in all the time she has been here, now he changes into a fresh, clean outfit. That can't be a coincidence. There must be a reason, and Elise was petrified it meant he was ready to begin rendering her so-called *transformation.*

'It's time, Elise.' He unlocked the door of her cage. She continued to shield her eyes and backed away from the door as she heard the hinge creak as it opened. But it was no use. What was the point? She recognised his voice, and that recognition struck a heavy blow. She was even more afraid now of looking upon him than she ever was before. She could no longer pretend that she did not know her captor. She relaxed her arm and looked upon Dale Bellringer. She remembered the man she had gone on a date with only a few nights earlier. He had been funny, charming her with casual, flirty banter, even managing to seduce her to the point she was prepared to go home with him. But no semblance of that man remained. In front of her stood a monster, poised with all the devilish charm of a viper, his menacing eyes set upon her like a hungry wolf. One look in his crazed eyes was all it took to know there was nothing she could say or do to appease the man that had locked her in a cage, starved her, beaten and raped her and let her stew in her own filth like a lonely, helpless animal caught in a trap.

But what else could she do?

'Please, Dale, I know it didn't work out between us the other night... I was being over-sensitive about Rachael, but please, we're friends...' She began to sob and hiccup. 'We've known each other for years. We sat together and ate lunch every weekday in the staff room. You don't have to do this!'

'That's the thing, Elise. Do you still not understand? I'm not doing this because I *have* to. I'm doing this because I *want* to. It is my purpose. It is why I am here on this Earth. Dale Bellringer isn't even my real name. That man you ate lunch with is just an empty shell. It's no use appealing to Dale Bellringer. He is nothing, nobody.' At first, he spoke tenderly, as if he were explaining a complex matter to a child in the simplest terms. But as Elise continued to try and barter for her freedom, he became agitated and that familiar sting presented in his voice, a sharpness that warned of the danger he was capable of if he wanted to unleash it. 'Stop it! Stop your begging and your whining!' He smacked himself on the side of the head with a sudden outburst of primal violence. 'Can't you get your dumb head around it? This is an honour! A great privilege. There is no greater gift than being liberated from this petty, pathetically fragile body in exchange for immortal life. You should be grateful!' He took her by the arm with great strength, but, as little use as she knows it to be, Elise isn't going to go down without a fight. She struggled against him, clawing at his hand with her fingernails, raising the skin and leaving bloody marks upon the back of his hand. He cried out with disdain. His hard, round fist struck her clean in the left side of her face, disorienting her senses, sending her reeling. She stumbled and lost balance, falling to the floor. Her hands desperately sought out some surface to cling to but came up short. He retook her by the arm and began dragging her. Whatever awareness remained, she understood that to go with him meant certain death, so she did everything she could to prevent him from moving her. She kicked, flailed her arms about, striking at him where she could, writhed, and screamed. As dazed as she is, she recognises the pressure on her arm. She tries to bite him; she beats at his arm, anything to wriggle free of his iron grip. 'That's it!' His thunderous shout bellows so loud it makes her ears buzz. A second blow collides with her head. Unlike the first, the force of it rattles her teeth. White specks impose themselves onto every surface as darkness invades her peripheral vision until it envelopes her entirely, and she fades beyond the realm of awareness.

    She blinks. There is a dull ache in her head. It feels as though her brain is swollen so that the whole pink, mushy organ is pressed against the interior of her skull, pressurised and desperate to erupt from beneath the bone. She can feel the beating of her heart, fast and heavy like a rock-and-roll drumbeat. Her body feels heavy. She is vaguely aware of her limbs being orientated against her will. A leg is being directed, then an arm. There is pressure on her wrists and ankles. The sensation of pressure is replaced by pain as if a snake has coiled itself tightly around her joints. She blinks again, salty tears leaking from her eyes. She realises she cannot move her arms or legs. Fearfully, she struggles against the bindings. A figure stands over her. A silhouette without detail, a face without features. Candles burn around her, their amber light like distant stars offering no warmth of comfort amongst a terribly dark and empty universe. Dark shapes creep along the walls around her by their light, moving in disturbing patterns. The same double spiral symbol Dale has tattooed on his chest has been painted in red paint on every surface in her visible range. The walls and ceiling are covered. In the ambience of the candlelight, they appear to shift and swirl, going round and round. Something tight is drawn over her middle. The final strap is made taut, the pressure making it difficult for her to draw breath.He presents the long, silver blade of a razor-edged knife to her fearful eyes. She shakes her head weakly. She tries to speak, but she cannot form any words. She blinks more tears from her eyes. He touches her forehead with a sympathetic hand. 'Poor, wretched creature you are. Don't worry, Elise, it will be over soon. No more pain, no more struggle.' His wild, hellishly crazed eyes are illuminated by a flash of bright light from a nearby window. She witnesses his alarm. He sets the knife down somewhere beside her. She tries to reach it, but her hands are secured firmly in place. She can only twist her wrists, and that serves no useful purpose. She turns her head as far as her neck allows and follows him as he hurries over to the window. 'Who the hell could this be?' he snarled. From the window, he can survey all the empty land beyond the front of his rural property for kilometres. In the distance, coming up along the dirt passage that connects his property to the main road, is a car. Two lone headlights penetrate the black night, slowly rolling towards the house. Already, the car has reached the cattle grid. He watches as a figure emerges from the backseat of the car and opens the gate, permitting passage for the vehicle onto the land he owns. His unexpected visitors would arrive at the front of his house in another half a minute. He retrieves some masking tape from a draw in the adjoining kitchen and gags her mouth. He leans in close and presses the blade of his knife firm against her cheek to drive home his threat. 'If you make even a peep, Elise, I swear, I will take my time and cut pieces off you while you're still alive to feel it. I'll make it last fucking *hours*. Do you hear me?' Startled by the terrifying promise and suffering the consequential shock it evokes, Elise nods her head to signify her understanding. He goes around the room, closes the blinds, then disappears somewhere behind her, beyond her field of view. It's too late to extinguish the candles. Their light will have already betrayed the truth to the unexpected arrivals that somebody is home. While he is away, Elise begins desperately tonguing the tape over her mouth, applying her saliva to the stickiness and wriggling her head, hoping she can loosen it just enough so that whoever is out there can hear her when she calls for help.

    He watches the car pull up to the front of his house. An unmarked, dark coloured sedan. Three people emerge brandishing flashlights. From behind the front door, he listens to the sound of their footsteps crunching in the dirt beyond his verandah. He is not afraid. He has never been scared a day in his life. He breathes slow and switches on the floodlights, bathing the front of his property In bright white light. He opens the front door, greeting the strangers with his well-practised, friendliest voice. 'Howdy!' He smiles effortlessly and waves a hand at the three people who are momentarily disorientated by the bright floodlights. One of the beams of light from a torch centres upon his face. He shields his eyes. 'Hey, you mind?' He sounds convincingly harmless. Whomever of the three had directed their torch upon his face warily removes it so Dale can see again. 'Can I help you, folks?' He takes in the visitors. A man and two women. The man is roughly his own height with a scruffy black beard and a dour expression on his ugly face. He's large-bodied, neither lean nor fat, making him appear squarish. One of the women is older than the other by twenty years and shorter by a head. The crone has a hook-shaped nose with leathery brown sun-damaged skin and hair that has almost all greyed out. The crowfeet wrinkles beside her eyes are deeply set when she squints, which is often. The younger woman is moderately attractive. She is taller and more full-bodied than the older women, possessing broad shoulders and thick thighs for someone her height. Her bleach blonde hair is tied back, and she leers at him with watchful, blue eyes. The youngest wears a Queensland Police uniform. The man and older woman are wearing grey suits. All three have Glock handguns holstered on their hips.

Cops. *How did they find me?*

'Are you Dale Bellringer?' asked the male police officer.

'Who's asking?' returns Dale.

The man produces a Detective's badge and police identification. 'My name is Detective Coltsworth.' The Detective gestures to the crone at his side, who displays her police ID and badge. 'This here is Detective Peters.' He points again to the blonde. 'And Senior Sergeant Price. We would like to have a word with the owner of the property.'

This Detective is clever, thinks Dale. Technically, the property is owned by a Trust, and the sole Director of the company that serves as trustee is Daniel Cassidy. Dale Bellringer has no connection to the house, and this Detective Coltsworth must know it. 'Why might that be?' Dale would answer every question with a question. Do as they do; gather as much information as possible and give nothing in return. The Detective approached cautiously, just a few steps, but enough to hold Dale's attention. Detective Peters shone her torch to the side of the property, tracing a line around the perimeter. Dale watched her, mindfully hiding his irritation.

The Detective explained. 'Queensland Police received a Missing Person notification. A teacher at Claremont College named Elise Arnott was reported missing a week ago. We were informed that the last person to see her was another teacher at her school, Mr Bellringer.'

This pathetic ruse wasn't fooling Dale. This missing person's report was a lie. If it were true, they would be knocking on Dale Bellringer's apartment door in Brisbane, not Daniel Cassidy's farmhouse in Buaraba. 'I'm afraid I can't help you with any of that, Officers. Now, if you don't mind, I'd like to invite you to leave. You're on private property, and this is trespassing.'

'That seems like a bit of a hostile reaction to a couple of innocent questions about a missing woman,' said Detective Peters. 'Do you realise it is an offence to fail to give Police your name when we ask for it?'

He levelled his gaze upon her and didn't bother to veil his contempt when he addressed her. 'With all due respect, Detective, I would put it to you that I am only obligated to give you my name so long as you have a right to ask for it. As I have done nothing wrong, I don't see how you could reason you have such a right. I have already told you that I know nothing about this missing woman or her disappearance and that I cannot help you in this matter. Therefore, it is inappropriate for you to remain here. I will ask you to leave now, please.' He shooed them with a wave. 'Be sure to close the gate again on your way out. It would be a shame if any of my cattle got loose and I had to go round them up because of your carelessness.'

'Sir,' said the one named Price, 'we came a long way, and we just want to ask a couple of questions. May we come inside for just a moment?'

Dale tilted his head and looked upon the youngest officer. The little mouse speaks. He answered resolutely. 'No.'

'It would just take a moment, sir—'

'Do you have a warrant?'

'Well, no—'

'I'm a little rusty on my legal knowledge, but I believe that, unless you have reasonable justification or a warrant commissioned by court, I don't have to admit you into my home. Isn't that right?'

'You're not wrong,' said Detective Coltsworth through gritted teeth. *This bastard knows his stuff*, he thinks resentfully.

'Well, in that case, good night, Officers.' Having defeated the would-be heroes in this exchange, he drove his supremacy home with a vindictive, contemptuous farewell: 'Take care on your way out. This place can be perilous in the dark.' Dale turned on his heel and made his way back inside, closing and locking the door behind him. He shut off the outside lights leaving the three officers limp and powerless in the night. Dale remained on the other side of the door for a minute, listening. He could hear them deliberating amongst themselves. He suspected they were talking about what to do next. It was with the most tantalising satisfaction that he had disarmed them of the only weapon they had at their disposal; the laws that sanctioned their policing powers. He heard the dirt and pebbles crunching underfoot as they returned to their car. He made his way to a window, peeping through a crack in the corner of the curtain and watched them. It was unfortunate that the farmhouse had been compromised. It had served stupendously as sacred grounds, a refuge from the world and a place of power for his rituals. Now that they had learned of Daniel Cassidy's familial home, he supposed he would have to burn it all down. He put the idea out of his mind. Tonight was about Elise's transformation. He waited so long for it and had been so patient. He deserved to embrace the satisfaction of finally indulging himself. Tomorrow, he would worry about moving on. The police could do nothing more tonight, not without breaking the law themselves. He turned to Elise.

He was a step too far away from the altar to reach her In time. While he had been dealing with the nuisance of the police, Elise had worked to liberate herself of the strip of tape over her mouth. She had managed to produce just enough of a gap that it allowed her to call out. He got to her a second too late. In the space of that second, the noise she produced damned him. She voiced a desperate scream.

'*He—!*'

He managed to cover her mouth in time to muffle the second half of the syllable, but the first half of her call for help was enough. The cops had their reasonable justification now. He could hear them outside, coming back to his door. It was over. They called to him through the door. 'Open up, Dale!'

He looked down at Elise with fury. He would enact his revenge upon her. He may not facilitate her transformation now, but she would never leave this house alive. The cops were banging on the door, ordering him to let them in. He ignored them. He put his hands on Elise's throat and throttled her. He watched Elise's wide, petrified eyes, staring up at him knowingly. He squeezed his hands around her throat until her cheeks puffed and turned blue, and her eyes bulged. 'Shhh,' he crooned. 'It's nearly over.' A few more seconds, and her feeble body will die. With agents of the law pounding at his door, there was no opportunity to perform the sacred rite of applying the Double Spiral to her flesh to ensure that her spirit would be bound to his own, so her death would have to suffice.

'We're coming in!' The Detective named Graham is at his door. Dale heard the sound of one of the officers discharging their firearm. The deadlock on his door was obliterated. Graham came rushing through the door, having forcefully charged at it shoulder first, breaking it from its hinges.

A bright cone of light penetrates the candlelit room. 'Let her go!' Dale squints at the light being shone in his face. He tilts his head away from the light and looks down at Elise. Beneath him, her eyelids are fluttering, and her eyes are rolling. Her limbs are stiffening. She's almost gone. A searing pain emerges in his shoulder while he registers the sound of a gunshot. He's unable to maintain his grip. The force of the bullet penetrating his shoulder causes him to fumble, staggering back two steps before he catches his balance. He lumbers forward towards his altar. The officers are barking orders, but the sound of their voices are mute to his ears. He sees the knife he left beside Elise and gathers it up.

'Put it down! Put it down!' They're mouthing commands with their guns trained on him. The blonde-haired lady-cop Detective Coltsworth identified as Sergeant Price is edging closer towards him.

She's saying: 'Turn around and put your hands on your head!' She's the youngest of the three. The least experienced. She is scared. He has elicited fear in others so often in his life, he recognises it so plainly. His shoulder burns, and the tension in the room is palpable. But he is calm. His mind is calculative, working tactfully. Every move they make is being astutely assessed.

Detective Coltsworth is issuing an order to Detective Peters: 'Check the girl's vitals! Price and I will secure him.'

Now is his moment. Detective Coltsworth takes his eyes off Dale for one second as he looks to Detective Peters when she steps towards Elise on the altar. Unaware of her mistake, the inexperienced Sergeant Price has stepped too close to him. Foolishly, she is reaching with one hand for handcuffs when she should have maintained both hands upon her firearm. She is within striking distance. The Detective's attention is elsewhere for only a moment, but it is enough. Dale acts without hesitation. 'No!' Detective Coltsworth's cry is full of hatred and mourning. It is the sound of a man who knows he has come undone. To Dale, there is no sound more satisfying. Dale withdraws the blade of his knife from Senior Sergeant Price's neck. The knife struck her carotid artery. Its removal sends blood ejecting from the wound like a geyser. With every beat of her racing heart, more of her life essence emits from the site of the injury. Dale shoves Sergeant Price in the back. Clutching at her neck, she lurches forward, staggering to the floor. Detective Peters is seeking to administer CPR to Elise. Detective Coltsworth is trying to attend Sergeant Price while she bleeds from the puncture wound in her neck. Dale turns to run. The window is only a couple of meters away. If he can make it there, he can jump through. He knows this land better than anyone. He can escape custody; he knows it. There is an earsplitting *bang,* and Dale feels the sting of a second bullet striking him in the back. It takes the breath out of him. All he hears is the deafening sound of the two Detectives discharging their guns until no more bullets remain in their magazines. He collapses to the floor just half a meter from the window, his body riddled with bullet holes. As he bleeds, his five Angels gather in a circle around him for a final vigil. He labours for every breath. They look down upon the man who anchored them to purgatory with rueful eyes. Theirs is a silent condemnation. As his consciousness falters, one by one, his Angels dissipate. He wants to ask them to bring him wherever they are going next. But he cannot. His lungs are punctured with holes just as theirs once were. His final, lonely plea is drowned by the blood that rises up his throat, spluttering from his mouth as the last of his five Angels departs this plane of existence, finally freed of the evil spell that shackled them to the man that deprived them of their lives.

    The Double Spiral Strangler dies alone and is committed to the beyond unaccompanied by any Angel.

Chapter Nineteen

Wednesday, 22nd December 2021 10:31 a.m

Was justice real, or had Colt only imagined it?

Colt sat at his desk at the North Brisbane Station, reading an email sent to staff members from the Queensland Police Commissioner:

To the dedicated staff of Queensland Police,

Last Friday, I was deeply saddened to learn that Senior Sergeant Price of Brisbane was tragically killed by Dale Bellringer, born Daniel Cassidy. Senior Sergeant Addilyn Price was a dedicated officer who protected her community with honour. The families of Daniel Cassidy's victims have expressed their gratitude for bringing justice to their loved ones, which is the lasting legacy that Addilyn leaves behind. In addition to the honours bequeathed upon her by Brisbane's State Premier and Lord Mayor, I would like to officially announce that Senior Sergeant Price shall be awarded the Queensland Police Valour Award for exceptional bravery in hazardous circumstances. Addilyn is survived by her parents, Susan and Richard Price, and her dog Jasper. My deepest sympathies go out to her family for their tragic loss. Addilyn was a valued member of our team and will be deeply missed.

His deepest sympathies… Colt rereads the words silently in his mind with enough cynicism to choke a satirist. A cop gives her life on the job, she's given a medal, and a salute and everybody is just expected to move on.

If that wasn't enough of a grievance, there was Superintendent La Pila to worry about too. When La Pila learned of what transpired at the farmhouse, she used her silver tongue to spin the whole incident in her favour. She convinced her superiors that she had been the one to commission the investigation undertaken by Colt, Peters and Price. The way she told it, she excused an off-the-books investigation because the department was being investigated for a potential mole. Given that the Ethical Standards Command was convinced the confidential information about the Double Spiral was suspected of being leaked to the media by someone in the North Brisbane Office, she could not risk allowing all her staff to be on the same page. By only offering information to various investigators, she could trace the source of the leak while also continuing to investigate the Double Spiral Strangler. As La Pila explained to her bosses, she chose to trust the real investigation with her most reliable Detective and his protégé while the rest of the team were made to maintain focus on the Dempsey case. While she had set out to achieve two goals; to identify the leak and catch the Strangler, sadly, her methods only satisfied one of these objectives. It was difficult for anyone, especially QPS leadership, to deny that identifying and apprehending the Strangler was the far more preferable outcome of La Pila's design. Unfortunately, Colt could not contest this version of events because all the investigative work that he and Price undertook together was off the books. There were no records in Queensland Police systems that demonstrated that Colt had any official link to the undercover investigation. Colt's work email was cleansed, as was Caroline Peters' in the days after the shootout. Likely, La Pila arranged for IT to delete everything so that even the record of emails between the two Detectives could not be referenced to disprove her assertions that she had masterminded the whole saga. Colt had to give it to her. She had outdone herself this time. Believing La Pila's story, the Queensland Police Commissioner credited La Pila's leadership as the reason QPS was able to take down the Double Spiral Strangler and bring an end to the reign of one of Queensland's most important prolific serial killers in modern history. The Commissioner promoted La Pila to the position of Chief Superintendent and granted her governance over all of the State's Special Operations. Finally, La Pila managed to climb one step higher on her ladder, reaching the lofty heights of State Command, making her one of the most powerful Officers in the State and, more broadly, the country. Never before had she wielded so much power over Graham, so it was no surprise that she had such a smug look on her face when she called him into her office for a private chat. She did not have to say the words. He could see it in her beady eyes and her satisfied grin. *I win...*

As Colt enters, he takes note of the new epaulettes upon her shoulder. There is also a recent photograph decorating her wall, hung in a prominent position behind her oversized desk. In the photo, she is shaking hands with the Commissioner with one hand while accepting a certificate correlating to her promotion with the other. Even from the picture, she appears to be lording it over him, as if she had that in mind when the photographer snapped the shot. 'Congratulations on the promotion,' says Colt dryly. 'I suppose I should call you Chief, now?'

La Pila answers only with a derivative snort, then gestures to the empty visitor's chair. 'Have a seat, Graham. I wanted to begin by saying that I'm sorry.' She *almost* sounded sympathetic, but Graham knew that whatever she said next would make any genuine sympathy she felt for Price's death moot. 'Price was a good cop. She deserved better. I warned her that she should have kept her distance from you, and look where it got her.' She leaned back in her chair. 'The thing is, Graham, you're a great Detective. One of the finest I have ever known. But you're fucking poison.' Her words stung, but he would let her have that one. Truth is, she is right. Since Price's funeral, Colt had been reflecting on his part in these events. On the day he received the Toowoomba case files, Price chose to partner with him in an unofficial and unsanctioned investigation. If Price had chosen differently, would she still be alive? What might have been if she had elected to report him to La Pila instead of joining with him? La Pila brushed her hair away from her face and crossed her legs. Was it disappointment or condescension he saw in her face? 'While you chose to disobey the instructions I gave you regarding the Dempsey case, technically, this homespun investigation of yours didn't breach any QPS protocol. It was clever of you to have Caroline Peters do all the police grunt work. I looked it all over. Everything that Detective Peters did during this crusade of yours fell outside the scope of my authority before my promotion, so I have no discretion to take any disciplinary action against her for the role she played in aiding your private investigation. Anyway, now, Peters is the hero cop who saved the life of the Strangler's last attempted victim. Elise Arnott wouldn't have survived if Peters wasn't there with you, and she's just a rinky-dink country-cop anyway, so there's no benefit to me in cutting her down.' She held out her hands, gesturing to the room but symbolically to the enormity of all the success that had come as a result of her persuasive storytelling. 'I suppose I can't think of her too harshly. She has as much to do with putting me on top as you did.'

'Yeah,' Colt snorted softly. 'I'm glad Elise Arnott is alive too.'

'Sarcasm aside, Graham, I wanted you to know that Ethical Standards Command never identified the source of the leak.' She eyed him suspiciously. 'But I think we both know that is of no consequence now. You covered your tracks expertly in that matter. I had hoped ESC Officers could pin it on you so firing you would be easily justified. Alas, it wasn't meant to be. And, although you will never hear me admit to this again, Graham, I have to concede that if it weren't for you, Price, and Peters, the Double Spiral Strangler might have gotten away with it. Elise Arnott would almost undoubtedly be dead, and worse still, the bastard might have been able to evade capture and continue killing were it not for the work you three did together.'

Colt wouldn't have any medals pinned to his chest or be credited any honours, but none of that mattered to him. Hearing La Pila acknowledge what he and Price and Peters achieved together was more satisfying than any accolade. 'Great. Is that all you wanted to say, *Chief?*'

'Not even close!' She laughed. 'As you know, I am now overseeing all the Special Ops divisions in Queensland. I couldn't terminate your employment for being the leak. There is no longer any evidence I have at my disposal to demonstrate your insubordination through this whole ordeal. However, none of that matters much now that I have been promoted. After careful consideration, I have decided that there is no place for an officer who conducts himself with such reckless regard for the safety of his fellow officers. The others here don't trust you, Graham. There's no room for mavericks on my team. Therefore, I am placing you on paid administrative leave for four weeks. That should be plenty of time for you to come to a decision.'

'A decision about what?'

'I am leaving you with one of two choices. When you return to work, you can either tender your resignation, or I'll arrange to transfer you far away from here.' She pretended to think on the matter for a moment before adding: 'North Queensland might be a better climate for you. City homicide has proven to be too burdensome for you. I think issuing speeding fines, breaking up bar brawls and settling domestic disputes somewhere rural and remote up north might be more your speed.'

'I think you're mistaken, Chief,' said Colt unemotively. 'I'm no fan of a humid climate. It's snakes who like hot temperatures.'

'Well,' she said contemptuously, 'this snake is giving you the boot, Colt. Consider yourself lucky I'm letting you keep your job at all. You antagonise me any further, and I'll be sure to introduce you to my bite.' She stared him down like he were a bug she wanted to squash beneath her heel. 'Your leave is effective immediately. You are dismissed.'

In the photo behind La Pila's desk, she smiles that sickening picture-perfect grin. A politician's smile. Unauthentic, insincere, but *just* convincing enough to appear warranted. 'You never bothered to ask, Lisa,' said Colt, looking back at his boss, 'so I'm going to let you in on something: it was Price who figured out the Strangler's kills all took place during school holidays. It was because of *her* that we found him.' He looked again at the photo. 'It's a nice photo, Lisa. When you look at it, I hope you're reminded that *Price* put you where you are. How sad it must be for you to know that nothing you have done of your own merits has afforded you the success you've attained.' Colt got up out of the chair and turned to leave.

'And I hope that *you* remember that if it wasn't for your actions, Price would still be alive today. Frankly, Graham, I don't know how you can live with yourself.'

'Funny,' he said as he got to the door. 'I was just thinking the same thing about you.'

Colt went to visit Joshua Dempsey at the Essence Suites Hotel. Anne Dempsey was leaving Josh's room as he came into the hall. Crossing paths in such a narrow corridor meant a collision was unavoidable. 'Detective Colt,' said Anne, 'er, I have just spoken with my husband, and he told me what you did. I heard about Sergeant Price in the news too. Josh tells me you two were partners. I'm very sorry for your loss.'

Colt forced a smile. 'Thank you.'

'This is kind of awkward…' murmured Anne. 'But, er, what you did for Josh, well, words just don't feel like they cut it. You saved my family from suffering incredible humiliation. I hate to think what kind of life my kids would have had to endure as the children of a convicted murderer…' She zoned out for a moment as the weight of that future, now foiled, sank in. 'Anyway, Detective. Thank you. My marriage is over, but Josh is still the father of my children, and I'll forever be grateful for what you have done for us.'

Colt wasn't sure what to say. It didn't feel right to be thanked for something that resulted in Price's life being snuffed out while she was still in her prime years. He said the only thing that came to mind: 'I was just doing my job.'

'No,' she touched him on the arm to show her sympathy and appreciation, 'you did a lot more than that.'

Colt knocked on the door of Josh's room. 'Anney! You came back—'

'Sorry to disappoint you,' said Colt as Josh appeared totally dejected to learn that Colt, not Anne, visited him next. Colt was invited inside by an unkempt Josh Dempsey, nursing a scotch and soda at 11.31 a.m. His eyes were bloodshot and watery, but Colt knew it wasn't the booze. Josh had been crying. Josh raised up his glass. 'You want one?'

'Sure,' said Colt. After all, technically, he was on holiday now anyway.

'She wants a divorce,' said Josh as he poured Colt a nip.

'Can't say I blame her.' Colt accepted the glass and took a sip, and the pair seated themselves at the table.

'I begged and pleaded for her to take me back, to give me a second chance, but she wasn't having a bar of it...' There was a silence between them for a moment while each man stared at the golden scotch in his glass. Breaking the silence, Josh said: 'Anyway, I, uh... I guess I should be thanking you.' Colt shrugged. 'No, I mean it. Really. If it wasn't for you, I would have been royally fucked. So, thanks. For everything. And for what it's worth, I'm sorry about what happened to Sergeant Price. She seemed like a good woman.'

'She was.' A tear came to his eye. Upon reflection, Colt had never wavered from his initial impression of Josh. A self-serving egotist with little regard for how his actions affected others. But, when push-came-to-shove, he had to ask himself: was he really any different?

'So, now that it's all over,' said Josh, 'can you tell me how he did it? How did he set me up?'

His career was over anyway, so Colt concluded there was no harm in revealing the information. 'Daniel Cassidy was a scientist. When forensics did a sweep of his farmhouse, they found bottles of homemade chloroform. It's how he could subdue his victims so easily and transport them from wherever he kidnapped them to his farmhouse. Among his personal effects, they found a lockpicking kit and highly detailed written accounts of you and your family's movements over the last few months. He knew your routine. Then, after he killed Rachael, he used her computer to send your wife an email from her Queensland Education email address. In it, he pasted a link to a passage from the bible. Our IT experts explained that once your wife clicked on that hyperlink, it would have temporarily disabled your home wifi because it infected your home network with spyware that enabled him to remotely observe all activity on devices connected to your router. None of you would have treated a dropped wifi signal as suspicious, but every device you reconnected to your home modem after that morning gave him direct access. That means he saw every message you ever sent Rachael. Every email, every text, every call. The sad fact is, he must have known how easily he could pin the murder on you. All he had to do was pick the lock on your front door and plant the evidence, and QPS took the reins from there.'

Josh listened intently, and with every detail Colt revealed, his jaw became a little slacker. 'I feel like a fucking puppet on strings…'

'After what happened at the farmhouse… I did a little digging. There are no death certificates for Daniel Cassidy's parents in the Births, Deaths and Marriages registry. I suspect they'll find the remains of the Cassidy family out there when they begin excavating the farmhouse. The point is: Daniel, Dale, the Double Spiral Strangler, his whole life was dedicated to manipulation and deception. He evaded capture and blended in masquerading as an ordinary bloke for a long time. He taught thirteen-year-old kids without ever raising any red flags. He killed five women, and probably more we don't know about. Nothing you could have done could have changed any of that.'

Josh breathed a remorseful sigh, heavy with regret. 'I've

been thinking a lot about that night, you know. When he broke into her apartment? It was just after she asked me to pretend to rob her, so when he showed up in the middle of the night, she must have thought it was me coming back to roleplay... God damn it, what if she had realised it wasn't me? What if she caught on earlier? Do you think she could have survived?'

Colt finished the scotch in his glass. 'When something like this happens, there's no use in playing the *what-if* game, mate. It'll only make you crazy. The fact is, when people go through this kind of thing, it's easy to want to look for the reason that explains all the mayhem. Why did he do it? Was he fucked up as a kid and grew into a monster, or was he born that way? What made him like this? In my experience as a cop with over twenty years under my belt, let me tell you: there's no grand mystery to be solved, no hidden meaning or secret to be uncovered... Daniel Cassidy was a killer because he wanted to and because he could. It's as simple as that. Nothing could be more rudimentary. It's the equivalent of you and I drinking this scotch at eleven-thirty in the morning. We want to. We can, so we do.'

'I 'spose you're right.' Josh scrunched his face as if Colt's words hurt to hear and finished off his scotch. Josh looked out the window with a contemplative expression. It reminded Colt of the story Addilyn had shared with him about when she used to look out the window during her time in the mental health ward at the hospital when she was a teenager. She talked about how she felt like an outsider, watching life happen outside her window as if she wasn't a part of the world but merely a spectator to it. Ironic that her actions in this case connected her so intimately to such a broad range of other people all these years later. The family of the Strangler's victims, the members of the Toowoomba Task Force, the Australian public, and most of all, himself.

Josh lamented. 'I fucked everything up. My marriage is over. I got sacked from work. I lost it all. My wife, my home, my career…' Josh ruminated for a second. 'Rachael too… All the things that made life worth living… And that bastard weaponised the trust Rachael had for me to kill her. It's my fault Rach is dead.'

'That isn't true.' Colt's voice was stern. Josh needed to know that for all his faults, he wasn't to blame for that. 'There's only one person to blame for Rachael's death, and it certainly isn't you. I've spent the last few days combing over every item in that farmhouse of his, and he had records that proved he was planning to kill Rachael well before she ran into you at that bar. Once he got a hold of your diary and read about your feelings for Rachael, you were just a convenient scapegoat.' Colt hadn't spoken the words aloud until now, but it was time he admitted the truth to himself. Right now, the only person who could really empathise with his guilt was seated right in front of him. Josh and Colt's actions had dire consequences for those closest to them. They shared in that unique burden. 'If you want to talk about blame, it's my fault Price is dead. *I* got her killed. I was supposed to mentor her. It was my job to look out for her, and I failed to protect her because I was too consumed with catching the bad guy when I should have been focused on doing what was best for her. Instead, I was too caught up in chasing my own ambition.'

Josh sunk low into his chair, completely deflated. 'I guess we both screwed up. It's just so unfair that the ones who ended up paying for our mistakes are the people we love. How do we atone for something like that? I mean… What are we supposed to do now?'

Colt considered the question for a moment. 'You ever heard that old adage, "the best revenge is to live well?" I don't think it's true. Revenge shouldn't be a motive for living well, but *justice* should. Justice is as much about healing for the victims of crime as it is punishing the wicked. You owe it to Rachael, and I owe it to Addilyn, to live the best life we can, and in that way, we honour what was stolen from them but remains to us. Live well for them. That's how we make amends. It's how we give them justice. It's how we do what's right.' He turned the empty tumbler glass over in his hands as he thought about the moment he watched Addilyn Price die in his arms. That image would haunt him the rest of his days. Her wide, unblinking eyes. The fear he saw in them. The pain. He hoped he would never forget it. He *needed* to remember every detail of that moment so that he never put anybody else's life at risk again. 'Nothing we can do can change the past. We both have to live with our choices.' The emotion swelled within. The guilt, the remorse, the self-contempt. They had become something hard inside his chest that made it hard to breathe. He cleared his throat. 'Well, speaking of making amends, I'll be going now, Josh. I have one more stop to make before I go home today.'

'Oh.' Josh offered his hand across the table. Colt shook it. 'Well, then... Thank you for everything...' He let go of the hand of the police officer who had saved him from a life of false accusations and public condemnation. 'Will I see you again?'

'I don't think so.' Colt stood and made his way to the door. Before he left, he offered one final comment to Josh: 'Take care of yourself. Remember what I said. Live well.'

Josh took one last look at the man responsible for his redemption. 'I will.'

Upon being contacted by Graham Colt, Addilyn's parents, Richard and Susan Price, showed no signs of any reluctance to meet with the Detective at their daughter's inner-city apartment. Before he retired, Richard Price had been a police officer and, knowing the job, still held fellow officers in high regard. That fact had relieved some of the hesitancy to meet with him. Colt had called them to arrange the meeting, explaining that he was the Detective who recruited their daughter into the Special Operations Unit. He only mentioned that he had something important to say to both of them on the phone. They invited him to meet them at Addilyn's apartment as they were beginning to collect her personal effects. Susan Price, in particular, was still so close to her grief that it took some urging from her husband to agree to the meeting. When he knocked on Addilyn's apartment door, he was greeted at the door by Mr Price, who shook his hand and invited him inside. Richard Price was still in great shape for a man aged in his sixties. He had an athletic build with thick legs, like Addilyn. His hair was white, as was his neatly trimmed beard. Colt expected to be greeted by Jasper bouncing at his legs and found it strange the dog wasn't around as he entered. Richard Price noticed Colt's reaction. 'Yeah, the dog hardly leaves Addy's room since she… Well, er, she didn't come home.'

'I see,' said Colt. The sound of Colt's voice was enough to provoke the Beagle's curiosity. His little head appeared at the edge of Addilyn's bedroom door. Upon spying Colt, his little tail wagged with some of its old enthusiasm, and the dog trotted over to the familiar, gruff man he had come to recognise. 'Hey, boy,' said Colt giving Jasper a pat on the head and a scratch on the back.

Addilyn's mother was on the small balcony, watering the plants that had begun to wilt in Addilyn's absence. 'Suzie, dear…' called Richard. 'Detective Coltsworth is here.' Addilyn's mother was likely a similar age to Richard, but her grief appeared to have aged her ten years in a matter of days. She walked with tiny, shuffling steps as if that were the best her legs could manage. Her face was sunken, and her back was arched as if she was burdened with a great weight upon her shoulders. But her eyes were just like Addilyn's, watery blue and expressively warm.

'Mr and Mrs Price,' said Colt as Richard helped his wife inside, and the pair took a seat on their daughter's couch. 'I'm very pleased that you agreed to meet with me. I am proud to say that I came to know your daughter rather well in the last few weeks. She was a fine woman and a talented police officer. As I said to you over the phone, I was the Detective responsible for recruiting Addilyn into homicide after she applied for a job in the Special Operations Division of the Queensland Police Service. I asked you to meet with me because there is something I think you ought to know, and I owe it to Addilyn to tell you the truth about why your daughter died.'

'Why?' asked Susan Price with understandable confusion. 'What do you mean, why? That evil man; he is why.'

'No,' protested Colt. '*I* am why. It's my fault that your daughter was killed. Despite what they might have told you, the truth is that the investigation Addilyn was part of that resulted in her death wasn't officially sanctioned by QPS. It was just me going rogue and dragging Addilyn along with me. I was investigating the man who killed your daughter without express consent from my superiors. When Addilyn learned what I was doing, I didn't try to dissuade her from joining me when she wanted to partner with me on the case.' Susan began to cry. Her husband took her hand into his to comfort her. Colt had to continue. He had to own it. 'Addilyn was young, and as you probably know, she aspired to become a detective in her own right. When she came over to Special Operations, she was eager to make her mark. She trusted me with her career and, more importantly, her safety, and I let her down. Her welfare was my responsibility, as was the choice I made to encourage her to pursue an investigation that did not have the department's support. I was selfish, thoughtless and reckless, which is why your daughter is dead. Dale Bellringer, the man born Daniel Cassidy, might have been the one to strike the blow, but it was me who put her in that farmhouse in the first place.' Richard Price fought to hold back tears. Sensing the pain in the hearts of those around him, Jasper joined in on the mourning with his own high pitched whine. 'Believe me when I tell you that I will carry the guilt and shame of my actions for the rest of my life. She was...' He found himself choking up. C'mon, Colt, he urged himself silently. 'Your daughter, Addilyn Price, was the finest officer I ever had the privilege of working with and one of the most beautiful souls I've ever encountered. She was thoughtful and kind, and funny. I miss her deeply. And I cannot possibly express how sorry I am for what I have done to your family. I hope that someday you might be able to forgive me for failing your daughter.' Colt wiped at his eyes, wet with tears for the first time in as long as he could remember.

Mrs Price looked Colt in the eye. He wasn't sure what was coming his way when she had her husband help her to her feet. She walked over to Colt and stood before him for a moment, looking him in the eye. Colt swallowed. Whatever came next, he would do the right thing and take it. Susan wrapped her arms around Colt and hugged him. 'We will miss our sweet Addy for as many days as we have left on this Earth, Detective Coltsworth. But, however many days are left to Richard and me, it is still fewer than remain to you. So, the real challenge will not be living long enough to earn *our* forgiveness but living long enough so that you might find a means of forgiving *yourself.*'

Colt didn't believe there were enough days within eternity for that to happen, but he was humbled nonetheless. 'Our Addy had a strong will and a keen sense of justice, Mr Coltsworth,' said Richard. 'I doubt anything you could have said or done would have deterred her from doing what she felt was right.'

Colt smiled, remembering the nights he spent cooped up in this apartment with Addilyn and Jasper going over the case. 'I can't say that isn't true, Mr Price. She was...tenacious.'

Addilyn's father wiped away a tear as a throaty chuckle burst out of him. 'Stubborn is what you mean! Just like her old man...' For just a fleeting second, everyone in the room privately reminisced on the woman they knew and loved, and their mutual admiration of Addilyn gave them a moment's reprieve from their grief. As Susan withdrew from Colt, the pair were disturbed by Jasper, who was clambering around their feet with one of Addilyn's socks in his mouth. Susan looked down at the dog at her feet.

'He seems very fond of you,' she said. She lowered herself just enough to give the dog a pat. 'You should take him.'

'Oh no, I couldn't,' Colt objected. 'Addilyn loved this dog; he should be with you.'

'No, no. I insist. We're too old to be chasing around picking up after him.' Tears welled up in her eyes as she looked at the little dog playing with the sock he had recovered from somewhere on the floor of Price's apartment. 'You would be doing us a kindness taking care of him. And if you're determined to blame yourself for what happened to Addy... Well, perhaps you could think of caring for the little fellow as your penance.'

Colt breathed a heartfelt sigh. 'Okay. I'll take him. It's the least I can do for her now.'

'Then it's settled. If you'll excuse me, I'll get his things ready for you.' Susan began to make her way around the apartment, gathering Jasper's toys and treats.

When Mr Price was composed, he looked Colt long in the eye before he spoke again. 'I want to thank you for coming here to speak with us today, Mr Coltsworth. A good man owns his mistakes and does what he can to remedy them. You believe yourself responsible for what happened to my daughter, but it would be an insult to her memory to suggest she didn't have the good sense to decide for herself the right thing to do. I think she worked with you on this case because she believed it was right, and she saw something in you that inspired her to follow you into the unknown. She was brave, like that. Wilful. I doubt you could have talked her out of it even if you tried.'

'So you know, Mr and Mrs Price, I *did* counsel her on the risks. She chose to partner with me on the case, knowing it flew in the face of what the department asked of us.'

'My word, that comes as no surprise to either of us, Mr Coltsworth! Our baby was never one to shy away from going against the grain.' Richard's proud words brought a smile briefly to his wife's lips. 'Thank you for your honesty. We appreciate it.'

'We do,' put in Susan.

Colt jotted down his telephone number on a page in his notepad, tore it off and offered it to Addilyn's father. 'You can reach me at this number if either of you ever needs anything. Anything at all. Or, you want to come to visit Jasper.'

'We'll keep that in mind,' said Mr Price as he accepted and pocketed the note with Colt's number scrawled on the paper. The veteran cop gave Jasper an encouraging final pat. 'On your way then, Jasp.' Then he shook Colt's hand. 'Take care, Detective.'

Colt looked down at the dog at his heel, who looked back up

at him with Addilyn's sock strung sidelong from his mouth. In the eyes of Addilyn Price's pet, Colt beheld an unspoken sadness identical to his own. I know, thought Colt, patting the dog; I miss her too. Mrs Price offered Colt the dog's lead and handed him a bag containing all of Jasper's goodies. Colt attached the lead to the Beagle's collar. His little tail began wagging excitedly at the prospect of going for a walk outside. 'C'mon then, Jasper,' said Colt, 'let's go home.'

Ingram Content Group UK Ltd.
Milton Keynes UK
UKHW011931300623
424349UK00001B/35